"Armstrong is a talented and evocative writer who knows well how to balance the elements of good, suspenseful fiction, and her stories evoke poignancy, action, humor and suspense."
The Globe and Mail

"[A] master of crime thrillers."
Kirkus

"Kelley Armstrong is one of the purest storytellers Canada has produced in a long while."
National Post

"Armstrong is a talented and original writer whose inventiveness and sense of the bizarre is arresting."
London Free Press

"Kelley Armstrong has long been a favorite of mine."
Charlaine Harris

"Armstrong's name is synonymous with great storytelling."
Suspense Magazine

"Like Stephen King, who manages an under-the-covers, flashlight-in-face kind of storytelling without sounding ridiculous, Armstrong not only writes interesting page-turners, she has also achieved that unlikely goal, what all writers strive for: a genre of her own."
The Walrus

ALSO BY KELLEY ARMSTRONG

A Stitch in Time time-travel gothic
A Stitch in Time
Ballgowns & Butterflies (novella)
A Twist of Fate
Snowstorms & Sleigh Bells (novella)
A Turn of the Tide
Ghosts & Garlands (novella)
A Castle in the Air

A Rip Through Time mystery series
A Rip Through Time
The Poisoner's Ring
Disturbing the Dead

Haven's Rock mystery series
Murder at Haven's Rock
The Boy Who Cried Bear

Standalone Horror
Hemlock Island

Standalone Romantic Comedy
Finding Mr. Write

Past Series
Rockton mystery series
Cursed Luck contemporary fantasy
Cainsville paranormal mystery series
Otherworld urban fantasy series
Nadia Stafford mystery trilogy

Standalone Thrillers
The Life She Had
Wherever She Goes / Every Step She Takes

Young Adult

Aftermath / Missing / The Masked Truth
Otherworld: Kate & Logan: paranormal duology
Darkest Powers / Darkness Rising paranormal trilogies
Age of Legends fantasy trilogy

Middle Grade

A Royal Guide to Monster Slaying fantasy series
The Blackwell Pages trilogy (with Melissa Marr)

A TURN OF THE TIDE

A STITCH IN TIME
BOOK III

KELLEY ARMSTRONG

Lines of poetry are from "On His Lady's Waking" by Pierre de Ronsard (1524-1585), translated by Andrew Lang (1888)

Cover Design by Cover Couture www.bookcovercouture.com

ISBN-13 (ebook): 978-1-989046-48-7
ISBN-13 (print): 978-1-989046-49-4

AUTHOR'S NOTE

The events of *A Turn of the Tide* center on a fishing village in North Yorkshire called Hood's Bay. The setting is inspired by Robin Hood's Bay, with its rich smuggling history and rumored subterranean tunnels. However, I was uncomfortable imposing a fictional history on a real small town, so I used Hood's Bay as the name instead, and my town and its history—and its people—are entirely fictional.

INTRODUCTION

*If you're new to my **A Stitch in Time** stories—or if it's been a while since you've read one—here's a little introduction to get you up to speed. Otherwise, if you're ready to go, just skip to chapter one, and dive in!*

There's a time stitch in Thorne Manor, hereditary summer home to the Thornes of North Yorkshire. As far as we know, Bronwyn Dale was the first to pass through, traveling from the twenty-first century to the nineteenth, where she met William Thorne when they were both children. Later, as a widow, she returned to find William still there. They're now married with two daughters. They live in Thorne Manor and divide their time between the modern world and the Victorian one.

Before Bronwyn returned to Thorne Manor, Rosalind—the wife of William's best friend, August Courtenay—accidentally went through the time stitch into the modern world, where she was trapped for four years, separated from August and their young son, Edmund.

Rosalind returned home last fall and reunited with her family, including her youngest sister, Miranda. Miranda Hastings is secretly a novelist, a teller of adventure tales and a bit of an adventurer herself, which meant Rosalind was definitely not telling her about the time stitch.

In Rosalind's holiday novella, *Snowstorms & Sleigh Bells*, Miranda discovered the locked door . . . along with a few oddities that suggested her sister was keeping a secret. In that story, we also saw the ghost of a legendary local pirate-turned-Robin-Hood. Miranda has the Second Sight, and while she can see ghosts, this particular phantom has only appeared in an echo of his death, his spirit long gone.

I magine that a locked door stands between you and the greatest adventure imaginable. It is not the sort of lock one might find on a safe containing such treasure but a mere interior door lock, easily opened with a hairpin.

What lies on the other side? A passage from the nineteenth century to the twenty-first.

Is any lock supposed to keep me from *that*?

The "time stitch"—as I have heard my eldest sister, Rosalind, call it—is located in Thorne Manor, home to William and Bronwyn Thorne, friends of Rosalind and her husband. From what I understand, Bronwyn is from the twenty-first century, where my sister was trapped for four years, having only returned to us last year. All this, of course, I learned only from listening to conversations I was not supposed to hear, as I endeavored to discover the secret of that locked door.

When I first figured out what lay behind it, it took all my willpower not to run to the house, burst in on the Thornes and dash through the passage right in front of them. I impatiently bided my time until they were in London, with Thorne Manor left empty. Then I set off.

I reach my destination around midday. Thorne Manor sits atop a hill overlooking the Yorkshire moors. Or, I should say, it perches there, a massive stone block of a house looking down on the village of High Thornesbury. Such a stern and forbidding abode should look as if it is watching the town with a judgmental eye, but the dark rectangles of windows seem more to watch over it, glaring into the moors at any who dare trespass.

I do dare trespass, entering the house through the kitchen door, which never closes properly. Halfway to the stairs, a movement makes me jump, but it is only a calico cat.

"Pandora?" I say, peering at it. "Or Enigma?"

The cat fixes me with a baleful look, and I smile. "Hello, Pandora."

She ignores me as I head up to the locked room. I open the door easily and walk into what is clearly an office. When I glimpse an open notebook on the desk, I must steel against the temptation to read it. I have a purpose, and it is—for once—more exciting than reading.

I look about for this "time stitch," but I see nothing.

My gaze turns to a stuffed bookcase, and I smile. What are books, if not doors into other worlds? That must be the source of this stitch. Open the right book, and I'll step into the future.

Heading for the bookcase, I veer past an awkwardly placed chest and—

I smack into the foot of a bed . . . where there had not been a bed moments ago.

I take a deep breath. Then heart tripping, I pivot to take in the wonders of the future and . . .

Well, that's disappointing.

Oh, I have passed through time. That is certain. I am standing in a bedroom instead of an office. And yet . . . is this truly the future? It looks like a bedroom in my own time. A rather dull guest chamber with a bed, a dresser, a night table and a wardrobe.

My gaze fixes on the wardrobe. Yes, the room may seem little different, but that is only because furniture may not change overmuch. Fashion is where I shall behold the first wonders of this new world.

I stride over, pull open the door and see . . .

Bed linens. The wardrobe is filled with very regular linens, ones that feel coarser than my own and are a nondescript beige color. I'm reaching to take out one when a clatter sounds from below, followed by an oath.

It is a male voice but definitely not William Thorne's. In my time, the Thornes employ a very small staff for their social station, but they do have a housekeeper. Perhaps their twenty-first-century one is male. I should like to think such a thing is possible—the dream of a world where a housekeeper can be a man and I would not need to write adventure tales under a man's name.

I close the wardrobe and tiptoe from the room. As I am leaving the time-stitch room, I note there is no lock on the door. That seems most odd. Would the Thornes not wish to lock the portal at both ends?

Another clatter from below pulls me from my thoughts. I continue to the stairs, which I descend with care, all the while tracking the noises, which seem to emanate from the kitchen. I crouch and slip into the parlor. Then I position myself behind the sofa and adjust until I am on an angle to see through the open kitchen door and—

That is not the housekeeper.

A man sits at the kitchen table, a cup at his elbow as he writes. His curly dark hair is cut very short. His sleeves are rolled up to show lean-muscled dark-skinned forearms, and he has a perfectly sculpted jawline. I am very fond of jawlines, being fonder only of eyes, and from what I can see, his are the richest brown.

Something about his countenance seems familiar. As I am thinking, I glimpse his footwear: a remarkable pair of boots, with gleaming copper buckles.

Those boots . . .

Where have I seen—

The man shoves back the stool with a squeak. He stands,

showing himself to be tall and well built, but my gaze falls to what looks like a sword hanging at his side.

I give my head a shake. That must be some modern implement. Even in my day, one hardly sees swords outside of a gymnasium, as I well know, having been training in the art for several years, lessons which I consider important for my writing . . . and great fun.

I lift my head just as the man reaches for something on the table. It's a bone-handled knife, tip wedged into the cutting-block table-top. He grabs the knife and flips it, nimble and confident. One last twirl, and then he drops it into a sheath at his side.

Is this a guest of the Thornes, invited to use the house in their absence? Would they dare such a thing in a house with a time portal, where a guest might walk into another century while simply looking for more blankets?

That's when I remember the open kitchen door. Is it still broken in the future? Could this be an intruder? He does not look like a thief. Also, I rather doubt a thief would write at the table before absconding with the silver.

I consider the matter. Then I take my pocketknife from my boot and slide it where it belongs—in a pocket. I design all my own clothing so that I might have pockets, and I have even converted my sister Portia to the wonders of pocketed skirts, though she insists on using hers for so-called practical items, such as pocket watches and pocket money. What is a pocketknife if not practical? Sometimes I despair of ever understanding my older sisters.

The man has moved to a spot I cannot see. There's a clattering of dishes that covers the sound of my journey from couch to doorway. Then a sigh and a struck match, as if he's settling in with a pipe or cheroot.

All goes quiet as he presumably smokes, and I contemplate my options. If he is a guest, I should leave, but I am not yet ready to venture into the wider world of the future. I must borrow some of Bronwyn Thorne's clothing first. Can I slip upstairs and—?

The cold tip of a knife digs into my neck.

"Do not move," a voice growls behind me. "I have no wish to harm you but—"

I swing around, my own knife raised. Or that is the plan, but he's too close for a proper "swing," and instead, I find myself pressed against the wall with *his* knife at my throat.

My word, he has gorgeous eyes.

That is *not* what I should be thinking, and yet, it is all I am thinking as I stare up into gold-flecked brown eyes ringed with enviable lashes.

"You have the most beautiful eyes," I say.

He blinks and pulls back. "What?"

I drop my gaze. "I am sorry, sir. That was very forward of me, but I could not help notice—"

I shove him, hard. As he staggers back, I dart to the side. He lunges to grab me, but I meet the attack with a push hard enough to send him flying backward over a footstool. His knife clatters to the floor, and I launch myself on him like a cat, landing on his chest, my own blade flying to his throat.

I tense, ready for him to throw me off. Instead, he only says, "I suppose I deserve this."

I'd heard his voice earlier, but I'd been too worried about my predicament to really hear it. Now that I do, it's beautiful, a light contralto with a French accent, made even more melodious by a wry lilt to the words.

"Yes, you do deserve it," I say. "Now—"

He bucks under me, legs flying up. I brace myself and stay where I am.

"I used a distraction trick on you moments ago," I say. "Do you really think I'd fall for one myself?"

He sighs and thumps his head back to the floor. "All right. You have bested me, fair maiden. There is a little money in my jacket pocket, which I left in the kitchen. It is yours."

I propel myself up, my free hand wrapped around the pommel of his sword. I dance away with it in my hand.

He only sighs and shakes his head as he rises. "Put that down, child."

"Child?" I sputter. "We are of an age."

"Hardly," he says. "I am six-and-twenty."

"As am I."

He smiles. "Does anyone actually believe such a story, child? You cannot be more than eighteen. Now put down that sword, or I shall be forced to take it from you."

I raise the weapon, and his eyes harden.

"Do not play this game, little one," he says as he comes toward me. "A sword is a dangerous weapon that requires years of training, and you will injure yourself if you attempt to use it."

I execute a perfect lunge and thrust.

He stops in his tracks. "My mistake."

"Evidently." I lift my chin. "I am not a *child*. I am Miranda Hastings, friend to the gentleman who owns this house."

"You mean Lord Thorne? The man whom *I* call friend? The man whose house you are burgling?"

"Burgling?" I squawk. "Do I look like a thief to you?"

He eyes my dress. "I am not certain. Your dress does seem unnecessarily ostentatious, whatever your intent."

"Unnecessarily ostentatious?" I stop myself with the reminder that I am not in my world, where my dress is quite fashionable. That's also when I get my first good look at what he's wearing. I see him, head to toe, and my stomach clenches with recognition.

I do know him.

Dear Lord, I know where I have seen this man before.

As a ghost.

$\approx$ 2 $\approx$

I have seen the ghost of this man walking along a road to his death.

Not his actual ghost, I remind myself. While I *do* see phantoms, his is what I call a death echo. I bear witness to the circumstances of his death, his spirit having long fled.

I have not stepped into the future.

I've fallen into the past.

A past where a man that I've watched die a dozen times is still alive.

"You are a pirate," I whisper.

The man blanches at the word.

"I am a *privateer*," he says, his face hardening. "Your English navy kidnapped me and pressed me into their service. But please, do call me a pirate. It puts me in such an excellent mood."

His words barely register. I can't stop seeing his ghost. Seeing his death.

"Wh-what year is it?" I manage to croak.

"I beg your pardon?"

"The year. It's seventeen . . . ?"

"Ninety," he says slowly. "The year is seventeen ninety."

That explains why so little has changed. The small differences

I'm seeing arise from the past, which would not have been so terribly different in a house occupied by the same family.

I look around. This wouldn't be the home of the William Thorne I know. It would be his grandfather's.

"You said you are friends with Lord Thorne?" I say.

"*Oui*." The man's voice is clipped with impatience now. "I am friends with Lord Thorne. He allows me to use his house when I need to take refuge."

"Which you do now," I say slowly, "because there is a warrant for your arrest."

His eyes snap. "A false warrant. I have done nothing—" He stops and clears his throat. "I will not lie and say I have done *nothing* to deserve it, but what I have done is not to further my own gain. If the law considers me a criminal, then a criminal I shall be, for the benefit of others."

"Robin Hood."

"I prefer Nicolas Dupuis," he says dryly, "if we are making introductions."

Robin Hood of the Bay. That is the legend—or what little of it I have been able to uncover, the facts lost to time. There is a town on the coast known as Hood's Bay. While it's been called that for centuries, the town is also connected to a young pirate—*privateer*—who temporarily made it his home.

In the eighteenth century, the bay was renowned for smuggling, and a young privateer embraced that while helping those who suffered under the rule of corrupt local gentry. That privateer was killed on a road now named after him—or his nickname: Hood's Lane, where history says he was betrayed and murdered by his allies. I know better. I've seen him die. He might have been betrayed by an ally, but his killers were members of the Royal Navy.

"You're going to die," I blurt.

His brows shoot up. "I believe we all are, child, but thank you for the words of warning."

I shake off the urge to say I'm not a child. Then I look at him. Truly study his attire. He wears form-fitting gray trousers tucked into tall, shiny boots with copper buttons. His grayish-blue vest also bears copper buttons. I have seen this exact outfit . . . on his ghost.

He mentioned a coat, and when I look about, I see through the open kitchen door. The same dark-blue fitted coat with tails that he wears in the echo. The same sword at his side, the weapon of a man who has learned to expect trouble. Only he did not expect it that day.

This day.

"You—you are meeting someone," I say quickly. "Today, yes?"

I expect his eyes to narrow, for him to ask how I know his business so well. Instead, his face relaxes in an indulgent smile.

"Ah, you practice the art of prophecy, do you, child?"

"Please stop calling me that."

He gives a courtly bow, one hand rising as he dips one leg. "As you wish, mademoiselle. But I must have something to call you."

"My name is Miranda."

That smile erupts in a grin, his eyes dancing. "Miranda, indeed. The intrepid would-be explorer, trapped on her island world and dreaming of more."

I startle, taken aback. Oh, I've heard my share of *Tempest* quotes. I was named after that Miranda, after all, which most people realize when they hear my sisters are Rosalind and Portia.

As a girl, I'd resented the connection. Miranda seemed a milksop, a naive girl batting her eyelashes at the first handsome man she meets. Only when I grew older did I understand the fullness of her, see her yearning and the frustration and the strength, traits I share.

Trapped on our islands and dreaming of more.

The man doesn't notice me falter. He's too pleased with himself for the literary allusion. And I'm too busy seeing him walking down a dusty road, whistling a tune as a figure raises a musket behind him.

"And you may call me . . . Well, in England, they are very fond of the diminutive Nick, but where I grew up, it was Nico. As we are friends—sharing the mutual acquaintance of Lord Thorne—you may call me Nico."

I am well aware of the irony here. The man—Nico—finding his footing as I lose mine, as I founder, my mind racing for a way to fix this.

My mind racing for a way to stop Fate in her tracks.

Prophecy.

My breath catches.

Yes, of course. Prophecy.

"You said I am practicing prophecy," I say carefully. "Attempting to foretell your future."

"Oui, and you ought to take care. They still burn witches in this land. Everyone loves to hear their future. Cross a palm with silver and learn what lies in the shadows ahead. I know many young women dabble in such arts, but you must take care."

"I do not dabble," I say, channeling Portia as I lift my chin. "I have a gift."

"I am certain you do, and I do not mean to tease you. You are quite correct that I have a meeting." He removes a pocket watch and checks it. "A meeting that I must rudely hurry off to attend."

He strides into the kitchen and takes his jacket. As he pulls it on, he picks up a rucksack from across the room. I see that rucksack, bulging with goods, and there is no doubt who he is truly going to meet: Death.

"Now, if you will return my sword?" he says as he returns to the living room, hand out.

I dance backward, and he sighs.

"You are a very fetching girl, and as much as I appreciated the diversion, I have business to attend."

"No," I blurt. "You cannot. You—you're going to die."

I flap my free hand, very aware that I look like a duckling attempting to take flight. For someone who makes her living from words, it is vexing how easily they abandon me, along with every ounce of poise I possess, leaving me squawking and flailing.

"Not someday," I say, quickly. "Today. You are going to die today, Mr. Dupuis."

Emotions flash over his face. Unfortunately, none of them

remotely resemble fear. Confusion. Wariness. And something like disappointment, as if I am so much less than he first thought.

"I see," he says.

"No, you don't. Please. Allow me to speak."

"Have I attempted to stop you yet, Miranda?" There's reproach in his voice, however gentle.

"You haven't, but I need you to listen without dismissing me as a child."

He dips his chin. "All right. Go on."

I walk over and return his sword, making him blink. It's a gesture of good faith. I trust he will listen without me holding his weapon hostage. I trust we can behave as adults.

"You are going to meet someone," I say. "You are taking them whatever is in that satchel. I don't know the details. The history— the future doesn't show me everything. I believe you are meeting a contact who will take those goods from you. Smuggled goods to be sold."

I raise my hands against protest. "That is only a guess. Whoever it is, they arranged the meeting on a certain road. It's not your usual route, but it's quiet, and that makes sense, as you have a price on your head, so you didn't question it. When you reach that road, though, you will be shot. Two men in naval jackets lie in wait. They intend to confront you, I think. Again, I only know what I see. A third man stays in the hedgerows. When you pass, he steps out behind you and shoots you in the back."

I wait for the look of shock.

Instead, he says, "I see," in the same tone, with that same look of wariness and an undercurrent of disappointment. I seemed an interesting young woman . . . and I have revealed myself to be nothing but a silly chit.

"No, you don't see," I say. "Am I not correct? Are you not meeting someone on a quiet road?"

"I am a smuggler, child. I meet many people in many quiet places. As for my pack and the valuables it contains?" He opens it to reveal fresh fruits and vegetables. "We have had a local outbreak of scurvy. I was trained as a doctor. My studies were interrupted, but I served as a ship's physician, and so I know how to treat scurvy. It is also a problem in seaside towns, where the diet is rich in fruits of the sea but sorely lacking actual fruits."

I stare into the satchel.

"Would you like me to empty it?" he says. "Prove there isn't gold hidden at the bottom?"

I pull myself back. "I did not say it definitely contained stolen goods. I said that was my guess."

"Is that not what prophecy is? Guesses?" He rocks back on his heels. "I am a man of science. Prophecy is not science. Fortune-telling is not science. They are fakery. I do not doubt that *you* believe this thing you are saying. Perhaps, in a dream, you saw a man die on a road."

"A man who looks like you? In North Yorkshire?"

"I am not the only dark-skinned man here, Miranda."

"I don't mean that. I mean that I saw you—dressed as you are, right down to that fancy sword and copper-buttoned boots. I saw you on that road. I saw you *die.*"

When he pauses, I quote another work of Shakespeare. "There are more things in heaven and earth, . . . than are dreamt of in your philosophy."

He pulls back. "Perhaps, but you cannot expect me to believe—" He stops short. "Why am I arguing when the solution is simple? You believe you saw me die on the road where I meet my compatriot. Therefore, we shall not meet there. We are to meet at a crossroads. I will approach from another direction. I may not believe you truly see the future, but why tempt fate?"

He snaps the sword in place. "It is settled. You may rest easy. I will not travel along the road where you saw me meet my fatal end."

"Good."

"I will be prepared for trouble."

"Good."

"Then allow me to bid you adieu and—"

"No need. I am going with you."

He raises one brow.

"I know exactly where you were set upon. I can be certain there is no confusion, and I can be there to assist, should anything go wrong. I have a knife. Two, in fact."

"*Naturellement.*" He peers at me. "I do not suppose I can dissuade you?"

"You cannot."

He checks his watch again and sighs. "Then you'll need to be quick about it."

"Quick about what?"

"Changing your attire, of course. It is a five-mile walk. You cannot do it in that." He eyes my dress. "I do not know how you do *anything* with all those petticoats."

I bite back a tart reply. When one has no choice but to wear "all these petticoats" one learns how to do almost anything in them. Still, he makes a valid point. As I recall, women's attire in this century is far less restrictive, which would work much better for both the long walk and any combat situations.

"I will be quick," I say.

He waves his pocket watch. "Fifteen minutes."

I almost laugh when Nicolas gives me fifteen minutes. Does he think I'm dressing for a ball? Even with the endless layers of nineteenth-century women's fashion, one learns how to disrobe and re-dress swiftly, at least for daily wear. It's not as if I employ a lady's maid.

Still, since he gave me fifteen minutes, I can take a little longer selecting an outfit. That turns out to be more necessary than usual, given that I am not in my own home with my own wardrobe. I open the one for the presumed Mrs. Thorne only to have my hopes plummet. William Thorne is a tall and sturdy man, but he did not inherit his size from his paternal grandmother. The only person I know small enough to fit into these dresses is Rosalind. I am my sister's height, but certainly not her weight.

I open the next wardrobe. Mr. Thorne's, it seems. They won't do me any good, even if he does appear to have been rather stout . . .

Wait.

When the solution hits, I let out a laugh loud enough that I'm surprised Nicolas doesn't come running to see what happened.

In my novels, heroines often dress as men. It is the only way to embark on such adventures. I have never done it myself, but if I was to start, is this not the perfect opportunity?

Lord Thorne is taller than me—most people are—so his clothing fits quite loosely. All the better to hide my true identity. My bust—flattened by extra corset tugs—forms a proper barrel chest. Admittedly, I will be somewhat short for a man, but a glance in the mirror shows that I ought to be able to pass for a youth. With smooth cheeks and blond curls escaping my cap, Nicolas will only have more reason to call me a child.

No matter. This "child" is about to save his life.

I find places for my knives—pockets! Glorious pockets!—and take the pouch with my notebook and writing utensils. Then I am ready for battle.

I march to the door, turn the knob and yank, only to have the knob slide from my grip, sending me tumbling backward.

The door did open inward, did it not? I try again.

The door does not budge.

The door is locked.

I take a moment to be certain of that, but when I peer through the doorjamb, I can clearly see that it is bolted.

Nicolas locked me in. He snuck up the stairs and locked me in and then left.

I want to tell myself I am being ridiculous, imagining myself in one of my own adventure novels. But the fact that I write such adventures allows me the advantage of seeing through machinations in the plot.

He does not believe in my "prophecy," but I wouldn't let the matter drop, so he promised to stay away from the spot. When that wasn't enough, he agreed—far too easily—to allow me to accompany him.

I should have seen through that in a blink, but I'd been too relieved to examine it more closely. I only cared that he wasn't arguing. I only cared that I could help him.

Yes, you may come, child. Oh, but you must change first. Quickly. I cannot wait longer than fifteen minutes.

Fifteen minutes? Ha! I did not need so long at all. That's what I thought, rather than wondering why he was being so generous with the schedule.

Because he wanted time to escape. To lock me in a room and ensure that, by the time I realized I was trapped, he'd be long gone.

Well, Dr. Dupuis, let us see about that.

I yank off my cap and pull out a hairpin. Within moments, the door is open. I step out and slide on something on the floor. When I look down, I see the key.

The key is on the floor. Just outside the room.

Because Nicolas left it there, where I'd eventually find it, snag it and get free. He didn't mean to trap me forever. Just long enough for him to escape.

I slap my cap back in place and adjust it as I stride out the door. Also, may I just say how much easier "striding" is in trousers? In my mind, I'm often marching with purpose, but when one is wearing five layers of floor-length skirts, striding is primarily a state of mind. Now I can actually walk with purpose, which is fitting, as I have rarely been in a mood to move quite so resolutely.

I am also, let us be honest, in half a mind to run like a mad creature and drag Nicolas from the Reaper's path, at sword point if necessary. He is walking to his death, and I cannot allow that.

I first saw the echo of his death years ago while accompanying Rosalind and August on a weekend excursion to Thorne Manor. I had been wandering the moors. If one is fond of wandering—as I am—there is no place better to do it. Cutting down empty bridle paths and following sheep across open fields, all the while surrounded by the sort of haunting landscape that inspires the latent poet in my soul. In those wanderings, I met Nicolas Dupuis.

Except I did not meet him at all, did I?

Here's the quandary I face. I have watched him walk down that road so many times that I feel entitled to think of him as "Nicolas," which is a shocking familiarity even for one who abhors the stiff formalities of society.

I have seen him on his mission. I have walked alongside him. I have even spoken to him, being glad no one was there to witness it. Pure sentimentality, as he was not even a ghost and able to hear me.

Merely an echo of himself, scorched onto that spot, as if the ground itself had been scarred by his untimely demise.

I have seen him. Spoken to him. Researched him. And, yes, I have shed tears for him. I'd hardly be a writer if I did not feel the tragedy of his passing. A dashing young man, dedicated to an idealistic cause, betrayed by his allies, shot in the back by cowards wearing uniforms they did not deserve.

I have the chance to save that man. The chance to avert the hand of fate and fend off the Reaper's scythe. The chance to protect someone I have come to care about.

Come to care about?

I've seen an *echo* of his *death*. I do not know him at all. It's a very pretty story, but stories like his rarely have more than a drop of truth in them. I have been well aware that, in real life, that man whose death I grieve could be a scoundrel and a thief. A proper pirate, which is a far cry from those I romanticize in my books.

I do not know the real Nicolas Dupuis. I never even knew his name. If he is so determined to die, what is that to me?

I could tell myself that . . . if he had not already shown himself to be exactly what I imagined. Idealistic. Passionate about his cause. A man who does good with his life and is about to be murdered for it, and I cannot allow that. I will not.

I do not catch up to Nicolas quickly, but I have time. It is a five-mile walk, and I am able to move briskly in trousers. The boots are another matter. The ones I found seem to belong to a boy— William's father, perhaps? They are still a little large, and so I have doubled up the stockings, which seems to help with any chafing. It does mean that my feet grow very warm, very quickly. By the time I'm closing in on Hood's Lane, my poor soles are screaming for respite. I only pick up my pace, as if to show them that such complaining will not be tolerated.

When I first set out, I told myself I had time because it was still daylight, and I know Nicolas is ambushed walking down a dark road. Yet I have only gone a couple of miles when I realize the sun is sinking behind the cloud cover. Also, those clouds grow steadily darker themselves, and the air crackles from an impending storm.

By the time I reach Hood's Lane, I am squinting to see my surroundings through the gloom and holding tight to my cap, lest it fly off in the gathering wind. I finally make out the signpost ahead. It's a decrepit stick of a thing, suitable for a rather decrepit country lane. It does not, of course, say Hood's Lane. That will come later, after this eighteenth-century Robin Hood dies here. But, if I have anything to say about it, it will never bear that moniker.

A tiny voice inside me whispers that I should have seen Nicolas by now. I know this route well, and I have walked as quickly as one can walk for five miles straight. Surely, he would not be traveling at the same pace.

No, but he is taller than me, with longer legs. He also had a head start.

What if I am too late? What if he already lies dead? What if—?

Enough of that. Just move, Miranda. *Move.*

I reach the signpost and peer down the long road. There is no sign of Nicolas, but I am not certain I would see him in this gloom. Brambles and gorse bushes line the lane, adding to the darkness and isolation. Anything could happen along such a road at night.

One thing I can see clearly is the road itself. The weather has obviously been dry and dusty, the earth in need of that coming storm. The lane unspools like a pale ribbon through the moor, and it is clear all the way to the rise farther down, which is beyond the point where Nicolas met his end. If I do not see his body, then he is not dead.

He has gone another way. He may not have believed me, but he was cautious enough not to tempt fate, as he said.

I stand at the mouth of the road, still peering down it, catching my breath and letting the sharp wind cool me.

The crisis has been averted.

What next?

Well, first, I'll want to rest, take off these boots and stretch my feet. Then I suppose it's back to Thorne Manor before this storm hits. Back to Thorne Manor and through the time stitch. My work here is done.

I tilt my head, considering that. I arrived in exactly the nick of time to save, well, Nick. Nico. Nicolas. I am not certain I believe in Fate. Yet this is more than mere coincidence. Some power conspired to put me here at this time, in this place, which is a truly wondrous thing and—

Thunder cracks, making me jump. Lightning flashes over a distant field, and for one moment, it is daylight again. In that moment, a figure crests the hill down the lane. A figure with a sword at this side and a rucksack over his shoulder. It's Nicolas. Walking the wrong way. Coming *toward* me.

I stare, certain I am mistaken. Then I remember how he said he was meeting his compatriot at a crossroads and, after my warning, he would take the other road to get there. He's circled around and come the other way, and now he's heading for that intersection, within sight of anyone lying in wait.

There's no one at the crossroads. Nicolas slows, as if that is not what he expects. After all, he's late, isn't he? First, I delayed him, and then he circled to come in another way. His compatriot should be there, waiting, and he's not.

Because it's a trap, Nicolas. You see that, do you not?

I don't stand there, gawping down the lane. I move quickly, ignoring my sore feet.

Look, there is a young lad strolling down the road. We cannot ambush young Dupuis in full sight of witnesses.

Nicolas doesn't see me. He's stopped in the intersection, peering down the other road, first one way and then the other. Thunder cracks again. Nicolas tugs out his pocket watch and shakes his head.

He does not see a trap. He sees only a missed connection. Has the other man left? Or has he not yet arrived?

I pick up my pace. Something moves ahead. Bramble bushes rustle at the roadside. Nicolas doesn't hear it. He's squinting back down the way he came.

Two uniformed figures step from the shadows.

I open my mouth to scream a warning when something moves in the hedge to my left. A figure steps out, a long-barreled musket in hand.

The assassin. Nicolas's killer . . . exactly where I'd seen him in the echo, a shadowy figure emerging from the bushes behind the young pirate, gun rising to shoot him in the back.

Only that gun isn't aimed at Nicolas. It's aimed at me.

❦ 4 ❧

I cannot see my attacker's face. I see only a slight figure, swathed in shadow, just as it is in the echo vision. The gun barrel rises. Rises straight at me.

I let out a yelp and start to run. My foot twists, and I stumble just as the gun fires with a deafening blast. White-hot pellets strike my arm, still raised as I fall.

A snarled shout erupts down the lane.

From where Nicolas is.

I have failed. All this, and I still failed to help him, and now someone has shot at me.

Someone is *still* shooting at me. As I scramble to my feet, the musket muzzle rises, reloaded and ready to fire again.

I run for the bushes. At the last second, I remember they are brambles. I don't care. Cannot care. I close my eyes, and I dive into them as the gun fires again. Then I am scrabbling through the thick, thorny brush.

Another shot fires. The pellets scorch past, hitting just enough to light my thigh afire. I keep going until I'm on the other side of the bushes. A dark and open field ahead calls, shouting for me to run, just run.

That would be entirely the wrong thing to do—race across an open field with my light hair a clear target for my assailant. While later—presuming I survive—I will claim that I had the presence of mind not to run into that field, what truly stops me is my leg.

My injured leg folds, and I stumble and fall. I glance down to see that it is, as I thought, only a scratch, barely bleeding. Yet I can *smell* the coppery stink of it. When blood drips onto my trouser leg, I realize that's where the smell is coming from. My arm. Which had been hit before I dove into the hedges.

Blood soaks my sleeve. Did one of the pellets pierce an artery?

I pluck at my sleeve with an interest devoid of any emotional connection, which can only mean one thing: I am in shock. As a doctor's daughter and a nurse's sister, I know all about shock, and I have the wherewithal to recognize that this is what I am experiencing.

The truly interesting thing about shock is that one is so numb that it is all too easy—if one is a writer who suffers from an addiction to new experiences—to simply stop mid-escape to ponder the moment. This is what shock feels like? How terribly interesting. Let me mentally document this moment for future stories . . . while I bleed out from a severed artery.

I do not think the artery is severed. It is bleeding quite heavily, though. Also, someone *is* trying to kill me, and even if I do not bleed out, I will surely perish if I sit here and ponder the matter much longer.

Thunder booms again. I don't see the lightning strike, but everything is illuminated for just long enough that I can determine a path.

I test my leg. It is sore, but it will move. Ignoring the screaming pain in my arm, I creep to the right, in the direction where Nicolas . . .

Lies dying by the roadside?

I dimly pick up voices, but my blood pounds too loud for me to distinguish words.

Stop and listen, Miranda.

How? I am being pursued by a killer.

Am I?

No, I'm crawling, bleeding, along a hedgerow of brambles. My assailant hasn't pursued me.

I force myself to stop and listen. Beyond the hedgerow, all has gone silent. I strain. Still nothing.

Is my attacker waiting on the other side for me to pop my head through? Or is he looking for an easier spot to come through himself?

I peer around. With the storm shadows, I cannot see well, but my memory fills in the missing pieces and tells me that the pasture divides with a stone wall, half-swallowed by more brambles. I brace myself to make a run for it, but as soon as I tense my muscles, blood streams down my arm.

I glance around. Then I remember the belt I put on to hold up the trousers. I yank it off and refasten it above the wound. Portia would be so proud of me . . . though she'd also feel the need to say that she's glad all my endless hours of pestering her with medical questions for my books actually proved useful. Of course, telling her about this would also require telling her that I was shot. So perhaps she does not need to know that I proved such a keen student of her teachings.

I cinch the belt as tight as I can, which is not tight enough, to my annoyance. I am rather light-headed, and I struggle to focus on the task at hand. I give myself a sharp shake and nearly pass out from the sudden movement.

I have lost blood. That is dangerous. Logically, I know that, and yet emotionally, I do not feel it, and that is what gets me up and bolting to that stone wall. I wriggle through a crumbling opening, and then I am crouched on the other side, listening.

The voices come clearer now. I still cannot make them out, but one is definitely snapping orders. Then I hear something that has my head shooting up. A word.

Pirate.

He's addressing Nicolas, which means Nicolas is alive. Alive and well and ignoring the man's orders? Alive and injured and unable to obey the man's orders?

It does not matter. He is alive. At least for now.

I crawl as quickly as I can while straining to hear more. There are two voices. Neither is Nicolas's. The one I thought was barking orders is asking questions. Demanding answers that Nicolas is refusing to give, and the other man is telling his compatriot to shoot Nicolas. That part I hear clearly.

"Shoot the devil and be done with it. He's a traitor and a thief. They'll hang him anyway."

I finally reach the spot. The men are on the other side of the hedgerow. I pull away the brambles until I can see through. There, on the road, kneels Nicolas, with his hands laced behind his head.

"Tell me who you work for," one man says. "Who is this Robin Hood of the Bay?"

That gives me pause. Is it not Nicolas himself?

"Tell us who you work for, boy, and we might let you go."

Boy? The men are about our own age.

"I work for no one," Nicolas says.

"Oh, look, he speaks!" the other man sneers. "The devil has a tongue after all."

"Tell us who this 'Robin Hood of the Bay' fellow is," the first man says, "whether you work for him or not."

"Work for him?" Nicolas says. "I *am* Robin Hood of the Bay."

The second man bursts out laughing. The first scowls and pokes Nicolas with a flintlock pistol.

"Do not mock us, boy. You are but one arm of the beast. We mean to chop off the head."

"But, good sir, I *am* the head." Nicolas's voice lilts, light and easy, as if he knows full well the men will not believe him.

He *is* Robin Hood of the Bay. I have no doubt of that. Yet they see only a pirate. A young man foreign in both his accent and his skin color, and so they presume he cannot be anything but a tool of their true target.

"Tell us—" one begins.

"I have. Do you wish me to lie? Lying is a sin. But I presume you must not know that, being in the employ of a man who lies as easily as he speaks."

"You call the king a liar?"

When Nicolas laughs, there's an edge to it, a bitterness he cannot disguise. "Oh, I have many answers to that question. Many answers. But you dissemble. You may wear the uniform of the navy, but you do not work for the king. Not unless the king is now employing former admirals to rob the poor of their livelihoods."

"We are members of His Majesty's Royal—"

"Yes, yes, but do you not draw pay from Lord Norrington? Answer carefully, *mes frères*, lest you be damned for your falsehoods."

The second man's pistol swings up, his finger moving to the trigger. And I do the one thing I can. I give the most "damsel in distress" screech I can manage, which is more genuine than I care to admit. I would much rather say I leaped out, sword in hand. But sometimes, screaming really is the right response, particularly as, even if I had a sword, it would not fare well against pistols.

Both men fall back at the sound.

"What the devil was that?" one says.

"It sounded like a woman," the other responds.

I crawl away from the hedge, staying well hidden.

"Help!" I cry out. "Please, help! I have been beset by brigands!"

When there's no response, I add, "I know I heard voices. Please help me, good sirs! We are wealthy travelers, and my husband shall pay you well for your aid." I sniffle. "If he has survived the attack. I fear he has not and I am already a widow."

A rich widow. A rich young widow. Surely, that is a tempting prospect. Unless, in my panic, I have overdone it. Yes, on second thought, I have definitely overembellished my tale of woe.

"Where are you, good lady?" A voice comes.

"I-I do not know. It is so dark and—"

As if on cue, thunder booms. Then there is a yelp. A shout. A gunshot.

I scramble behind the low wall. A figure appears at the hedgerow. Diving *through* the hedgerow.

It's Nicolas. I push myself to standing and wave my arms over the low wall. He sees me, stops short and then veers my way. He reaches the wall, vaults over it and drops.

"Thank you, lad," he whispers. "I—"

A bolt of lightning illuminates my face. His eyes widen. "You!"

"Yes, *me*," I hiss. "*Now* do you regret not listening to me?"

"I listened—" He cuts himself short and motions for me to do the same.

"Where did he go?" a man says.

"Through a hedgerow, obviously. Unless he is truly a devil and vanished in a puff of sulfur."

"I know he went through a hedgerow," the first man snaps. "I mean, which side of the road."

"You go that way. I'll go this."

Nicolas lets out a curse in French. I would love to ask the translation, if the world weren't tilting, darkness edging in from all sides.

"Come," he whispers. "We must get farther—"

He blinks at me. I follow his gaze to my blood-soaked sleeve.

"I was shot," I say. "There is a third man. I do not believe it struck an artery, but I feel a bit light-headed."

Nicolas lets out a string of curses now, some English, some French.

As he opens his mouth to say more, the clouds finally split, and the rain comes, pounding down, as if punishing us for its imprisonment. Nicolas speaks, but I hear only the rain and the wind, and even those become muffled and indistinct.

"I-I fear I feel rather unwell," I say. "We should take shelter soon."

I rise to a crouch. He reaches to pull me down again, gesturing at the road, and I frown. Why should I not stand if I am able? It is storming, and we really ought to take shelter.

Men. Guns.

I blink. However did I forget that?

Nicolas's mouth is moving, but no words reach my ears.

"I really do feel quite odd," I say. "Faint, even. I do hope I do not swoon. That would be terribly—"

I swoon, straight into his arms, and the world goes dark.

5

My eyelids flutter open. I did swoon, didn't I? How terribly embarrassing. I turn to apologize to Nicolas, only to find I am in . . .

I am not certain where I am.

I'm lying down, for one thing. When I inhale, I smell hay and dried manure. I try to push up, and my hand comes down on straw. A coarse blanket covers me. I tug at it to discover it is a burlap sack, ripped open into a rough sheet. Rain pounds a wooden roof.

I squint upward to see a dove peering down at me from the rafters.

"Oh, bother," I grumble. "I *did* swoon, didn't I? And then I needed to be carried and nursed back to health."

"You sound quite annoyed at that. Most young ladies would swoon again at the very thought."

I snort. "If you believe that, then you are acquainted with very few young ladies. There are many who would prefer to avoid the embarrassment of being rescued."

"Even by a charming and notorious pirate?" His tone is light, teasing, as he walks from the shadows, an apple and knife in hand.

"I thought you weren't a pirate?"

He shrugs. "Charming and notorious *privateer* does not sound quite the same, so I will allow myself the title of pirate, just this once."

"And the title of Robin Hood? You are the one they seek, are you not?"

He peels a strip off the apple, pops it in his mouth and chews. I wait for my answer, but he only motions for me to lift the sack from my leg.

"I must examine this wound as well as the arm," he says, "to be sure it does not fester."

When I lift the sheet, my leg is bare. That gives me pause. I am not prudish, but I have been raised in a world where even a doctor will avoid unclothing a lady. Nicolas doesn't bat an eye at my naked leg. He munches another slice of apple, hands me the rest, wipes his hands on his trousers and goes to work.

As a testament to my mental confusion, there is a moment where I think it is excellent that the future world has overcome excessive modesty. Then I remember that we are in the past, and I must acknowledge, with chagrin, that my century's notions of modest are largely our own. In this time period, a doctor obviously thinks nothing of asking a woman to bare her thigh if that's where she was wounded.

I also reflect that, while Nicolas claims his studies were interrupted, he seems as much a doctor as my sister, which is to say fully trained and only lacking the formality of an education. That might also explain the sword. I recall my father jokingly lamenting that he did not live a century earlier when doctors often carried swords as a sign of their status.

"Thank you," I say. "You have saved my life."

"It is only fair recompense for you saving mine."

He doesn't look up from his ministrations. Pain throbs through my leg, but I nibble at the apple and ignore the pain as he works.

"You appear on the road to full recovery," he says as he straightens. "You are strong and very healthy."

I tense and force myself to say, coolly, "Yes, that is one way of putting it."

He frowns, as if confused, but I do not explain. I have certainly heard such comments often enough.

Well, you are certainly a healthy young lady.

By which they mean, of course, that I am plump. At one time, that was considered a measure of health. Now, though, insult always taints the words, and perhaps I am being sensitive, but I have had one too many doctors chortle about how *healthy* I am after only a cursory glance at my figure.

"I am in very good health," I say as I flip the sack-blanket over my leg again.

"Healthy and fierce," he says. "In my business, we often do not use our real names, and so I shall call you *crécerelle*. It is a small hawk I saw in the Americas, which they call a kestrel. It is very small and very fierce."

He is complimenting me, at least on the fierce part, and yet I am still annoyed about the healthy comment, and so I find something else to grumble about. "You locked me into a closet."

"It was for your own—"

"If you are about to say it was for my own good, I beg you to reconsider, Dr. Dupuis, for *your* own good."

I expect a scowl. That is my usual reward for such "impertinence."

Nicolas only smiles and shakes his head. "Having seen you with a sword, I shall heed the warning," he says as he stands. "If you feel ready to move about, there is a cart in this barn. I will use it to convey you back to Thorne Manor. Then I must be off. I have lost a day I could not afford to lose."

"A day?"

"That sounded uncharitable. You were in dire straits, and you did save me. I appreciate the warning, however it arose, and I have sworn not to question you on that. Your reasons are your own."

"My reasons?"

He gives me a hard look. "Come now, crécerelle. We both know you cannot see the future. You came upon the information another way. Perhaps by accident. Perhaps by involvement."

I prop myself on my elbows. "You think I am *involved* with the scoundrels who tried to kill you?"

"More likely Lord Norrington himself. He is not known to consort with pretty young maidens, but I suspect even he would make an exception for one such as you."

He waves off my squawks of protest. "I have said I will not pry, and so I shall not. I am only thankful that you chose to warn me, in however a convoluted manner."

"Convoluted?" I straighten. "Fine. You do not wish to argue, and neither do I. As you said, you have tarried long enough. Be off with you. I can manage from here."

He sighs. "You are easily offended, crécerelle."

"You accused me of being involved with this Lord Norrington."

"I did not mean to suggest you are a woman of loose morals. He is a man of wealth and social standing, and a fine catch of a husband, I am sure."

"So I am a scheming girl, set on a wealthy husband. That is *worse* than calling me a tart. My indignation comes from you presuming I have aligned myself with a villain. I came about the information innocently—"

"And I acknowledged that possibility."

"Perfunctorily."

His lips twitch. "Perfunctorily?"

"If you tell me I am a clever girl for knowing such big words, I swear I will run you through."

"With that apple?"

Before he can blink, I have the knife he used to carve the apple.

He looks from me to the blade. "I would applaud that graceful move if I did not think you might take it as condescension."

"A wise choice." I cut a slice from the apple. "Now you may leave."

"May I?"

"Yes." I eat the slice. "I presume you will deal with the man who betrayed you? So I will not need to rescue you again?"

He shakes his head. "Lord Norrington's men must have

followed my associate to the meeting place. Seeing them, my associate fled. As I was late, my associate presumed I had warning of the ambush."

I open my mouth to argue. Then I shut it. Could history be wrong? I cannot be certain enough to pursue the matter, not when he is so set on his answer.

"All right," I say. "I will only ask you to be careful, sir. Now, I shall take my leave."

He puts out a hand to help me up. "Your cart awaits."

I accept the hand but shake my head. "I do not need that." My leg shakes, threatening to brand me a liar, but I find my balance before he sees the falter. "You have business to attend to."

"You are not walking five miles after being shot in the leg."

"Then I shall crawl." Catching his look, I sigh. "That is a joke, Dr. Dupuis."

"It is Nico, and your joke will become a reality if you attempt it. Stop being stubborn." He walks into the dimly lit barn. "Enough of this, or we will argue until nightfall. I am a man of honor who feels a debt is owed, and so you must allow me to repay it."

"Then you may repay it by gifting me your sword."

His laugh drifts out from the darkness. "That is a fine effort, crécerelle. But my sword is my own, and I will not gift it to any woman. Or man."

"That seems a pity," I murmur.

Silence, and then a sharp laugh as he reappears, one hand pulling a cart, the other waggling a finger at me. "I heard your riposte. Yes, I walked into that one, I suppose. The sword I carry at my side is not for gifting."

I start to ask whether any of his swords are for gifting. He was not shocked by my innuendo, and so I want to enjoy a few moments of risqué repartee with such an attractive man. Any of my heroines would. But the words dry up, and I can only sigh and say, "You are no fun at all, sir."

His mouth opens, and a rejoinder flashes in his eyes. Perhaps something about how he can be quite fun? But he stops, and I swear I see him mentally divert course, as I did.

"You shall not have my sword on so short an acquaintance," he says finally. "But you shall have my cart. Now, alight, fair maiden, so that I may carry you from this wretched place."

"I'm walking."

He slumps dramatically against the cart and sighs deeply enough to startle a dove overheard. The bird wings off into the barn rafters. Another follows. Then another.

"See?" Nicolas says. "Even the doves are disappointed with you, crécerelle. Impressed by your pluck, but in the end, disappointed."

"My *pluck*?" I glower at him. "If the next adjective from your mouth is *feisty*, you may need your sword."

"I was going to say *spirited*. Is that acceptable?"

I'm about to answer when I catch a noise. I lift as high as I can on my tiptoes, bringing me close to his ear. "Something startled the birds, and it was not me. I heard a horse whinny."

"A horse. Near a barn. *Quelle surprise!*"

I frantically motion for him to be quiet.

He tilts his head. Then he must hear something. His mouth sets, and he strides toward the wall. I follow as fast as my injured leg will allow. He presses his eye to a knot in the wood. I find one lower down and do the same.

At first, I see nothing but an old stone wall and a lone sheep. Then, beyond the wall, I spot a trio of horses. They could be simply grazing . . . if they were not wearing saddles.

Nicolas pulls back sharply, only to hiss through his teeth when I am not where he left me. He glances about and stalks over to me.

"We must hide," he whispers.

He wraps his fingers around my forearm as he glances about. I look up into the hayloft. He presses his lips together and shakes his head.

"You are too badly injured," he whispers.

I tug from his grasp and hurry to the ladder where I start to climb, ignoring the pain in my arm. I am prepared for him to grab my leg, in which case I would be required to climb faster, but he seems to have already realized such restraint is unwise . . . or simply futile. He settles for helping me up, which seems to require putting his hands on my bottom to steady me, and I have to bite back a laugh thinking of how Portia would react to such a familiarity. I also must admit that when one is wearing men's trousers, one can actually feel someone's hands on one's bottom, and it is quite pleasant, at least when that someone is a handsome young man.

Nicolas prods me up, and soon I am scrambling across the hay just as something creaks below. Nicolas scampers after me, grabbing my ankle to stop me. As I turn, light floods the dark barn. Someone is holding open a door.

"It's a barn."

The man's voice echoes through the cavernous space. Is it one of the duo who confronted Nicolas the day before? I believe so, though I cannot be sure.

"An empty barn," he continues.

"Which is why we are looking for him here." That *does* sound like the first man from the day before. "He has gone to ground in some hole or other. He is injured and in hiding, and I am not telling his lordship that we lost him again."

I glance at Nicolas. He has settled in beside me, both of us stretched out on our stomachs. His hip presses against mine, and while I realize it is not the time for such thoughts, I must reflect that if this is how things were in the past, I wish they were so again. It is lovely to be with a man and not need to worry about—gasp!—touching, even in the most innocent way.

"There is no sign of him here," the second man from yesterday says.

"No? Then explain this half-eaten apple, not yet browned?"

Nicolas closes his eyes in a wince. I whisper an apology, but he waves it off.

"I thought we were safe," he whispers, his breath warm against my ear. "They do not usually pursue with such vigor."

I turn my mouth to his ear. "It will not take them long to come up here. There is a hole in the roof behind us. We ought to climb out."

"Why did I know you were going to say that?"

"Because it is the only escape route. Unless you would like to fight our way out." I perk up. "There are only two of them. You have your sword. I have . . ." I pat my pockets and brandish one of my knives.

He shakes his head. "First, crécerelle, there are three horses. That means three men, presumably also the one who shot you. While I have my sword, I am never eager to fight. It is too easy to kill a man, and then I shall hang. As of now, a trip to the gallows is only a possibility. I would hate to make it an absolute."

Below, the men are searching. A third has indeed joined. We are fortunate that the barn is both large and in poor repair, meaning there are many places for them to search.

We creep to the hole. It is not overly large, but we should be able to fit through. I grab both sides. Nicolas clamps a hand on my uninjured arm.

"Have you looked first, crécerelle?"

I have not, admittedly. Now I do, and I map out my options. When I do ease through, he does not try to stop me. I climb onto a narrow ledge and then lower myself with care to a crossbeam. I am poised there, flexing my feet, when a voice inside says, "I'll check the hayloft."

I glance up to see Nicolas coming through the hole. He's halfway onto the ledge, but he can proceed no farther while I block the way down.

I grab a vertical board and slide my hands down it, wincing at the inevitable splinters. When I reach as far down as I can, I hook my fingers into knots in the boards and then lower my legs. My injured arm will not let me suspend my body weight, and my feet are still a yard from the ground, but there is nothing else to be done. I release my fingers and let myself fall.

A sharp breath sounds from above in that brief moment during which I seem to hang in the air before I fall, backward, arms pushing as if I am propelling myself through water. My bottom hits the ground. Pain ignites my injuries, but I am too busy wishing I had looked to see where I would land. On open ground—yes—but is it rock? Or dried grass that will crackle and give me up again? No, to my relief, I struck down on soft heather, and the only sound is the dull thump of my landing.

I scramble up and run, bent double, to the other side of a jutting boulder. Then I drop there, and I've barely drawn a breath before Nicolas lands beside me.

"Are you all right, Miranda? Have you reinjured your arm?"

I want to tease that he's using my real name, but he is in such a state that I say nothing as he examines my arm's binding.

"It is bleeding again," he says, ending with a French curse. "The wound has reopened."

I take his hands and gently pull them from my arm. "I am fine."

"You are not—"

"I am not lying sprawled on the heather with a broken back. Nor sprawled and riddled with bullets. Therefore, I consider myself to be fine, sir."

"Sir?" He gives a sharp shake of his head and then manages a strained laugh as he squeezes my hand. "You are never going to call me Nico, are you?"

I shake my head. "I heard mention of a warrant, and you said something about hanging. Was that in jest? I am attempting to ascertain the seriousness of the situation and how determined these men are to kill you. To kill *us*, if necessary."

All humor drains from his face as he rubs his cheek. "A day ago, I would have said no danger at all. Not of death. Imprisonment, yes. Humiliation, certainly, if at all possible, because that is the gravest crime I have committed."

"Humiliating Lord Norrington. Or should I say, Nottingham?"

The faintest quirk of his lips. "You are not the first to make that jest. *Mais oui*, I have undermined his authority by daring to feed his people. That is not, however, a hanging offense. I will explain more later, as you seem not to know the story, but as to the question, I cannot answer it except to say that, given that you were shot twice, we must presume they intend us grave harm."

"Thank you. One more question, how far can muskets shoot?"

"About fifty yards, with very poor accuracy."

"Good. Then we can safely steal one of their horses and ride off without being shot in the back."

"Steal a horse? You really do want me to swing, don't you?"

He's teasing, but I see his point. "Let me do it." I peer at the trio. "The flanks on the bay mare bear marks of recent abuse. I will not truly be stealing her, but liberating her, in recompense for her aid in our escape." I look at him. "Unless you have a better idea?"

"*Non*. That poor mare has obviously endured abuse, and now, having seen it, we cannot ignore her plight."

"Nor ours."

A faint smile. "Nor ours. All right, let us free the poor beast."

6

We arrive at the horses just as the men realize we are not in the barn. Nicolas helps me onto the mare, who does not seem the least concerned about being boarded by strangers. Any resistance has, I fear, been whipped out of her. Nor does she complain at the second weight added to the first, and we take off across the open moor just as a shout sounds behind us. A musket blast follows, but we are too far gone to be in any danger.

The poor mare must realize we are not the only ones escaping our fate. She runs like the wind, despite having both of us on her. We fly over the moors, with Nicolas taking the reins as I cling to him, perhaps more tightly than is necessary, but the mare *is* in full gallop, and I must have a care for my safety.

Nicolas expertly steers her through hill and dale, cutting a path that our pursuers cannot easily follow. If they *do* follow, we never see it. We are long gone, having veered past every wall and building and shrubbery stand that might hide us.

When Nicolas is certain we have lost them, he stops the mare and swings from her back to walk alongside her. I try to do the same —arguing she needs the rest—but he insists I ride, and I must admit he is correct. That brief run to the horses set my injuries afire. I

cannot risk further inflaming them when I may need their coopera-
tion again soon.

"Are we returning to Thorne Manor?" I ask.

Nicolas shakes his head. "While Lord Thorne is a friend, I
attempt not to involve him in my affairs. His family name will only
shield him from Lord Norrington's wrath for so long. They are
already at odds over Norrington's behavior in Hood's Bay, and
Thorne does not know the half of it."

"May I know the half of it?" I ask. "Perhaps even the all of it?"

I glance down at him when he does not answer.

"I have nothing to do with this Norrington, Dr. Dupuis. I do not
even know the man. I am from London, and I only came north for a
visit. As for how I knew you were in danger, I fear you would find
the truth more outlandish than the lie, and so I would prefer not to
speak on it further. I can assure you that it did not come from any
association with your enemies."

He dips his chin. "All right, then. Norrington is a former Navy
admiral. On the death of his father, he returned home. Now, while
Whitby has its share of smugglers, the true center of it in these parts
is here. The late Lord Norrington preferred to manage his farms. He
turned a blind eye to smuggling on his coastal lands and in his ports
and even on his ships. A suitable arrangement for all."

"Until the new Lord Norrington put a stop to it."

Nicolas's laugh startles a plover. "Norrington had no intention of
stopping anything. He simply wanted a bigger cut. Impossibly
bigger. When the smugglers refused, Norrington cast the net of his
displeasure far and wide, over even innocent fishing families and
local trading ships. He has all but shut down Hood's Bay. Anything
coming in or going out is subject to his secret tariffs."

"And you are helping those innocent victims."

He makes a face. "There are many good people helping. I am in a
unique position to do more, on account of my history and my lack
of local ties. Norrington cannot threaten my mother or sister or wife
or daughter if I have none."

"None at all? Or none here?"

"None here." He wags a finger at me. "If that was a hint to reveal my past, it falls on deaf ears."

"Still, it must be a very interesting past, all things considered. You are hardly a likely candidate for Robin Hood of Yorkshire."

His gaze cools. "You refer, of course, to the color of my skin."

"No, I refer to your accent. I doubt there are many Frenchmen among British privateers."

He relaxes. "You would be surprised. As for my past, I shall address it briefly. I am from Martinique, not France. My grandfather was a French marquis who settled in Martinique and fell in love with and married a freed woman of color. Then my father married a woman of color who had been freed as a child. They arranged for me to complete my medical education in France. I was on my way there when war broke out between my country and yours, and my ship was captured. I made the mistake of proving my medical skills and found myself pressed into the service of the English king."

"I am sorry you were captured."

He shrugs. "I could have escaped, but with the revolution in France, it was hardly the time for a marquis's son to visit. I stayed with the privateers by choice and sent letters to my family assuring them I was fine."

"Until you were not."

"Oui. Until I was not. We were docked in Whitby. I was ashore helping with a typhus outbreak when the news came that my captain had been accused of treason, my crew captured. My captain and three crew members were hanged, with the others being sent south for trial. A warrant was issued for my arrest. Given my accent and my skin color, I could not hope to slip away. Families I had helped with the typhus passed me along to others in Hood's Bay for safekeeping."

"And so in return, you now help the people of Hood's Bay."

"Oui. I *will* leave England—Lord Thorne has devised a way—but first, I must repay the village by helping them against Norrington."

"Who has a warrant on your head as well."

"Yes, it seems now I have properly earned my criminal reputation."

"Yet they do not believe you are Robin Hood of the Bay. Even when you claim the title."

"Which is to my advantage. I can tell the truth and still not be believed because, clearly, a man of my color cannot act of his own volition."

"That must be frustrating," I say. "Even if it aids your cause for them to *not* believe you."

"True enough. My only concern is that they may decide an innocent man or woman is the real Robin Hood."

I shake my head. "Not a woman. It would be the same if I were Robin Hood of the Bay." I add quickly, "Which is not to equate our situations. I only mean that women can also get away with much mischief that no one presumes them capable of."

"Also true, and while I appreciate that you do not fully equate our situations, there are similarities, and so I take no offense at a comparison."

He pauses by a spring and unhooks a cup from the mare's saddle. I slide to the ground. While the mare drinks, he fills the cup. When he tries to hand me the cup, I wave for him to drink first.

"You deny me my small acts of chivalry? Whatever would my mother say?"

"She would credit you for the attempt, which is what truly counts. I am very fond of chivalry in theory, but in practice, I fear it too often casts women in the role of weaker. Which I know you did not intend."

"I did not, but I understand your position, and my mother would credit you with *that*, so we both remain in her good graces. And your mother? Is she distant?" He lifts his gaze from the cup. "See how skillfully I slid that in? Nudging conversation to your own secret past?"

"Well done, sir. However, I do believe we have talked quite enough."

"About *me*. Now it is time—"

At a sound behind us, we both turn sharply, only to see a brace of game birds take flight.

Nicolas sighs as he passes me the water. "And that is a reminder that, however much I wish to know more about you, we ought to be on our way. My cave is nearby."

"Cave?"

His eyes twinkle. "I hope you did not expect a grand manor. I am a fugitive after all."

I drink quickly, and he takes the cup when I have finished, and we are off.

7

"**B**efore we reach the cave," Nicolas says, "I ought to make a stop in case my associate has left a message for me. It is not far from our destination."

I want to ask whether this is the same "associate" he was supposed to meet yesterday, the one I fear betrayed him. From his wording, I suspect it is, and I tense before reminding myself this is not an argument I can pursue.

We take a bridle path, and as we near a road, Nicolas asks me to wait with the horse and to remain out of sight.

The meeting point seems to be across the road and down an extension of the riding path. I tie the mare where she can reach a patch of grass, and then I set out. I promised to remain out of sight, but I need to be sure he isn't walking into another ambush.

I barely cross the road before voices drift my way. One is Nicolas's, unmistakable with that accent. The other is a young woman's, and on hearing it, my stomach tightens. I chastise myself, but my heart still sinks when I peer through the brambles to see him standing with the young woman. She's no more than twenty, dark haired and beautiful, and she's leaning toward him, speaking urgently, her fingers on his arm.

This is not a chance encounter. This is a woman he knows. From the little bit I can hear, it is also the person from whom he expected to receive a message.

There is no reason why Nicolas's "associate" could not be a woman, and of all people, I should allow for such a possibility.

I look at her, leaning toward him, her gaze fixed on his.

Maid Marian, I presume?

I want to say it lightly. Of course this Robin Hood would have a Maid Marian or three. He's far too charming and decent and handsome to lack that sort of attention.

"You must take more care, Dr. Dupuis," she's saying. "We heard about the attack. My father is beside himself with worry."

There's little of the Yorkshire accent in her voice. She sounds city bred and educated. Her dress is simple—with a rust-brown bodice and light-brown skirt—but it is obviously not meant for mucking out a stable.

"I am fine, Miss Jenkins," he says.

"Then why is there blood on your cuffs?"

"It is not mine," he says. "It belongs to a small hawk I found, injured. I believe a hunter shot her in the wing. It was most unfortunate, but she survived."

I bite my cheek at that. Not entirely a lie, at least not as long as he insists on calling me by that ridiculous name, which admittedly, I'm rather proud of.

I shall call you crécerelle. It is a small hawk I saw in the Americas, which they call a kestrel. It is very small and very fierce.

"You are so kind," she says. "That poor creature."

"She would have been fine without my intervention. She is a strong little thing. Now, I presume if you are here, you have a message for me?"

A movement behind the pair has me snapping to attention, and I miss Miss Jenkin's response as I notice a man standing twenty feet from them.

I start to lunge forward, ready to race down the path and warn

Nicolas and his Marian, but the man is making no effort to approach them. No effort to hide, either. He stands openly on the path behind Nicolas.

Because he is *with* Maid Marian. She can see him, and Nicolas could, too, if he turned slightly to the left.

Yes, a young woman of Marian's status and age would not be roaming the moors alone. The man is at least fifty and seems, from this distance, well dressed, meaning he is a member of her family or her household staff who has accompanied her to this rendezvous.

Nicolas and Marian continue speaking, their voices now too hushed for me to distinguish more than the occasional word. Marian leans closer to her Robin Hood, gazing up at him with such obvious adoration that if she *was* the compatriot Nicolas was meeting yesterday, then history is wrong. This girl did not betray him.

Having no excuse to linger—and not particularly wishing to see any parting kiss—I return to the mare. I settle in to wait for Nicolas while insisting that I am not the least bit upset at this turn of events . . . and knowing I have rarely told myself a greater lie.

Nicolas says little when he returns. He assures me all is well, and then we are off with the mare. Once we reach the coast, Nicolas stops. As he helps me off the mare, he says, "I propose we release the horse nearby, where there is both grazing land and water."

I look around. "Your cave is nearby?"

"Non, but the skiff is below."

"Skiff?"

"It is similar to a rowboat," he says.

"I know what a skiff is, but I am not sure of the application in this context."

His brows rise. "Do you intend to swim to my pirate cove, crécerelle? I would not advise it, the water being terribly cold."

Of course. He said he stays in a cave. Where does one find a cave in these parts? Along the ocean bluffs. History tells of countless ones in this area being used for smuggling.

As he releases the mare, I say, "We ought to have sent her with your sweetheart."

His brows shoot up so high I almost laugh.

"I apologize," I say. "I was concerned for your safety, and so I snuck after you. When I realized you were with your sweetheart, I withdrew."

"Presuming you mean Mademoiselle M . . .?"

That is not the name I heard, but as he said, they do not use their own names in this business. I must look confused, though, because he continues.

"The young woman I met," he says. "She is the daughter of my associate. I would consider her a friend, perhaps, but sweetheart?" He shakes his head. "She is even younger than you. A mere child."

"I am six-and-twenty, Nicolas."

"Did you call me Nicolas? Well, that is a start. As for your age, if you are truly six-and-twenty, pray tell, what year were you born?"

"Eighteen—" I stop short.

He laughs. "You were born in the future? You are even younger than I thought."

"Fine," I say. "I was born in 1765, which makes me twenty-five. But I will be twenty-six this year, and I do not appreciate being called a child."

"I called Mademoiselle M a child. I have not called you thus since our first meeting, after which I realized I had underestimated your age due to your petite stature and deceptively innocent appearance. I will accept you are five-and-twenty, then, which means you are six years older than Mademoiselle M, and I am seven. There is no romantic entanglement between Mademoiselle M and me."

The girl is clearly enamored of Nicolas, and he'd seemed quite comfortable with her attentions. Either he doesn't want to admit to a romance, or they are still merely circling the possibility.

"All right," I say. "She is not your Maid Marian."

He chokes on a laugh. "Non, crécerelle. I have no Maid Marian. I am not in a position to form such entanglements, being a man with a price upon his head."

8

Nicolas's cave is damnably difficult to get to, which would be the point. His hideaway is not an abandoned barn or even a cave just below the bluff's edge. No, to get to it, we must find a hidden skiff and then row to a cave barely above the high-tide mark. As it is not high tide, we must climb the rock face to that cave. Or I must, while he takes the skiff to a spot farther down.

It is an adventure; I must say that, and I must also say how delightful it is that he only once asks, "Is your arm all right to climb?" Then he allows me to ascend unassisted . . . though he does wait below, should I fall. Yes, my arm is throbbing by the time I make it to the top, but if I had been in danger, I would have accepted help.

I climb into the cave and make myself at home there while he hides the boat and returns.

The cave is more comfortable than I expected. Or, I should say, Nicolas has made it thus, with pillows and throws and furs to ward off the chill. The sea has infused the fabrics with the faint odor of must, but it is masked by the smell of salty brine and the scent of lavender.

When Nicolas arrives, he finds me settling onto furs near the back of the cave, and he brings food—dried fish, fresh water and apples.

As he checks and redresses my arm, he says, "I fear I do not have a change of clothing for you. That will need to wait for tonight."

I arch one brow.

His eyes glint as he grins. "I have an adventure planned for tonight, crécerelle. One I think you will enjoy. Only if you are up to it, of course. I must make the journey myself—to fetch supplies that Mademoiselle M has told me are much needed—but you do not need to join me."

"Are we to raid Lord Norrington's storehouses?"

Nicolas shakes his head. "You have an interesting idea of what I do, crécerelle, and the risks I take. No, I fear it is not a midnight raid. Not even a meeting with smugglers. The goods are already obtained, and I simply need to fetch them. It is where I must fetch them *from* that you may find interesting, if you are feeling—"

"Yes."

"We must go under cover of night. You may not wish—"

"I do."

He smiles. "All right, then. The day is already growing late, so I will suggest we rest." He holds out a waterskin, and when I shake my head, he has a sip and says, "As we rest, I will expect some reciprocation for my own history-telling. Let us begin where we left off as I asked after your parents."

I hesitate, and then I say, "I fear they passed when I was thirteen."

He chokes on the water. "Oh! I am sorry. That was very clumsy of me. I did not think— Well, I did not think, and I apologize."

"No need. I am quite accustomed to both the question and the response. They perished in an accident."

"And you had family to raise you, I hope."

"My eldest sister was nineteen, and she kept me from the worst of our situation. Our parents were very kind and loving but not the most prosperous of people. Our father, like you, was a doctor, and he did not believe in charging more than people could afford."

"Charity is a temptation that does not always lead one along the safest path."

"True, but it is still a virtue to be admired and pursued. I would rather look back on my father as a good man than as a rich one. His daughters have done well in spite of their lack of money."

"Or perhaps because of it."

"Yes, that is my feeling exactly." I take the waterskin from him and drink. "Rosalind—my eldest sister—opened a bakeshop in London. Terribly scandalous, but she is an incredibly talented baker, so society allowed it. My other sister, Portia, pursued our father's profession and yours."

"She became a doctor?"

"No," I say. "Like you, she has the training but not the formal education. In her case, being a woman, that education is not possible, so she is a nurse who pursues further education however she can."

"And you?" He takes the empty waterskin and refills it. "Do you have a profession as well?"

"I am a writer of novels."

I say it before I can stop myself, and I brace myself for the inevitable response, the verbal equivalent of a pat on the head for a child intent on mastering a craft beyond their capabilities.

You are trying to write a novel? How lovely!

You are scribbling stories in your journal? How lovely!

Perhaps someday, you can polish them and share them with your children as bedtime stories.

"A writer of novels?" Nicolas says. "Might I find one in the bookshop?"

I relax. "They are not yet available publicly, but they will be." Which is true, given that we are nearly a half-century before they will be published. "I secured a publisher who has paid me quite well, making this trip possible." Also true.

"Will they be under your own name?" he says. "Miranda . . . ?"

"Hastings, but no. They will be published under Randall Hastings."

His brows shoot up. "You write as a man. Is that necessity or choice?"

"Necessity if I wish anyone to read them."

"Are they about men, then? Adventures, I hope. You do not strike me as a woman to write poems about posies." He stops and clears his throat. "But if you do, I am certain they are enchanting poems."

I laugh. "No, they are definitely not poems about posies. They are adventures about women, which does not make it any easier to publish as a woman, particularly . . ." I clear my throat. "There are racy bits."

His smile broadens to a grin, dark eyes glittering. "Racy bits? Miss Miranda, how very shocking. Also, may I say I am less surprised by that than I ought to be."

"I take that as a compliment. Yes, they have both bloody bits and racy bits, and neither is appropriate from a woman, particularly an unmarried one. Randall Hastings may be a bachelor, but if Miranda Hastings, a maiden, wrote them, it would be far more scandalous than my sister's bakery. However would this maiden know about such things to write them?"

"The racy bits or the bloody ones?"

That makes me sputter a laugh. "I suspect no one would think to ask about the bloody bits, though they certainly should. I believe in writing what I know, and Rosalind says she fears the day I turn my attention to murder mysteries."

He pauses, and it takes a moment to realize what I've implied. That I write the "racy bits" from experience.

My cheeks heat, and I clear my throat. "That is to say, I do not always write *entirely* from experience. I have an excellent imagination."

He frowns and then bursts out laughing. "That part did not give me pause at all, crécerelle. As a gentleman, I would have drawn no attention to it. As a Frenchman, I would not have thought twice about it. The English can be ridiculous about such things. Still, I wonder at those who would question your right to pen such scenes.

First, it is none of their business. Second, surely everyone can relate the experience of intimate pleasure, whether there is a partner involved or not."

I choke on my own laugh. "So one might hope, but sadly, I have met many a young woman who goes to her wedding bed expecting nothing pleasurable about it."

"That is a shame. If one expects nothing pleasurable, one might find nothing pleasurable."

I open my mouth to reply. I want to pursue this conversation. Desperately want to pursue it. Not only to flirt with Nicolas but to engage in an even rarer opportunity—openly discussing sex.

I can talk to Rosalind about sex. Even Portia, though she would be more reticent. I also have friends willing to discuss the matter. Yet I am always the bold one, the one leading and pulling others along in my wake. Here, I have met my equal, and better yet, it is a man, who will offer a perspective I crave.

While I want to continue the conversation, I do not know how. It is my turn to speak, and when I do not, he deftly—and erroneously —takes the hint and changes the subject.

"When I paused," he says, "I meant that I have not heard of these 'murder mysteries.' Are they a new literary fashion?"

They are . . . fifty years from now. The so-called sensation novel, which Rosalind—presumably borrowing from the future—calls murder mysteries.

"It is a joke my sister makes," I say. "I do not think anyone pens such books."

"Then perhaps you can start," he says. "So long as you do not require personal experience of murder to do so." He glances out the cave entrance and pulls a face. "And now, as much as I am enjoying this conversation, I must allow you to properly rest. We will set out when the sun has dropped and the moon is full."

I SPEND THE REST OF OUR RELAXATION TIME CURSING MYSELF FOR fumbling that conversation . . . while also chastising myself for lamenting such a thing, considering the circumstances. And yet I cannot help but grieve the loss of the moment. I sometimes feel as if I am an anomaly among women when it comes to matters of a sexual nature. I am not. Rosalind has an active and, I suspect, very adventurous intimate life with her husband. Two of my friends sought out sexual encounters with "unmarriageable" young men, partly to satisfy curiosity and partly to ensure, when they did marry, that they would know what they did and did not want in a lover.

If I feel different, it is because my own curiosity has been frustrated and thwarted at every turn, half by my partners and half by myself. My first lover was also my first suitor. My sisters both thought him unworthy of me, and I thought that terribly sweet of them. He was the sort of young rake so common in popular fiction. Handsome and wild, with a devilish grin and a string of past lovers almost as long as his string of not-so-past gambling debts. My only excuse is that I was dreadfully young. Also dreadfully eager to experience the sort of carnal delights such a man could surely offer.

I have no intention of ever marrying and having children. Yes, my parents had an enviable marriage, as does Rosalind, and if I could have such a thing, I would not refuse it, but I consider it too lofty a goal to actively pursue. As much as I adore my nephew—and cannot wait for Rosalind's impending second arrival—I see myself as a doting aunt rather than mother.

All this means that I was not the least bit concerned about "saving myself for the marriage bed." If I ever did find a partner for my life, he would not expect such a thing.

So, while my first lover did not remotely qualify as life-partner material, he was my ticket to exploring all the fun parts of relationships—from intimate conversations to intimacy itself. After all, if he had a reputation as a rake, he had experience.

Experience, as I swiftly learned, does not equal expertise. I wanted a gradual introduction to the world of physical intimacy, complete with all the grace notes I had read in those books I was not supposed to find. Instead, I got . . .

I flinch. Four years have passed since I ended the relationship, and I still do not know how to put words to what I got. The memory is pure emotion, and that emotion is not disappointment. It is grief and fear and anger with myself for not ending the entanglement sooner.

Looking back, I realize he took advantage of my naiveté. At the time, I blamed myself. I had not been clear about what I wanted. I had not set limits. I had not explained. Yet even if that were true—and I do recall being quite clear in my expectations—he still took advantage. Our first time, I thought he was only pushing up my skirts to touch me. After all, that is what he said. "I want to touch you." Instead . . .

There were no "grace notes." It was animal rutting, and I am endlessly shamed to admit I did not end the relationship forthwith. I told myself he'd been overcome by passion, as he claimed. I told myself it would get better. I told myself any mistake was mine, and this was ultimately what I wanted, so why was I complaining?

It did not get better. He had no interest in making it better. Why would he? He got what he wanted.

I have had two lovers since. Both were single-night affairs. One was an older man who promised me "delights" and delivered little better than my first lover. The other was a young man who'd been most enamored of me, and with whom I finally saw the door to true pleasure open . . . only to have him slam it shut by declaring there would be no more of that until I agreed to marry him.

I do not know whether Nicolas was extending a discreet invitation to intimacy. He seemed to be discussing sexual matters as easily as he might discuss the weather. Or as easily as men might discuss it amongst themselves.

No, I *had* caught the currents of flirtation there. It was not a frank and analytical discussion, but it was still only risqué flirtation, of the sort the French are famous for. I still wish I had pursued it.

9

The moon is *not* full. I suspect if it were, Nicolas would not be making this nighttime journey. It's another overcast night, with a quarter moon, and we are in the skiff again, headed north toward Whitby. No lantern lights our way, but Nicolas navigates with expert skill.

We pass the seaside town and continue heading north until I spot a ship moored in a cove.

I turn to look at him. "Is that . . . ?"

"A pirate ship?" He smiles. "Oui, crécerelle. It is indeed a ship of the sort used by pirates—or privateers. More specifically, it was the one sailed by me." He wrinkles his nose. "Well, no, I did not sail it, beyond assisting when required. It is the ship sailed by my crewmates."

"What is it doing here?" I gaze around. "You cannot tell me it is hidden. We are scarcely five miles from Whitby, and that is far too large a ship to conceal."

"Mmm, you would be surprised at how well we could conceal it, when such concealment was required. *Mais non*, it is docked here for a much more banal reason. A legal battle."

"Ah, over ownership, after the crew was accused of—" I clear my throat. "Nefarious deeds which they did not commit."

He smiles my way. "You need not be so circumspect. The officers were accused of treason. I believe them innocent, but only a fool would stake his life on such a thing."

"As the charge was treason, though, the Crown seized the ship."

"It did. All her goods were forfeit. The ship, however, is owned by my captain's benefactor, and that is the bone of contention over which they battle. By this point, I suspect both sides have lost interest, and so she sits in this cove, slowly rotting."

He steers the skiff around to the side, where it disappears in the shadow of the huge galleon ship. She is a glorious creature, rising from the water, her sails tight against their masts, the curve of her jutting prow like a proud chin lifted against the night.

Nicolas steers to where a dark rope hangs hidden in those shadows. He gives a pull, and down comes a rope ladder.

"You hide your goods here?" I say.

"It is the last place they would expect to find them, non?"

I laugh softly at that.

He gives the ladder a tug, making sure it's secure. "It is safe, and it is dryer than my cave."

He motions for me to climb the ladder. I do, and he holds it steady. My arm gives a brief complaint at being asked to climb again, but it does no more than that. Once I am on the deck, Nicolas starts up, leaving the skiff secured. I wait until he is on the deck with me before I look around.

Look around? No, I scamper around, my leg feeling rested and well. She is not a new ship by any means. Every surface is worn with the patina of age, touched by a thousand fingers. The deck is rough underfoot, which keeps it from being slippery in the mist. I examine the navigation room and the sterncastle and the many masts and ask a hundred questions, all of which Nicolas answers with patience and good humor.

"Would you like the below-decks tour?" he asks when my stream of questions finally slows.

"Please."

"There are a few areas that are not safe for exploration. I do not exaggerate when I say she has been left to rot. The North Sea is not kind to abandoned vessels. I have applied what minor remedies I can, but the patient, I fear, is not long for this world."

"That is a shame," I say. "I am certain she has many stories to tell, and many more she *could* tell."

"Many stories, indeed, and a life cut short before her time." His eyes twinkle. "Perhaps you can immortalize her in prose?"

"If you will tell me a few of those stories."

"I will tell you stories until you beg me to stop, crécerelle. Now, let the tour begin."

৩≈৩

WE TOUR THE SHIP. SHE HAS A NAME, OF COURSE. THE *TEMERITY*. AS Nicolas said, she is in ill health, and there are areas—such as the galley—that he cannot show me. He has sectioned off storerooms for his goods, and that is where he has concentrated his preservation efforts.

As for those goods, he is acting as a middleman between smugglers and the shopkeepers who would sell and distribute exotic items. He is also storing more mundane goods to avoid Lord Norrington's tariffs, which are one part for the Crown and one part for his pocket.

Nicolas and his confederates buy goods from the shipowners wishing to avoid the tariffs and then sell them to the villagers who could not afford those tariffs. It is more complicated than that, but the exact mechanics do not concern me as much as the fact that, whatever laws Nicolas is breaking, he is doing it for the good of others and not to line his own pockets.

Speaking of pockets, we end the tour in a storeroom filled with clothing, some of it exotic in nature and some merely imported from other parts of the British Isles.

"Your wardrobe awaits, my lady," he says, waving his lantern at the crates. "Find something that suits you better than that dreadful outfit."

I bristle. "You mean find myself a pretty frock?"

"Not at all, crécerelle," he says mildly. "Unless that is what you wish. You certainly may select a dress, but I must warn that you would likely find it inconvenient for climbing in and out of caves and pirate ships."

I dip my chin. "I apologize for the undeserved presumption." I look around. "There is much to choose from."

"Might I make a true presumption and offer my aid, as one more accustomed to male attire?"

"Please do."

⚜

NICOLAS FINDS ME AN OUTFIT—A LOOSE SHIRT AND TIGHT TROUSERS and a pair of knee-high boots with polished silver buckles that make my heart skip. He leaves me to dress and knocks when he returns. I open the storeroom door and strike a pose.

"It seems to fit," I say as I turn. "Yes?"

He pauses.

I stop turning. "It does not fit? It seems to."

I look down at the shirt, on which I had to leave open a couple of buttons for my bosom.

"I did not mean to imply it does not fit," he says. "I was pausing to consider my response and fashion it in a way that did not make me sound like a libertine. I will only say that you are proof that women really ought to wear trousers more often. They show off your figure admirably, as does that shirt, which . . ." He clears his throat. "I believe I ought to stop there."

He lifts a bottle from his side. "Do you drink, crécerelle? I thought that, as we are on a pirate ship, you might care to indulge in that most piratical of spirits. Rum, direct from the islands."

"I have never had rum."

"Non?" He waggles the bottle. "Do you wish to rectify that oversight? Share a bottle of rum with me on the deck of a pirate ship, gazing up into the night sky?"

"Will you tell me a story?"

"I will tell you many stories, crécerelle, as promised. The first one shall be the origins of this particular bottle."

10

F or perhaps the first time in my adult life, I have no idea what I am doing. Yes, to others, it seems that when the patron goddess of practicality bestowed her gifts, she passed me by entirely. Yet that is only in comparison to Rosalind and Portia, who fairly bristle with practicality. I am the youngest Hastings girl, and as befits my junior status, I am the wild one, the unfettered one, the dreamer and the fantasist. Even in my wildness, though, I have a plan. I always have a plan.

I planned the relationship with my first lover, pursuing the goal of carnal education. One might say that went very poorly indeed, but one might also say it went very well—teaching me lessons about the dangers of that pursuit. I planned my career as a novelist, pursuing it even more ardently and determinedly. I pursued my goal of crossing the time stitch to see the future. When I ended up in the past, I simply switched goals. I had a privateer to save.

Now I have done that. Nicolas is alive, and so I'm . . . Well, I have no idea what I'm doing.

I'm torn between wondrous delight and abject terror. I am on a pirate ship, drinking rum with a man who makes my head swim even more than does the alcohol. It is night, and we are alone, and I know that should be dangerous, but it does not *feel* dangerous. Or, I should say, it does not feel dangerous in *that* way. It does feel very dangerous in another way. Because I know exactly why I am here.

I am falling for Nicolas Dupuis, and until he sends me off, I am staying right where I am, at his side, drinking in his every word like a besotted maiden.

I am drunk. That is the answer, obviously, because I have known this man for two days, for half of which I was unconscious, and therefore I cannot possibly have fallen into anything approaching love.

Can one fall into *like*? Can one fall into fascination? One can certainly fall into lust. Desire fits better here. I have fallen into ardent desire and cerebral fascination and—

And I am drunk. Let us leave it at that.

I am drunk on rum and drunk on Nicolas Dupuis, the music of his words and the wit of his stories and the beauty of his face in the moonlight.

There is indeed a moon now. She has slipped from her cloudy cover, throwing out a carpet of stars for us.

"And so," Nicolas says, "naturally, I had no choice but to challenge the man to a—" He stops, his eyes going wide. Then he sits up abruptly.

"Is everything all right?" I ask, sitting up, too.

"Non. It is most certainly not all right. I was on a mission belowdecks to fetch you a gift, and I saw the rum and forgot my purpose. Inexcusable."

He pushes to his feet. "Wait here. I will get it."

He sets out, staggers and stops to peer around. "Is the sea becoming unsettled?"

"No, you are becoming drunk."

"Bah. I hold my liquor better than that. It is the tide. Now, wait there."

He disappears, still walking unsteadily. I'm stretching onto my back when I catch a movement by a hatch. I jump up. There's nothing there. I watch the spot, squinting, tensed for a rat. Nothing.

Moments later, Nicolas returns with something behind his back.

"I have brought you a gift," he says. "The thing you want most in the world."

"Peace and prosperity for all?"

That makes him laugh, music in the night. "Agreed, *chérie*, but sadly, I cannot grant wishes. This is merely a gift. Earlier today, you asked me for something, and now I am delivering it to you."

"Uh . . ." I struggle to corral my tipsy thoughts.

"Think, crécerelle. In the barn. I said I owed you, and you asked for . . . ?"

"Your sword."

His grin is pure devilry, and it makes my insides quiver.

"Yes, you asked for the gift of my sword. So I am delivering." His brows shoot up. "Why is your gaze dropping *there*, crécerelle?"

"What? No. You are holding something behind you, and I was trying to see what it was."

"Then how did you know to what I was referring? From that squawk of protest, one would think I had mentioned a certain part of my person, when all I said was—"

"You brought me a sword."

"You are changing the subject."

I meet his gaze. "Am I?"

His grin grows. "I should warn you, crécerelle, that the sword may be somewhat more . . . petite than you hope."

"It is not the size of the sword that matters, but the expertise of the swordsman."

He laughs again, the sound ringing out. "This is true. Expertise is the most important part of the art. Not experience, per se. One can be very experienced and still possess no definable skill."

"Oh, I do know that." I realize I've spoken the words aloud, and my cheeks scorch. I open my mouth to twist my meaning back into the context of sword fighting, but the same inebriation that made me speak so boldly now keeps me from withdrawing the sentiment.

"I am sorry to hear it, crécerelle. That is most unfortunate, but not uncommon, I fear. Men mistake experience for expertise, in all forms of swordplay. I consider myself . . ." He pauses. "And there I tread into uncouth territory, as if I am petitioning for a post with a letter of reference."

I sputter a laugh. "Please tell me you carry letters of reference."

He rubs a hand over his face. "I truly have had too much to drink, have I not? Non. There are no letters, though now I cannot help but imagine such a thing."

"It would be terribly convenient. I shall certainly need to write it into a book. A man who provides letters of reference to his . . . dueling partners."

I put out my hand. "Best hand over the sword, Nico, before you dig this particular hole any deeper."

"Did you call me Nico?"

"I am drunk. Now give me your sw— Argh. The sword. Give me *the* sword."

"You do not want *my* sword?"

"Only if it comes with a letter of recommendation. I believe I shall begin demanding that, now that you have put the idea into my head."

"As you should. However, as an alternative, perhaps I could offer a written guarantee of satisfaction?"

"Or you will refund my money?"

"Hmm, that does not work as well, does it? If not a letter or guarantee, then perhaps an offer. I will—"

He stops and shakes his head sharply, leaving me hanging, waiting for the rest, conjuring the rest with my excellent imagination.

"Enough of that, Nico," he says, as if chastising himself. "Swordplay is a dangerous sport to engage in when one or both parties are inebriated and perhaps unable to properly agree to the duel."

"Agreed. Now, *the* sword, sir."

I put out my hand. From behind his back appears a small blade in an elaborate hammered steel sheath. My breath catches.

"Is that . . . ?" I manage.

He twirls the sheath in his fingers. "A very old short sword. It is in need of sharpening, but the scabbard is quite pretty."

I snatch it from him so fast he laughs.

"It is only an old blade, crécerelle."

I pull the sword from its sheath with the reverence another might display toward the crown jewels themselves.

"Wh-where did you come upon such a thing?" I ask as I turn it over in my hands.

"A farmer found it in a field. West of here, I believe."

"By the old Roman road?"

He frowns. "I do not know exactly. Only that the farmer thought it a pretty relic that a nobleman might wish to display, but it was so old, none wanted it, and I bought it. The man was in dire need of the money."

"This is a Roman gladius," I say.

"Were they rare?"

"At the time? No. Every soldier had one. Nowadays? They are rare indeed. The sword may seem in poor shape, but the ones I have seen in the museum are little more than rusted remains. This one, as you say, needs only sharpening."

I return the gladius to its sheath. "I do not know what geological conditions preserved it, but this is worth a fortune, Nicolas."

"Then it is ample repayment for my life, which I consider also worth a fortune, at least to me."

I shake my head. "I cannot take such a thing. It must be in a museum."

"Bah. They would see piles of gold and secretly sell it to a nobleman who would put it upon his wall. The nobility had their chance to buy it, and they did not see its value. Nor did I. Therefore, it should remain with the person who did."

"I truly cannot keep it," I say. "But if I may borrow it, that will be gift enough."

"Then you may borrow it. I shall expect it back in fifty years. Until then, it is yours."

I shake my head, but I don't argue. This truly is a piece fit for a museum. Yet if I am careful, there is no reason why I cannot enjoy the temporary use of it.

I gingerly withdraw the sword. The sheath is indeed the fanciest part, as it was with such swords, each infantry soldier attempting to put his own stamp on a standard-issue weapon. This one seems to have been wood on the inside, but that has all but rotted away, leaving only the metal exterior.

I carefully set the scabbard on the deck. Then I examine the sword. It is barely longer than my arm. The stout blade is as wide as three of my fingers. Both edges are sharp, and the end is pointed for stabbing. The blade itself is steel, with little sign of damage, which makes me wonder whether it was encased in more than the sheath. Perhaps it was new, never seeing warfare, secreted away in something that kept it from corroding.

I am well aware of the history of the Romans in Britain. They were invaders, and the Celtic people suffered greatly under them, just as others suffer under my queen's ever-expanding empire. I have no reverence for those invading Romans, but as a student of swords, I can admire the breathtaking history of what I hold in my hands, and I can craft myself a new story for it, where the gladius was stolen by a Celtic warrior maid who used it to fight off the invaders and save her village.

"You are thinking," Nicolas says.

I smile. "I am making up stories."

"May I ask to hear them?"

I tell him the history of the blades, and the meaning of the Roman invasion and my fanciful alternate story of this gladius's origins.

"I believe you are correct," he says. "Clearly, it was the sword of a Celtic warrior maid, and Fate has now passed it on to you. Do you know how to use a short sword? I fear I do not."

"I am still learning swordsmanship," I say. "I began with fencing but found it quite dull. My instructor has let me try his short swords."

"Has he?"

I waggle the blade at him. "None of that. My instructor is a gentleman, who is very enamored of his wife, and I have nothing to fear in that regard."

Nicolas sobers. "I ought not to jest. I am certain it would not be easy for a young lady to find a sword-fighting instructor who is both respectable and respectful."

"I have been fortunate. To return to the question, I know a bit about short-sword fighting. The problem, of course, comes when fighting against a longer sword, such as yours."

He walks to where he left his, having removed it once we were safely on the ship. He takes out the blade and returns to me.

"If I initiate . . ." I feign doing so. "The sheer length of your sword . . ." I wave the gladius at him. "And no comments on that, sir."

"I would not comment. My sword"—he lifts it in the air—"is of a middling length, perhaps only slightly longer than average, which suits me, being a man of just above average height."

"Yet your sword is much longer than mine, and if I initiate attack, and you retaliate . . ."

We attempt it, showing that his sword will easily reach me, while mine falls short of any target other than his arm.

"I could go for your hand," I say. "I am better not to initiate offense and instead allow you to do so."

He does, and I stop his sword with mine and then feign stabbing with my smaller pocketknife.

"Ideally, this would be a dagger," I say. "Or a buckler, with which I could bash you while your sword is stopped."

We continue on like that, sparring as I explain, until I manage to get him backed into the mast. That's when I notice the rigging lines blowing in the night air and the crow's nest far above.

"How does one reach the crow's nest?" I ask.

"One climbs," he says, returning his sword to its sheath.

I tug a rope experimentally. "I should like to do that."

"You are asking to climb my mast, crécerelle?"

I wave my blade at him. "You are a terrible flirt, Dr. Dupuis."

"Am I? I thought I was rather good at it."

"You are, which makes it all the more terrible."

His eyes glint as his mouth opens to say something. Then he stops and shakes his head. "And despite the bracing night air, I am still inebriated and unable to stanch my flow of ribaldry. I will do so, however, if you wish. You have been a good sport about it, but if it makes you at all uncomfortable, you may tell me to stop."

"Thank you. There have been times when I have laughed at something I did not find amusing for fear of seeming overly sensitive. I no longer do so, and if a man flirts with me and I do not wish it, I will let him know, at first by gentle withdrawal from the conversation and, if that does not work . . ." I lift the gladius. "There is a reason I am learning sword fighting."

"I do not doubt that you need such weaponry to beat off your admirers. I can only imagine—" He clears his throat. "Mais oui, crécerelle. You may climb the ship's mast if your arm will permit it."

"I believe it will, and I should like to try."

"Do you require instruction?"

I pause long enough that he waggles his forefinger at me. "Not that sort of instruction."

"I was thinking of the ship's mast, Nicolas. Deciding whether I want to be instructed or to figure it out for myself."

"In my experience, there is an appeal to figuring it out for oneself, but also an advantage to instruction, though the latter can be hard to come by."

"Not at all, if one knows where to look."

His mouth opens. Shuts. He lifts one brow so comically that I sputter a laugh, and then he says, "I am endeavoring not to ask for details, as much as I desire details. Are there instructors in such things for young ladies? I know there are for young men, as my uncles introduced me to them at the appropriate age, but I was not aware of any for young ladies."

"I mean *books*, Dr. Dupuis. That grand repository of knowledge, which one might utilize without significant cost or significant risk of, ahem, disease."

"There are books on climbing ship's masts?"

"If there are not, then I shall write the first—a detailed description in my next novel. Now, if you are quite done flirting with me . . ."

"I do not believe I shall ever be done flirting with you, crécerelle. It is the most delightful entertainment I have had in a very long time."

"The mast. The ship's mast. I should like to climb it."

He looks up. "That is very adventurous of you. Also very ambitious. It is exceedingly big."

I rap him on the arm. "Enough. The rum's effect is fading, and I fear when it does, we shall both realize what a dangerous endeavor this is. Now, are you going to show me how to climb a ship's mast or not?"

He takes hold of the rigging. "Let the lesson begin."

11

"You are reaching the last of it," Nicolas says from the rigging just below me. "Whatever you do, do not look down."

"Why does everyone say that?" I grumble as I pause, catching my breath before reaching for the next rope. "Do they not know that as soon as they say not to do a thing, one will do it out of pure curiosity?"

"Perhaps that is only you, crécerelle."

"It is not, I assure you. You say not to look down, and I immediately want to look down. It is evil temptation at its worst."

"All right, then. Look down, my fair Miranda. Look upon the raging sea below, waiting to swallow you and deposit your lovely form on a beach, a mermaid flung from the ocean for all to admire."

"My lifeless, bloated and fish-nibbled naked form? Anyone who admires such a thing ought to be taken to prison on the spot before they commit some horrible atrocity."

"It seemed much more romantic in my head."

"Then I fear for your sense of romance, Dr. Dupuis."

"All right. I would prefer you not to look down because I would prefer you not to die. Is that more romantic?"

"Much."

While my arm is still giving me trouble, I am determined to reach the crow's nest, and I do. I am also pleased to know I am not the only one who finds the climb exhausting, as Nicolas pauses for breath. It is not merely the climb but also the wind, her tendrils tugging most insistently.

Nicolas directs me on how to climb into the lookout. Then I am there. In the crow's nest of a galleon, gripping the railing and gazing out to sea.

"Careful you do not lean against that railing," Nicolas says as he stands.

"I won't." I turn to look east, and from this angle, I see nothing but the ocean meeting the starry sky. A light wind catches a tendril of hair, and I pull off my cap and let my hair catch the wind as I tilt my face into it, the smell of the sea washing over me.

"I wish I were a woodcarver," Nicolas says. "I would fashion you as a figurehead for the finest ship on the sea."

I turn my head, hair blowing in my face as I grin at him.

He stares. Only stares, and I'm about to ask if all is well when he says, "You are . . ."

I know what the next word will be. *Beautiful.* I have heard it often enough. I would not be so vain as to say I *am* beautiful, but rather that I believe men feel honor bound to say it, perhaps in recognition that—despite being plumper than is the fashion—I am still conventionally attractive.

"Remarkable," Nicolas says. "You are remarkable, Miranda, and I . . ." He swallows and then shakes it off with a wry smile. "I do not believe I am quite as sober as I thought."

"Do you only offer compliments when you are drunk?" I say.

"Non. I would say the same sober, but I fear that tonight I may say more than I should and embarrass both of us."

"Well, then, let us share the future embarrassment as I return the compliment." I meet his gaze. "I find you equally remarkable."

He moves closer, hand rising to smooth blowing hair back from my face. "I should very much like to kiss you, Miranda."

"And I should very much like to be kissed by you, Nicolas."

He pauses only a moment, gaze locking on mine, as if to be sure I'm not simply playing the flirtation game. Then his mouth comes to mine. It is tender, light as the kiss of the wind, and yet it steals the breath from me, and I stand there, quivering, unable to breathe as I wait in hope of more. His lips part against mine, the kiss deepening once he is certain of its welcome, and . . .

Oh, this is a *kiss*.

In my novels, my intimate scenes are considered quite scandalous. They are pure innuendo and allusion, with no frank detail—that would be pornography, and while I am quite fond of the sort written secretly by women, it is not the purpose of my stories. I still include great sensual detail on the act of lovemaking . . . and none at all on the act of kissing. I write "they kissed," and then I carry on to the more exciting parts. There is nothing exciting about a kiss. I have had dozens, and they ranged from repugnant to tolerable, and so, having clearly experienced the full spectrum of kisses, I could declare them worth no more than those two words: they kissed.

Nicolas's kiss does not land on that spectrum. I cannot even *see* that spectrum from where it does land. This is a kiss that demands I track down each and every copy of my books and expand those two words to a chapter at least, and yet I cannot imagine how I would put such a thing into words. Simply put, for once, I lack the language.

Perhaps I could find the language, but I will not try. I have lived my life compiling experiences as fodder for my novels, and this is not one of those. This is mine, and mine alone, and I shall only say that I do not believe, before this moment, that I have been properly kissed. Nor that I have properly kissed someone in return, having no model to follow. Nicolas provides that model, and I throw myself into the study of it, and when I break for breath, he is gasping and glassy eyed, and I will take that as a sign of my success.

Nicolas strokes my hair and murmurs something, and I strain to catch the words, only to realize it is not the low tone that makes them elude me—it is the words themselves.

"I do not know French," I say.

"Good." He smiles as he brushes my cheek.

"Then I do not know what you are saying."

He leans in, his lips coming to mine. "Good."

He says more, the words spilling out, and I make a noise of frustration.

"Did you *growl* at me, crécerelle?"

"It is rude to speak in a language the other does not understand."

"*Terribly* rude." He says something else, in French, and then kisses me softly. "Would you like to know what I am saying?"

"I believe that is the gist of my complaint."

"Then I suppose you shall need to learn my language. It should only take a year or two. By then, perhaps, I will be ready for you to hear what I have said."

I pull back and glower at him.

He taps my nose. "You are the most adorable crécerelle. So small and yet so fierce."

"Also strong."

"Very strong."

"Strong enough to dangle you over the railing of this crow's nest if you continue to mock me."

"I am not mocking. I am provoking you. Just a little." He leans down, forehead touching mine. "I will teach you French, and until then, you can be certain I shall say nothing you would find insulting. Unless you would be insulted by admissions of admiration, ones I am not drunk enough to say in a language you understand."

"Mmm."

"So I am forgiven?"

"That depends. Are you going to keep talking? Or are you going to kiss me again? It is getting cold up here, and if you are not going to warm me, I shall need to descend to the deck."

"We would not want that." His mouth lowers to mine. "I will keep you as warm as you like, crécerelle. You need only say the word."

"You're still talking."

A sharp laugh, and then he is kissing me again, his arms around me, pulling me to him. He turns me toward the mast, my back against it.

"Do not worry," he murmurs. "I will do nothing except kiss you. I only did not want to push you against the railing."

He lifts me, my back against the mast, and I discover yet another advantage of split trousers. I can wrap my legs around his waist, which feels wickedly sinful, despite the layers of clothing between us. He leans into me, groaning against my mouth, and I adjust my hips, just a little and—

Oh!

Oh, that *is* wonderful.

I break the kiss in a gasp, and he buries his face against my neck, murmuring in French as he presses against me and I entwine my hands in his hair, unabashedly enjoying the incredible feel of him—

Something moves on the deck below. Nicolas is returning to the kiss, and I'm shifting to meet him when I look down and startle. I pull back with a very different sort of gasp as I scramble free.

"Miranda?"

"Th-there is someone on the deck," I whisper.

He wheels so fast I start to fall, and he grabs me with a whispered curse in French, paired with what I presume by the tone is an apology, but he's too agitated to realize he's still speaking French.

When he goes to step toward the railing, I tug him back, and he leans instead, scouring the deck.

"I see no one, crécerelle," he whispers. "Was it one man? Several?"

I can still easily distinguish the figure below, looking up at us.

"One man," I say. "He is right there. On the forecastle deck."

Nicolas frowns. "I do not see him."

I look again. The figure has a slight build, and he stands near shadows, but he is plainly visible in the moonlight.

"To the left of the foremast?" I say again. "You see no one?"

"Non, Miranda. I do not."

"Then it is a ghost."

He looks at me sharply.

"I have the Sight," I say. "What we call the Second Sight. It means I see ghosts."

He continues to stare.

"And you do not believe me," I say, my stomach sinking. "Of course you do not. Earlier, I claimed to be able to see into the future, and I admitted that was a lie. This is not. I swear it. The Sight runs in my family. My grandmother had it, and my young nephew does, too. We see ghosts." I meet his gaze. "We truly do."

"My expression was not one of doubt, Miranda. I was only being clear I heard correctly, and you were not teasing. Or feeling the need to come up with an excuse to stop what we were doing."

"That would be quite the excuse. I should hope I could do better."

"And I should hope you would not feel such an excuse is needed." He kisses my cheek. "As for seeing ghosts, I come from people who believe very strongly in the spirit world. Only a few can see them, but we know they exist, and so if that is what you see, that is what you see."

He peers over the edge. "It is a man, you say?"

"Slight of stature, yes. He is looking up at you. It is all right. In my experience, ghosts do not mean us harm. They only wish to communicate, when they are able."

"That is what I have been taught as well. Although there are spirits who are angry or even evil, most only seek to communicate, as you say."

I nod. "I will attempt to do so, if that is all right with you."

He gives a short laugh. "I would much rather return to our previous occupation, but we can hardly do that now, knowing we have a spectral audience." He walks to the edge and turns to descend. "I shall go first, if that is acceptable."

I agree, and we begin making our way down.

12

I know I am not supposed to look down, but that is even harder now as I want to keep an eye on the ghost. If he leaves, I need to know where he goes so I may follow. I will not chase. I would never do that without cause. Yet there is, as far as I know, no way for a ghost to realize that I can see him, and so he may leave when we are no longer providing risqué entertainment from the crow's nest.

I wait until I am halfway descended. Then I glance in the ghost's direction. It is a young man. He's still too far for me to tell more than that, but he looks as real as a living person. Ghosts always do, which leads to terrible confusion and more than a few mistakes such as the one I just made, pointing out a person who isn't there.

I have learned tricks to avoid such mistakes, which I have been teaching my nephew, Edmund. My only excuse tonight is that I am still somewhat inebriated. Also, kissing a handsome man in a pirate ship crow's nest is bound to unsettle the most sober young woman.

No, let us be honest. I spoke the truth—both about seeing someone below and then admitting I can see ghosts—because I am comfortable with Nicolas. Unreasonably comfortable, and he has given me no reason to be anything else.

I continue down, glancing every few moments to be sure the

ghost is still there. I also hope he will see me watching and know I can see him and that we might communicate. Yet he has not so much as glanced my way. His attention is entirely upon Nicolas.

I descend a little farther, and then the angle is exactly right for me to see the ghost, and I stifle a gasp. He is little more than a boy.

Oh, I am certain he would consider himself a "young man," but he is about fourteen. He wears what seems the correct clothing for the period, though simply made. He carries a dagger at his waist, and his feet are bare.

A ship's boy? A cabin boy?

As I consider that, a terrible thought strikes.

This boy knows Nicolas. That is why he is staring at him. He is from the ship's crew. Nicolas will know *him*.

I am opening my mouth when the boy launches himself. He is there, gaze fixed on Nicolas. Then he is hurtling toward Nicolas, letting out a strangely hoarse cry.

"Nico!" I shout.

Even as I say his name, I chide myself for overreacting. It is a ghost flying at him. Nothing more substantial than—

The ghost hits him, and Nicolas inhales in a sudden gasp. His head jerks back, and all I see is the whites of his eyes. His body convulses, and his hands release the rigging.

"Nico!"

He falls. There seems to be an impossibly long moment where he is suspended in midair. A moment where it feels as if I could grab him if only I moved faster. I *am* moving, but it is not fast enough, and he is already plummeting toward the deck, a half-dozen feet below.

"Nico!"

It takes every ounce of my practicality not to release my own grip on the rigging. My heart shouts that it would be the fastest way down. Let go and drop. My brain knows better, and instead, I scramble down, hand over hand, ignoring the pain in my arm, until my toes brush the deck.

I let go and drop beside Nicolas. He's sprawled motionless on the deck. My hands fly to his neck first. His pulse beats strong. Then I bend to check his breathing, and his eyes snap open, eyes staring into mine.

"Did I swoon, crécerelle? Please tell me I did not swoon."

I can't bring myself to even smile at the joke. I am too busy looking at his eyes, being sure they seem focused. They do. When he tries to rise, I stop him.

"You fell from the rope," I say. "Do not move yet. Please."

He cocks his head. "I think I am fine."

"Are you actually a doctor, Nico? Because if you are, you should know better. Lie *still*."

His lips curve in a smile. "You called me Nico again."

I sigh and run my hands along his neck. "Tell me if anything hurts."

"It all hurts."

"How hard did you hit your head?"

"I do believe I am fine, crécerelle. I have heard it said that alcohol consumption can reduce physical damage from a fall. The theory is that, if inebriated, one does not have the wits to tense before landing."

He rolls his shoulders. "I am very sore, and I suspect I will be even more sore come morning, but I believe I can rise."

"Carefully."

"Oui." He sits up and tests his arms and then his legs. "The worst injury seems to be to my pride. I do not know how I lost my grip like that."

"You . . . don't recall what happened?"

He glances up at me as he gets to his feet. "I was descending the rigging, and I slipped."

"You did not feel anything unusual?"

"Non. Why?"

I look out over the ship's deck, which is now empty. "It was the ghost. He charged at you. Flew into the air and ran you through. I saw your face. You looked terrified."

"Interesting . . ."

"That is not the word I would use, Nicolas."

"Nico. You know how to say it, and so I now expect it."

"Even calling you by your first name is scandalous enough, Dr. Dupuis."

"Then embrace the scandal fully by employing my diminutive of choice." He takes a few tentative steps, wincing and rubbing his back. "You say the ghost rushed at me? I do not remember anything, but that would explain my fall. Is he still here? Can you ask him why he did so?"

"He is gone."

"Hmm, that is poorly done. Attack a man from the back and then flee." He raises his voice. "Out with you, sir. Do not hide your face. I demand recompense. Failing that, I would accept an explanation."

I shake my head.

"Did it say anything?" he asks.

"No. It did make a rather strange noise when it rushed at you. A guttural sort of sound. It seemed a noise rather than a word. An exclamation of—"

I cut myself off, remembering what I'd thought just before the ghost attacked. That the boy knew Nicolas.

"Miranda?"

I turn away as if surveying the deck. "While ghosts are usually harmless, they can be angry, and they can misdirect their anger at anyone who comes within their sights."

"So this ghost uttered a noise of anger as he attacked me. I would not expect him to utter a noise of joy."

"Precisely. Now, as you have been injured, you should sit here and allow me to find and speak to this ghost."

"I will do nothing of the sort. I do not fear further attacks. I understand that the anger is not directed at me, and the specter is blindly lashing out . . ."

He trails off and then peers at me. "You think otherwise."

"Of course not."

"Ah, I understand now. You saw the ghost of a man on a ship I once sailed, and you fear I know him. Fear that I am responsible for his demise? I am not a saint, chérie. I have dueled, though I insist on doing so with swords rather than pistols. I duel to first blood only, and I have never taken a life in such a manner. I have seen sailors die in raids. I have taken a life myself, in self-defence. However, the most likely scenario, if this ghost blames me, is a sadly more common one, where my own crewmates were injured, and I could not save them. I have lost four patients in such a manner. Three were beyond my help, and one was beyond my skill. I suspect this is such a case, and if so, then I appreciate the opportunity to allow the deceased to say his piece and blame me if he must."

I do not say such deaths are not his fault. Nicolas strikes me as a man who would feel each medical "failure" deeply but would also realize he had done his best and lay blame, correctly, on the inadequate medical knowledge of his time.

"It is a boy," I say.

His brows furrow. "A boy?"

"Of about fourteen."

He relaxes. "Ah, then it is neither one of my former patients nor anyone I knew. There was only one cabin boy on our ship, and he escaped capture. He was spotted in Whitby after the captain was arrested, and a family hid him and got him safely from the town. He is working outside York, I hear, apprenticed to a wainwright."

"Good," I say.

"Excellent, really. He did not belong on a ship. He was a stowaway. I found him myself, shortly after I was pressed into service. I tried to persuade him to go to shore, but he insisted on staying, and the captain took him on. He will have a better life in trade."

Nicolas starts for the ladder leading below. "This young man must be a local boy. I hope he was not drowned swimming to the ship. I know it must have provided ample temptation to the local children, but I did not ever see signs that they found their way aboard. There was one in particular who was most persistent. I do hope . . ."

He glances over. "The boy was not light haired, was he?"

I shake my head. "Dark haired."

"Not the same boy, then."

Nicolas opens a door and pokes his head through, only to laugh as he withdraws. "I am not certain why I did that, as I can hardly scout the way for you."

"I appreciate the sentiment, but yes, I ought to lead."

I slide down the stairs. Nicolas left a lantern belowdecks, and I take that and light it. Then I hold it up and peer down the hall.

"Hello!" I call. "If you can hear me, young man, I wish to speak to you. I saw you above deck, and I know you are a spirit."

No answer comes. I start down the hall with Nicolas right behind me. With each room we reach, I open the door to peer through. I am backing from one when a face shoots in front of mine so fast and so close that I let out a yelp and stumble back into Nicolas, who catches both me and the lantern before I drop it.

I shake myself and push upright from his grip.

"I am not your enemy, young man," I say briskly. "Do not pull such tricks on me, please. Not unless you wish to squander the rare opportunity to communicate with one who can hear you."

"What did he do?" Nicolas asks.

"I am fine. However, I think you should carry the lantern, to be safe."

He holds it up for me as I continue down the hall. There is no sign of the boy who attacked and then disappeared. I am braced now for such shenanigans, or so I tell myself, but when he does it again, I still yelp and fall back. Then I stamp my foot.

"You are being rude," Nicolas calls to the ghost. "I cannot hear or see you myself, but I can tell you are being most ungracious. Miss Hastings is offering her assistance. If you do not wish it, have the courtesy to say so."

Silence. I peer around and resist the urge to listen as well. Unless the boy speaks, I will not hear him as ghosts make no sound when they move.

I take two more steps, and he lunges from a closed door farther down. I tense, ready for attack, but he stays there, poised in the hall, his glare fixed on Nicolas.

I see the boy clearly now, and what catches my attention most is a terrible scar across his throat. Could that be how he died? I have never seen a ghost with signs of its passing still evident, but those who have say they see the wounds as they were at the time of death, and this one seems healed.

"Hello," I say. "I know you are angry but—"

He flies at Nicolas again, and I have only time to wheel and start to call a warning when he strikes. He runs right into Nicolas, and Nicolas's head jerks, his eyes widening in that same look of abject terror. He falls back, staggering, and the lantern crashes to the floor, the glass breaking, the fire igniting dried bits of rotten wood.

I run and stamp out the flames as Nicolas slumps against the wall, hands to his chest. Fire out, I steady him, but he's already recovering, breathing deeply.

"Do I wish to know what happened?" he says.

"You were attacked. Again. I fear this is a fool's errand. The boy is angry, and if he has never done this to you on your visits, then perhaps I am acting as some sort of conduit permitting physical attack. Either way, we cannot remain, or I fear he will give you heart failure next time."

I pick up the lantern and light it as best I can. The damage means it casts only the faintest illumination.

I raise my voice as I look up and down the empty hall. "Do you hear that, young man? We are leaving. If that is what you want, then you shall have it. If it is not, you have moments to speak. I know you have suffered. I saw the injury to your throat. But we did not cause that. We came to help."

"Injury to his throat?"

"A scar. I believe it is an old injury but . . . Nico?"

Nicolas braces himself against the wall, and I glare about for the ghost, but there is no sign of him.

"He has not spoken, correct?" Nicolas says, his voice low. "The ghost. He has said not a word."

"Only that noise."

"A guttural sound. Because it is all he can make."

Nicolas swallows, and when he speaks again, his voice is low. "He was attacked as a boy on the streets of Cartagena. Attacked and left for dead, but someone rushed him to a cloister, and the nuns were able to save his life. They could not save his voice. He is mute."

"Oh, Nico," I whisper. "You do know him."

Nicolas nods. "His name is Andrés."

13

B efore I can speak, Nicolas pushes from the wall, straightening.

"Andrés?" he calls. "It is Nico. I know you can hear me, and I know you are angry and—" His voice catches, grief clogging it until he must clear his throat, and even then, there is such pain in his voice that I feel as if I ought to retreat, that I am spying on a private moment.

"I do not blame you," Nicolas says. "Not for being angry, nor for being angry with me. I vowed to protect you."

A shape shimmers down the hall. It solidifies into the ghost, but he is too far away to see clearly.

"He is there," I whisper. "He hears you."

"I do not know what happened to you, Andrés. I knew that you were taken south. I knew that you were safe, and that was enough. It was not safe for you if I joined you or even checked on you. I wanted to, but others rightly dissuaded me. There is a price on my head, and you were safe."

The boy—Andrés—takes a few steps closer.

Nicolas continues, "I presume you died in some accident or misfortune, and you returned to your home—this ship. I am heartsick to know you are no longer in this world, yet you must not remain here. There is a better life waiting for you. I am certain of that."

Andrés continues forward. When I can see him, I suck in a breath at the anger on his face. He is bearing down on Nicolas. His lips move, and he makes a noise. I do not understand until he has repeated it thrice. Then the sound and the movement of his lips tell me what he is saying.

You lie.

I leap between them. "No, Andrés. Whatever happened to you, Nicolas could not prevent it. He was here, in Whitby. He could not go to you for your own safety."

Andrés's lip curls in a snarl.

You both lie.

"What is he saying?" Nicolas asks, his voice tight. "He is communicating in some way, yes?"

"I can make out a few words if he mouths them clearly. He says that he does not believe you, but I do not know why. Communication is difficult."

"He has a slate. I bought it for him and taught him to write. If we can find . . ." He looks around and then shakes his head. "That will not matter, will it? He cannot touch anything in this world."

Nicolas sidesteps to move past me. "Andrés. I swear that I am not lying about anything. I would like to know what you think I am lying about. May we do that? We will play the game of questions."

Nicolas looks at me. "I ask him a question, and he will nod or shake his head. If there is not an easy answer, he will raise his hand, and that means I need to be more specific in my—"

"Andrés!" I say. "Wait!"

I jog after the boy as he walks away. "Nicolas is trying to speak to you. To clear up what is obviously a terrible misunderstanding."

I pick up speed, and the boy shoots forward, disappearing behind a closed door.

"He went in here," I say as I grab for the handle.

Nicolas catches my hand. "That is the galley. It is not safe."

"But that is where he went."

Nicolas hesitates, his hand around mine. When he speaks, his voice is tentative. "In your experience, can spirits be malicious? I have heard it is possible. That they may not act in death as they did in life if they are consumed with anger."

"I-I have not encountered that, but I . . ." I look up at him. "You think Andrés may be leading us in there *because* it is not safe."

"The boy I knew would do no such thing."

"But he might if he were not himself."

"Oui."

I look at the door. "He is clearly angry. Angry with you, which does seem unreasonable. You were close?"

"There are dangers for a boy on a ship, as much as for a boy on the street, and I protected him from that. I treated him as I would my young nephews."

"Then yes, you were close, and if there were a misunderstanding, and he thought you had betrayed him, that would be far more devastating than the betrayal of a mere acquaintance. You say he once lived on the streets? Badly injured, obviously. I would presume he was not a boy who gave his trust easily?"

Nicolas nods. "The others called him my stray pup, but he was more of a wildcat. I still bear the scars from his scratches. As I said, life is not easy for a boy—or a girl—in such situations, and he was convinced I wanted . . ." He clears his throat. "Well, there are some men who take advantage of children in ways that no child should be . . ." Another throat clearing.

"They interfere with children in a despicable way, and Andrés was accustomed to men being kind only because they wanted something."

"Oui. Which is to agree that he did not trust easily, and so, if I understand your meaning, he would be even more angered by what he saw as a betrayal. In other words, he may be himself and *still* be trying to harm me, in his anger."

I nod. "So we can walk away and thwart his attempt at revenge, but if we do, then we leave him as a tormented spirit suffering under the mistaken belief that his protector failed him."

Nicolas swallows. "Is it mistaken? I was his protector, and if he is dead, then I did fail him. I wanted to go down to York. I wanted to assure him that I was well and assure myself he was, too, but others —rightly, it seemed—dissuaded me from doing anything that could place Andrés in jeopardy. If I could have helped him . . ."

"You had reason to stay away, but he is young, and he may not have seen it the same way. I would like to follow him, taking as much care as possible. I think it is important for both of you to set this right."

"I do not relish putting you in danger, Miranda."

"I do not like to interfere in your private business, but as only I can see him, leaving me out of it is impossible." I motion to the door. "Would you open this, please?"

He nods. "Then I will, of course, go with you."

14

The galley is in ruins. It seems that when the ship was being moved to this cove, a beam broke, and no one bothered to repair the damage. The entire ceiling has collapsed, and a huge cast-iron caldron fell through the floor. We must pick our way through the debris, with the weak lantern light guiding us.

The entire floor caves in toward the hole left by the caldron. One slip, and we'd plummet into the belly of the ship. It does not help that the floor is slick with mist from the damaged roof and that the rot has sprouted mold. Nicolas advises me to keep a hand on something at all times, lest my boots slide. We stay as far from the hole as we can, but with the collapsed ceiling, we must sometimes venture close to it in order to ease past the broken beams.

I am well aware that we face double danger here. Not only can we slip and fall—or slip and impale ourselves on broken boards—but there is a ghost who may wish us harm, and this is the optimal place to do it. Leap out at me and send me tumbling. Pass through Nicolas and give him that sudden shock that will send *him* tumbling.

I let Nicolas choose our path, which allows me to keep as much attention as possible on our surroundings. There has been no sign of

Andrés, and I want to believe that means he does not wish harm on Nicolas, but I fear it only means he is waiting for us to lower our guard. When he finally does peek through a closed door, I nearly do lose my grip, despite the fact he does not "pop" out or seem to be trying to startle me.

"He is there," I say, pointing at the closed door. "Andrés? Can you hear me?"

The boy turns my way for the first time. His long face is unreadable, but there is no fury in his eyes. Only grim determination. He steps through the door but remains just beyond it. Then he waves for me to follow, and the gesture seems almost reluctant.

"He wishes us to follow him into that room," I say. "He is still angry, but he is ready to give us a chance."

"Andrés? Would you come back into the hall, please? It is dangerous in here, and Miss Hastings has done nothing to deserve whatever punishment you might wish to inflict upon me. She is only trying to help us communicate."

Andrés meets my gaze. He holds it, and I see suspicion in his eyes. A natural suspicion.

He shakes his head and points at the closed door.

"He really does want us to follow him in there," I say. "Is there something inside that you wish us to see, Andrés?"

His mouth sets in a hard line. Then he nods abruptly and disappears inside.

"He says yes," I say. "He has gone into that room, whatever it might be."

"The pantry. It was also his quarters. He had a bed in the corner. Part of his job was to keep rats away from the foodstuffs, and that was more easily done if there was a person staying in the room. Or that is what the cook said, though I think he was just allowing the boy a warm and safe place to sleep, one with late-night food at hand."

"If it was his room, then there is probably something he wishes you to see. Or wishes you to have. That would make sense."

"It would."

Nicolas climbs over a broken ceiling beam. "Is there something in the pantry you wish me to see, Andrés?"

"He isn't here," I say. "He has gone inside."

"Wait there, please, crécerelle," he says when I start to follow. "It is not safe here, most of all. The floor is gone, and I must . . ."

He grunts as he swings over what I now see is a hole, as if something else smashed through the floor. On the other side, he grips the wall while balancing on what remains of the floor in front of the pantry door. It is little more than a ledge, and my heart stops on seeing it.

Do not trick him, Andrés. Please. Whatever you suffered, Nicolas was good to you. I know he was. Tell me you did not lure him into that precarious spot to harm him.

I stare at the door, focusing all my energy on it, ready to warn Nicolas if I see even a shimmer. There is none, and Nicolas grunts again as he positions himself better. Wood has fallen in front of the door, and he must move it aside. He's doing so when he stops. He's tugging one thick plank, and it isn't moving.

"It is stuck." Another tug, sharper.

"Careful, Nico. Please. It must be wedged in. Find where it is sticking."

He runs his hands along the plank. Then he goes still.

"It . . . it has been nailed on."

"Nailed . . . ?"

"Nailed over the door. On both ends."

His hands move over the plank. Then he grabs another and pulls, only to have it stay in place.

"This one as well. Also one below. Three planks have been nailed in place to keep the door shut. That makes no sense."

"It does if there's treasure within."

He glances over at me and then relaxes in a laugh. "Yes, of course. I did not dare approach the ship while she was in the harbor. She sat there for months. Someone must have secreted treasure in the pantry and nailed shut the door. Then the ship was moved, and the galley damaged. Either they could not get to the treasure, or they thought it safe."

As he talks, he is prying loose the nails with a pocketknife. He removes each board, talking as he does.

"Does this mean you understand, Andrés?" he says. "You understand that I did not abandon you, and so you are showing me this? It is not necessary. I need no treasure, and I would prefer to have the chance to speak to you through Miss Hastings, but as this seems important, I shall look."

He finishes removing the boards. Then he tries the knob.

"Locked, of course. Luckily, I have the key."

He takes the galley key from his pocket, which also fits into this lock. He turns it and pulls open the door. A smell rushes out. A smell that has my hand flying to cover my mouth and nose. Evidently, without a cabin boy sleeping in the pantry, the rats returned and found themselves locked in, dying amid the—

Nicolas lets out a cry. It is a horrible, anguished cry, and I lunge forward so fast I almost stumble into the hole.

"Nicolas? Nico!"

"Non." The word comes as a whisper. "No, no, no!"

Another cry, this one choked with rage, and I leap over the hole before I fully understand what I am doing.

I slip and scrabble and manage to grab the doorknob. Then I pull myself upright and push into the room to find Nicolas kneeling with his back to me. In front of him—

"Oh!" I say, and for a moment, I cannot breathe.

Nicolas doesn't hear me. He doesn't notice me there, no more than he did when I slipped, and I would not expect him to. Right now, he hears nothing but his own ragged breathing. Sees nothing but the figure curled up on the floor.

It is Andrés. His body, long dead, lying on the pantry floor.

Tears spring to my eyes, and I look around for the boy's ghost, only to see him in the shadows beside Nicolas. Watching Nicolas kneel over his mortal remains.

"I am so sorry," I say.

At first, Andrés does not look my way. Perhaps he presumes those words are for Nicolas, for his grief. But when I say them again, Andrés looks. Our eyes meet.

"I am so sorry, Andrés," I say. "This is . . ." Tears stream down my face. "It is . . ."

I cannot find words. In that moment, I do not want to be blessed with imagination. I do not want to be a writer who has learned the art of putting herself in another's place, imagining their lives. I am not imagining Andrés's life here. I am imagining his death. Locked in, with plenty of food but no water, pounding on the door for help that never came. It is too horrible to contemplate, and I can do nothing but cry as quietly as I can so I do not disturb Nicolas's grief. When I am able, I move behind him and kneel and lay my head on his back.

"I am sorry for you, too," I whisper. "Sorry that you saw this." I look at Andrés. "But you needed him to see it, didn't you? You needed him to know."

"Someone killed him," Nicolas says, barely able to get the words out. "Someone locked him in this room and nailed shut the door and . . ." His entire body shakes with rage as he pushes to his feet. "I will kill whoever did this. I swear that to you, Andrés. I will find him, and I will kill him."

There is satisfaction on Andrés's face. The satisfaction of knowing he is mourned, and of knowing someone vows revenge. After a moment, though, he shakes his head. He looks at me and shakes it again, mouthing no.

"He says no," I say. "I think he means he does not wish you to kill his murderer but only to bring him to justice. Is that it, Andrés?"

The boy nods. He makes a motion, as if putting a rope around his neck.

"He wants his killer to hang," I say. "Let him die as he should, branded a murderer."

"How did it happen?" Nicolas asks, looking in Andrés's direction as he helps me to my feet. "Did you return from York? Were you looking for me? You must have come here to fetch something from your quarters. Was someone on the ship? Not me. You know that, do you not? It was not me." His eyes round in horror. "You did not think it was me."

Andrés shakes his head emphatically.

"No," I say. "He did not. Is Nicolas right, Andrés? You returned from York to fetch something and—"

The ship lurches. For a moment, I think Andrés has attacked again. Nicolas falls against me, and I gasp, catching him even as I slam into shelves behind me. Then the ship jolts again, and I see Andrés standing where he has been the entire time, his head tilted as if listening to something above.

I hear it then. A low moan, followed by a scraping sound.

"Wh-what's happening?" I say as Nicolas rights himself and helps me do the same. "Is the ship collapsing?"

"It is not in such disrepair as that." His gaze sweeps the room. "Andrés? Would you do me a favor, please? We cannot safely leave this room in case the ship moves again. Would you see what is happening?"

The boy takes off, half-running and half-flying, through the door and then gone. An ominous creak sounds from somewhere in the belly of the ship. Then an odd flapping noise that has Nicolas's head jerking up.

"Is that a sail?" I say. "Did we knock one loose in our climb? Is the ship fighting against her moorings?"

"It takes more than a nudge to break a sail free, chérie. Yet it does sound like one. And it feels . . ."

He braces his feet as if testing. Beneath my boots, the floor seems to sway. It's barely noticeable until I try to take a step and my knees wobble.

"Are we moving?" I say.

"Yes, that is what I was just thinking. It has been a long time since I have been at sea, and I thought I might be mistaken, but no, we seem to be moving."

"How is that possible?"

"I have no idea."

Andrés reappears, his face animated for the first time since I've seen him. He glances about wildly. His gaze lands on something, a slate with chalk. His slate for communication.

The sight pokes at me, saying something is wrong, very wrong, something I was already working out. I cannot pursue it, though. Not when something far more critically important is far more critically wrong.

Andrés turns from the slate, which will do him no good in his current form.

"The ship is unmoored, non?" Nicolas says when I ask what Andrés has seen.

He's right—without that slate, Andrés must be asked questions answered in the affirmative or negative.

This one is affirmative.

"It is," I say quickly for Nicolas. "The ship has ripped from its moorings? Broken from its anchor?"

Andrés shakes his head.

"Breaking from the anchor is not possible," Nicolas says. "The chain is too thick, and I check it regularly. If it is undone, someone has undone it. Someone has raised the anchor."

Andrés nods emphatically.

"There is someone onboard?" I ask.

Andrés shakes his head and motions with his hand, as if showing someone running and then climbing.

"Someone *was* onboard," I say. "And they have raised the anchor and the sails?"

Andrés nods.

"We are at sea?" I say, twisting to face Nicolas.

Nicolas isn't there. He's striding across the pantry. In the doorway, he pauses, his hands braced as the ship rocks. He looks down into the hole. Then back at me.

"Come," he says. "I will help you over. We must get to the skiff."

I grab the shelves for balance as I make my way to him. "Can we not steer the ship? Lower the anchor and stop her?"

He gives a humorless laugh. "I am sorry, crécerelle. I do not mean to laugh. A ship like this *can* be steered by a small number of sailors, should tragedy decimate the crew. But two people cannot keep it on course, not when we are neither of us truly sailors. And we cannot drop the anchor while she is in motion."

My cheeks heat. I have written pirate stories, but admittedly, I skip past the parts about actually operating the ship. There are experiences a "lady" of my station cannot have, not unless she emulates my heroine and dresses as a boy to join a crew. I have considered that, but it does seem extreme for the sake of verisimilitude. Now, though, I wish I had done exactly that.

"We must get to the skiff," he says as he helps me over the hole. "Quickly."

"Before she heads to sea," I say. "Or crashes into the shore."

"She will do neither before we are in the skiff."

I steady myself and then reach out to help him across after me, but he waves me off and jumps before I can protest. When one of his feet slips, my heart nearly stops. I grab for him, but he recovers his balance.

As I turn to continue on, the plank beneath me cracks, the sound loud as a shot. I slide, flailing. Nicolas catches the back of my shirt, but I am falling, and he is going to fall with me.

I fall into the hole, and he drops to the floor before I drag him with me. He's still holding me, my shirt wrapped in both his hands. His lower half remains on solid floor, and I clutch the edge of the hole in both hands.

"I am going to back up," he says. "I am secure. Wriggle onto the floor as best you can, and then I shall haul you out."

"If you begin to slide, you must release me. Promise me that you will—"

He shimmies backward, hauling me from the hole as I pull myself out, wincing against the pain in my arm. When I am on the solid floor, we scramble to our feet, and I nudge him farther from the hole . . . and nearly push him into the bigger one in the middle of the galley. We catch our balance, and then we start making our way around that larger hole.

A creak sounds overhead. Then a noise to my left, and I look to see Andrés waving wildly to get my attention. He jabs a finger at a rotted and broken beam. It groans, ready to snap right over our heads.

I snatch Nicolas's arm and launch myself, shouting a warning just as the beam gives way. We hit the floor, with him atop me, debris raining down on his legs.

"You must stop saving my life, crécerelle," he says.

"Did you not just save mine? Also, it was not I but Andrés who saved your life this time, by alerting me to the breaking beam." I look over to where the boy is watching us. "Thank you, Andrés."

He motions with both hands, telling us to get moving before we become ghosts ourselves.

15

W e are above deck, clinging to the railing as we make our way along it. I am behind him, and he seems to fear I will slide straight into the sea. He has insisted, therefore, that I hold his left hand as we both use our right to grip the railing. His insistence is not as ridiculous as it seems. The lurching is worse now as the ship reaches open water beyond the cove. The wind has picked up, the mainsails snapping.

"She should be sailing straighter than this," Nicolas says as the ship sways. "She is damaged worse than I realized. I tried to keep her afloat, but I am not a shipwright."

"Could someone have damaged her?" I say. "While she was docked in Whitby?"

"I have considered that. The galley should not have collapsed as it did. Vandals must have set upon the ship . . ." He trails off, as if he's realizing what has just occurred to me.

"Someone did it after Andrés . . ." He swallows, the sound still audible even with the water smacking the side of the boat. "He did not return to the ship from York. The damage was done after he was nailed in that room. Someone did not want him found, his body discovered, and so when I returned to the ship and found the galley impassable, I left it."

"His slate was on the shelf," he continues a moment later. "It was where he always kept it. If he returned from York to fetch something from his quarters, he would not have brought it along and put it there—"

The ship lurches again, and this time, we both slip and smack into the railing. Nicolas's hands cover mine as we wait for the ship to even out again. Then we carry on in silence. When we reach the spot where he hung the rope, he peers over the side.

"Miranda?" he says, his voice strained. "Do you see a rope in the water?"

I lean, gripping his hand and the railing, and I squint down to see the pale snake of a rope whipping along the side of the ship.

"The skiff," I whisper. "They found the skiff."

"Found it and cut it loose."

The ship makes a sound. A terrible, low creak that has Nicolas's head jerking up. He scrabbles to his feet and looks around. Andrés appears, running across the deck. He's motioning wildly at the ship.

"Something is wrong," I say. "Something is breaking."

Andrés nods and continues gesturing, telling us to get off the ship and quickly.

I turn to Nicolas. "Andrés is here. Tell me what I can ask him to know what is wrong."

Andrés shakes his head, his gestures turning panicked.

"Non," Nicolas says. "It does not matter what is happening. We cannot fix it."

Andrés nods emphatically. He runs to the side and looks down. When he glances back at me, his eyes are huge.

"Yes, the skiff is gone," I say. "Is there another lifeboat? Another way off the ship?"

Both shake their heads.

"Can you swim?" I ask Nicolas.

He gives a harsh laugh. "I swim as well as I walk. But this is the North Sea. We would perish of the cold before we made it to shore."

I squint over the railing. I can barely see the shore. When I turn, the lights of Whitby are fading to my left. The abbey looms on the hill. We have passed the town already.

I'm turning back to Nicolas when I see another light. This one is behind us. At sea.

"A boat!" I say. "There is a boat right there. A night fisherman."

I start to make my way back to the rear of the ship. Nicolas grabs for me, but I wave him off and keep going. The small boat is no more than a hundred feet off the stern.

"It is following us," I say. "It sees we are in distress. We need to let the fisherman know there are people aboard. Then we can descend the rope, and they can pick us up."

Nicolas says something, but the wind whips away his words. I stand at the railing and wave my arms over my head. The small craft is even closer than I thought. And there is a man on the front of the ship, arms crossed. I wave more.

He gestures back. A gesture that even I know is a rude one.

I stare, my breath catching. Then my cheeks heat in shame.

"That is not a night fisherman, is it?" I say as Nicolas moves up beside me. "It is not a fishing boat."

"Non, chérie."

"It is the men who set us adrift. Which they did not do accidentally while you were aboard."

"Non, chérie. They knew I was here." He turns to look behind us. "Andrés? Are you there?"

"He is," I say as the boy runs over.

"Are these the men who boarded the ship?"

Andrés leaps onto the railing, nearly giving me heart failure until I remember he is no longer bound by the limitations of our world. He leaps again, this time onto the stern.

When he returns, he nods and gestures.

"He says, yes, it is the boat he saw beside the *Temerity*, and two of the men are the ones he saw onboard. The one in front is not."

"Because he sent his lickspits to do his bidding. As he always does."

"That is Lord Norrington, is it not?"

"It is."

I squint out at the man. It's the one who made a rude gesture to us. At first, I thought he was elderly. Now I realize his white hair is a wig. We are in a time when men, particularly those of noble birth, wore them. The other two wear their hair long and pulled back, like the two who confronted Nicolas in Hood's Lane. Are they the same men? I cannot tell from here.

"If we did jump in to swim, they would come after us," I say.

"Oui."

"And not to save us."

A wry smile. "Non, crécerelle. Not to save us, I fear."

"Norrington is making certain you do not escape this fate. Being set adrift in the ocean."

"It is a convenient way to rid himself of an inconvenient man, non? I am *most* inconvenient. A pirate who may be innocent of the charges, even if his shipmates were not, as I was only the ship's doctor. A man of color, which should make it easy to cast me in the role of brigand, but also French, which is inconvenient. I am also of noble birth, which is *very* inconvenient."

"You are not an unknown ship's hand he might easily see hanged, so he is trying to kill you another way. Ambushed by brigands on a dark road. Or disappearing along with your ship."

"I am still not entirely convinced the men in the lane wanted me dead," he says. "Without a doubt, this is a much more convenient fate, and Norrington is ensuring I do not escape it."

I won't point out that he's wrong about the intentions of those men in the lane—I have watched him die too often to question it. At least now he understands that Norrington will not settle for merely arresting him. He wants him dead. Dead not for piracy but for kindness—for helping those who helped him.

Norrington is sentencing Nicolas to a fate worse than hanging. To being adrift at sea until he perishes, alone and helpless. The same way a fourteen-year-old boy died beneath our very feet. A boy who committed no crime at all.

Rage fills me, and I stare at that wigged man as if I could shoot bullets from my eyes. Then I stop, and my gaze drops over the side of the boat.

"Those cannons," I say. "Do they still fire?"

"I believe so, but . . ." Nicolas trails off and then breaks into a grin. "Why, crécerelle, I do believe I love you. I hope you are suggesting what you seem to be suggesting."

"We need to get rid of Norrington's boat if we wish to escape."

"We do indeed. Yes, the cannon should work, and better yet, I know how to fire it." He reaches for my hand. "Come. Let us send the lord a message of our own."

۞

NICOLAS READIES THE REAR CANNON AS ANDRÉS BOUNCES WITH GLEE. I do not ask whether these could be the men who murdered him. That will come later. Let him have his delight at this moment, which I heartily endorse.

We raced off the deck as quickly as we could move with the lurching ship. If Norrington has any inkling that we were *not* fleeing, we see no sign of that. His boat remains to the port side of the stern, his men steering and sailing to keep it there.

Once the cannon is readied, Nicolas turns it toward the small boat, and then we all get a few moments to bask in the panic on Norrington's face as he sees that cannon swing their way.

Norrington shouts orders to the men. The boat begins to turn. Nicolas is ready to fire the cannon, and for a heartbeat, as he pauses, I think he has changed his mind. But no, he is only waiting for the correct angle, because he is a decent man, even when dealing with those who seek to kill him.

Nicolas fires when the smaller ship presents her starboard side. The cannon booms, and the ball blows a hole through, near the stern.

More shouts, rising above the wind. The men clamber over the deck and disappear belowdecks. Their boat turns in a lazy circle as our ship pulls away.

We stand there until we are certain their craft is disabled.

"Will they sink?" I say.

"Not if they can get her to shore in time, which they appear to be doing." Nicolas backs away from the cannon. "That was a most pleasant diversion. However . . ."

"It does not change the fact that *our* ship is heading out to sea."

He motions for me to follow him back above deck. Once we're there, he lets out a curse in French.

"Non," he says. "We are not heading to sea. We are heading to shore. To dash upon the rocks." He turns. "Andrés? You know more than I do about navigation. How do I steer her toward shore and slow her progress?"

"Steer her *toward* shore?" I say.

"I would prefer to simply run aground, but at worst, we could jump if we were close enough to shore."

"Ah, I see. Yes, that makes sense."

Andrés motions that he can help instruct Nicolas on how to steer and slow the ship, and he does, showing me the correct riggings to use and how to turn the sails, which I pass onto Nicolas as we do it together. Soon, while we are still heading for the shore—the *rocky* shore—we have slowed.

Nicolas continues working on the sails. Through the spyglass, he sees what looks like safer shoreline ahead.

As he navigates, I talk to Andrés. It is not uncommon for ghosts to be bound to the site of their death, especially when it is something like a ship. If that is the case, I need to ask my questions now. Should the ship run aground, we may not be easily able to return for my questions.

We will return—of course—to set Andrés free. First, I must know who killed him. That is the key. I must name his killer, and I cannot make a mistake or I risk condemning him to life as a ghost.

I ask questions, and he answers in nods and shakes of his head and through pantomime. He must stop now and then to give instructions for Nicolas, when the ship does not behave as she ought, but otherwise, we are left to our discourse. Soon, I have a picture of what happened to him.

I find Nicolas at the helm.

"The rudder is not operating as it should," he says. "We seem to be on course for that stretch of shoreline, though. It will be a rough landing, and we may need to swim, but we will not crash."

"Good. Crashes are far more fun in fiction than reality."

He smiles over at me. "Agreed. Now what did Andrés tell you?"

I relate the story, as best I could determine based on simple yes and no questions. When the crew was taken, Andrés was indeed in town, presumably spending his earnings from the enemy ships they had "liberated" of their fortunes on the high seas.

He was supposed to meet up with Nicolas, but he was late, and he arrived to see the crowd at the dock, the captain and some of the crew arrested. He fled and took shelter outside of town.

At the time, he presumed Nicolas had been taken with the others. When he returned, he found the hanged men, with Nicolas not among them. He snuck onto the ship to look for Nicolas. I do not tell Nicolas this part—he does not need to know that Andrés had been looking for him, relying on him.

As much as I want to set Andrés's spirit free by naming his killer, in some ways, I think that knowing his protector did not abandon him is equally important. Nicolas's story makes sense to Andrés. This is the man he knows—who would neither abandon him nor endanger him.

Of course, the question now is, Who told Nicolas this? I can't ask that yet. Not as we are fighting for our lives. There will be time for that difficult discussion later.

After Andrés could not find Nicolas, the boy returned to the ship, likely hiding out there for the same reason Nicolas later made it his storage spot. No one would expect the crew to go near that ship again.

At that time, it was in dock, and Nicolas had indeed not dared get near it. The ship stayed in dock as the authorities decided what to do with it. All that time, Andrés was aboard.

One night, he overheard voices. None were any he recognized, so he quickly retreated. He was spotted and pursued, but he seemed to lose his pursuer and made it to the pantry. When he heard banging outside the pantry door, he braced for capture, but no one came.

Before he could try the door, another sound came, that of someone sawing wood. Sawing through a beam, as we know. The galley collapse was not accidental. Someone cut the beam, and the roof caved in, and Andrés huddled in the pantry and counted himself lucky that his own roof had not collapsed. Then he discovered the purpose of that hammering. He was trapped.

He tried to get free. He banged about and made what little noise he could. No one heard him. No one could get close enough to the pantry, which was intentional.

It was all intentional. So unbelievably intentional. Someone didn't lock Andrés in that room temporarily. They locked him in and then ensured he could not escape or be rescued.

There is cowardice in that. Monstrous cowardice. Killing Andrés outright would have been despicable, but it was still better than sentencing him to a slow death with no chance of survival.

I do not believe that the killer wanted to torture Andrés. What could a boy do to deserve such a horrible death? Nothing. They killed him this way because they were too cowardly to murder him outright.

Kill a fourteen-year-old boy? No, that is wrong. Let us simply lock him in a room and ensure he cannot escape. Let nature take her course.

Just like Lord Norrington attempted with us, setting the *Temerity* out to sea.

Back to Andrés. After the galley was destroyed, the ship was towed to the cove. That may have been the impetus for the move. She was rotting and falling apart—or so it appeared—and the court case seemed unlikely to be resolved soon.

Did Andrés's killer have a hand in the decision to move the ship? It is a very good question. Either way, the *Temerity* was moved, and by the time Nicolas got aboard, Andrés would have been long dead.

"I have asked whether he saw his killer," I say. "He did not. He was too busy fleeing, and they never said a word, so he cannot tell us anything about them. I asked about those he heard talking. Again, he could not identify them. He thinks he may have heard Lord Norrington. The man had been onboard before, during the day, and he recognized him just now in the boat. He thinks he heard his voice that day, but he cannot say with certainty."

"They thought he overheard something," Nicolas says. "They came onboard in the night for some nefarious purpose. Someone spotted Andrés. They thought he had seen or heard their plotting."

"He did not."

"Yet they killed him anyway. Lord Norrington would not have nailed up the door himself. He'd have given the order. Can we still name Norrington as Andrés's killer?"

"We could if we were absolutely certain that is what happened."

"We need proof. Confirm it was Lord Norrington. Confirm he ordered Andrés's death. I am certain of it, but we cannot chance erring. We must—"

The ship lurches. Nicolas grabs for me as I stumble. A howl, as if from the heavens themselves, and the sails snap.

"The wind," Nicolas says. "She is picking up."

He starts to run when another lurch knocks him to his knees. I hurry to him and help him to his feet, and we get to the sails, trying to lower them, but the wind catches, and the ship changes direction. It is a small change. One that would be unnoticeable on the high seas. Here, though, this close to the rocky shore, it is catastrophic.

"We cannot bring her around." Nicolas shouts to be heard as the wind whistles. "We do not have enough room!"

I peer over the side. The craggy shore is less than a hundred yards away, and we are headed straight for it.

"Can we swim?" I say. "Or prepare to?"

"Prepare to, oui." He turns. "Andrés?"

I point. "He is here."

"I am not abandoning you," Nicolas says to the ghost. "I am leaving the ship, for obvious reasons, but I will return. Whatever happens, I will return and free you."

"He is waving for you to stop talking and go."

Nicolas gives a short laugh. "He is wise. Yes, I am going. I will find who did this to you and return. I promise you that."

16

We debate leaving our swords on the ship. Mine is small enough to pose no encumbrance, so I will take it. Nicolas's is longer and heavier, and it may impede swimming, but he is loath to be weaponless when we reach the shore. In the end, we keep both.

We lower ourselves on the rope we used to climb onto the ship. I am quite an avid swimmer, being fonder of physical activity than is good for any woman of childbearing years. Or that is conventional wisdom, which my father considered utter nonsense. As children, we were encouraged to be as active as we wished. My childhood veered between the extremes. Days spent running wild at a holiday house on the coast, gone from sunup to sundown, along with days spent never leaving my room, my mind traveling to the worlds I discovered in books. Yet there is a great difference between leaping twenty feet from a cliffside and plunging from a vessel the size of the *Temerity*.

The first problem is the wake. The ship is careening for the coast, and we risk being caught in her wake and sucked underneath. The second problem is my unfamiliarity with the water. My mother taught me to dive, and the cardinal rule there is to always understand the water into which you are diving. Know the depth. Know the conditions—rocks or kelp or any other hazards. That is impossible here. It is dark, and we are leaping into murky water, and we must jump from high enough to avoid the wake yet low enough that we do not dash ourselves on rocks.

Nicolas goes first. Please note that I do not agree to let him go first. He wisely doesn't ask. He jumps while I am positioning myself to do so, and thus he takes the risk, and I will refrain from chiding him about that later, just as I will refrain from letting him know I find his chivalry unexpectedly charming.

He jumps into the water and lands easily, but the wake begins to pull him under. Every impulse in me screams to jump in and help. I know better. This, too, is a lesson from my mother. If someone is caught in an undertow, you cannot save them by jumping in after them—you'll both drown. You need to stay on firm ground and throw something to pull them out.

I scramble onto the ledge over the railing and prepare to throw the climbing rope, but Nicolas has already freed himself. A few strong strokes, and he's safe.

Now it is my turn. Nicolas gestures for me to jump farther than he did, which I am already calculating. He swims alongside the ship as I crouch, check my trajectory and then throw myself from the side of the ship with as much force as I can.

I hit the water. It is not a dive—that would be unsafe—but rather an awkward jump, and I plunge under the surface. The ship's wake yanks at me, firm and insistent, but I focus on getting my head above water. Fingers touch mine. I take two long strokes in that direction, until I am certain I am free of the wake. Then I let Nicolas take my hand in a quick squeeze.

"You are well?" he says.

I nod, and we begin the swim for shore. As strong a swimmer as I am, even without my injured arm, Nicolas would be stronger. He insists on staying behind me, which is infuriating but, yes, also very considerate. I swim as quickly as I can for the rocky shore, my teeth chattering, fingers going numb.

Then my leg strikes sharp rock. It's the same leg that was shot, right above the same place. I gasp, and my mouth fills with water, and I begin to choke. Between the pain and the choking, my mind blanks, and I flail.

Something grabs me, cold as ice, and I flail again, only to realize it's Nicolas. He holds me above water. The night air, pleasantly cool before, is like being taken from an ice bath and plunged into ice itself. I convulse but force myself to breathe.

When he tries to swim with me under his arm, I wriggle out and continue on. My arms barely move now. I no longer feel the pain in my leg, because I no longer feel my leg. My perfect strokes have turned into the flails of a drowning soul, and it takes all my energy to propel my dead-weight arms up and over my head. Then my knee hits something else, and I brace for the pain. None comes, and I presume that is the lack of feeling, but then I realize my other knee is also touching something.

I am on sand. I am nearly at the shore, yet I can barely feel the ground under my knees, and when I put my hand down, I only know it is touching the earth when it stops moving. My entire body is numb, and yes, I panic at the thought of that, of the effect such cold can have, but I force myself to crawl on my numb limbs until I am out of the water.

Nicolas is right behind me, and as I sit there, teeth chattering, he wraps his arms around me. At first, it is like being held by a dead man. Then I feel the barest flicker of warmth. With icy hands, he moves mine up under his armpits, where that warmth leaps out, a flame in the ice.

I gesture for him to do the same with his hands, and we huddle there, perhaps the most intimate embrace I have ever shared, the two of us entwined. While I'm sure I will look back on this later, right now, it is devoid of any sensuality. We are freezing—quite literally freezing—and this is survival.

When he can finally speak, his teeth still chattering, he says, "I was attempting to haul you to shore, crécerelle, but you insisted on doing it yourself, and it is most vexing. If I cannot save you, however will I make you swoon for me?"

"I am certain you will think of a way or two."

I say it simply, no double entendre intended, but his face lights in a grin. "Oh, I am certain I can think of a way or two as well."

"Excellent, but at the moment, my only interest is in getting warm."

"That is what I mean, crécerelle. A way to make you very warm."

He waggles his brows, mock-seductive, and I can only sputter a laugh that turns into a full fit of the giggles, spurred by the overwhelming relief that we have survived. We are off the ship and safe on shore and alive.

He leans over and gives me a kiss, his touch cool but not horribly so, and when I kiss him back, his lips part to the most delicious warmth. I wriggle closer, kissing him deeper, drinking in that warmth. His hands slide over my waist, beneath the soaked shirt and along the skin under my corset. Heat trails in their wake. His breathing picks up, fingers traveling up my corset to the ties before stopping himself.

"That is enough of that, Nico," he murmurs. "There are more appropriate—and efficient—ways to warm a lady in serious danger of freezing."

"I am not the least bit concerned about appropriate," I say. "But, in this situation, efficiency may be called for. Other warming methods may follow at a more suitable time."

His grin sparks again. "I will remember you said that, crécerelle."

"I am relying on it, sir."

He laughs and embraces me one more time. Then he rises, his legs still wobbly, and peers about.

"I see a sheltered spot in the cliffside, perhaps a hundred feet that way, if we can manage it. If we see driftwood—or dried seaweed—we ought to gather it for a fire."

"And rocks to spark the fire?"

"Chérie, I am a sailor." He lifts a pouch on his belt. "I have waterproof matches."

"Perfect."

WE FIND NOT ONLY A NOOK CARVED INTO THE ROCK BUT, JUST A FEW feet away, a cave that will provide complete shelter. Nicolas starts the fire at the opening to let the smoke escape. Then we hunker down beside it.

Nicolas clears his throat. "I realize that I was being playful earlier with my flirtations, and in light of that, my next suggestion may seem more of the same. I make it with the assurance that it is not. We have been exposed to a dangerous cold, and we are warming ourselves now, but as long as we continue to be clothed in cold and wet attire . . ."

"You are suggesting we should disrobe."

His skin tone does not permit an obvious blush, but I am still certain he does exactly that. His voice loses its usual confidence. "Y-yes. That is to say, we ought to remove some of our outer layers, at least until we are warmer. I will turn my back, of course, and avert my gaze as much as is possible, to allow you your modesty."

"If anything I have said or done has led you to believe I am a woman of modesty, then I have given entirely the wrong impression. Would I be comfortable sitting naked at the fire? No. I wish I were, but I am not yet that woman. Would I be comfortable in my underthings? Certainly, and if you still wish to avert your gaze . . . or if you wish me to do the same, then we shall do so."

He relaxes. "That is very practical of you, crécerelle, and I appreciate it."

"Oh, there is no practicality at all. I simply wish to see you in your undergarments."

He laughs, relaxing more, as I assure him I am teasing and he may undress as much or as little as he wishes. I do turn my back for that part. I cannot help it. I might abhor the ridiculous degree to which I am expected to hide myself, lest my bare skin inflame male passions, but I have still internally recognized my society's limits and the perils of ignoring them altogether. So I have my back to Nicolas as I strip off my outer garments, leaving on only my bottom layer of clothing—my corset and drawers.

I turn to see Nicolas studiously gazing upon the cave wall, which is very sweet, particularly in that it affords me the opportunity to enjoy the sight of him without being seen doing so. He has taken off both his shirt and undershirt, leaving his upper body bare, and it is . . . Oh my, it is a sight to behold.

One of my friends, who shares my interest in carnal matters, is fond of working-class men. Stable hands and blacksmiths and such. She waxes rhapsodic about their physiques. My lovers have been men of my own class and higher, not given to athletic endeavors more strenuous than a good fox hunt. I will admit I have admired the muscular forearms on a groom or dockworker, but I presumed that was mostly because it was more exposed skin than I would see on a man of my own class.

I was mistaken.

Nicolas's class is above my own, so *that* is not the explanation. While I *have* seen powerfully built men of nobility, I never see them in anything except long sleeves and buttoned collars. I will also say that Nicolas is not constructed like a strapping dockworker, with forearms the size of my thighs. His build is slighter, and as such, it is perfection in its lines and symmetry. His bare back and arms show a man fond of athleticism and not afraid of hard work, the result being a physique that has me growing very warm, despite being in wet and cold underthings.

I have seen such male physiques before, but they have always been sculpted in marble . . . and are usually missing a limb or head. Nicolas, from the rear, is perfection, and I find my mouth dry just looking at him. My mouth dry and my body hot, growing warmer by the minute as my gaze drops to his hips, his skin visible through the wet ivory fabric of his drawers—

"Crécerelle?" he says. "May I turn?"

I want to say no. *Sorry, but no, I am suddenly very shy, and you must sadly continue facing the cave wall . . . so that I might continue staring at you.*

"Yes, of course," I say, and drop my gaze, not out of modesty but respect, lest I be caught gaping.

He turns, and out of the corner of my eye, I see him tense. He clears his throat quickly and sits nearly as quickly, and I am left standing there, almost naked, feeling as if he barely bothered to look at me. Worse, fearing he got just enough of a look to decide he didn't want a longer one.

"Would you be more comfortable if I pulled on my shirt and trousers?" I say.

He gives a laugh in a tone I can't quite decipher. "More comfortable, oui, but that is hardly the point, which is to ensure you are warm and as dry as possible."

My heart sinks, and the heat evaporates in a blink. "I do not mind dressing if the sight of me is repellant."

"Repellant?" He twists to face me. "I thought I knew what that word meant, crécerelle, but clearly I do not."

I sit quickly, pulling my knees in. "I am sorry if that sounded as if I were fishing for compliments. I understand that the situation is uncomfortable."

"Not in the way you seem to think." He stretches to lean over far enough to kiss my bare shoulder. "I am trying to be a gentleman and not gape at you with proof of my interest making itself obvious."

When I frown, he smiles and kisses my shoulder again. "If my meaning is not clear, I will not explain further and only be glad I did nothing to embarrass either of us. And I know you are not fishing for compliments, so I will only say . . ."

He meets my eyes and switches to French, letting loose a torrent of it that has my eyes narrowing.

"That is most unfair," I say.

"Is it? I would not wish to be overly forward in my flattery, particularly considering your current state of dress and the fact that it is for necessity, and not for my viewing pleasure."

I roll my eyes.

"Would you like me to say a few words of admiration in English?" he asks.

"Not now," I say. "The buildup has been too great, and the moment has passed. I will say only that I ought to apologize for having taken so long to tell you to turn around. I was caught up in admiring the view, which is, I must say, quite perfect. You are an excessively handsome man fully clothed, but quite devastating in your drawers."

His mouth opens. Shuts. Opens again. Pauses a moment before he says, "And so you deliver a breathtaking compliment in such an efficient manner that I am not certain how to respond."

"As you said, efficiency is the order of the day." I turn to face the fire again and inch closer to it. "And in light of that efficiency, no response is required."

"All right, then, let me skip past a response and move straight to my own words of admiration—"

"No."

"No?"

"The moment has passed. You missed it. I am quite bereft. Now, let us discuss the ship."

"Wait. Allow me to tell you how—"

"How we are going to warm ourselves quickly—and efficiently—and then see whether the ship has crashed close enough to shore to salvage your goods? Excellent."

He says a few words in French.

"I do not think that was a compliment," I say.

"Oh, it is, my crécerelle. A compliment wound in a blasphemy, and my mother would be shocked and appalled, but I stand by the sentiment. As for the ship, at this very moment, I am not overly concerned about my goods."

"Well, I am. So let us warm ourselves and then go investigate."

⚜

THE SHIP HAS INDEED CRASHED, ABOUT A HALF MILE AWAY, ON EXACTLY the sort of craggy shoreline we'd feared. We can see her in the darkness, which remains dark enough that we can be relatively certain no one heard or saw the wreck. She's at the base of a steep cliff, which will help keep her secret until morning.

It is a very long walk. Oh, the shore is flat enough up near the cliff, and now that our underthings have dried, it is not terribly cold. No, the problem is Nicolas. He does not stop talking the entire way, which would not be a problem if I could understand a word he's saying. He's speaking French. From the cadence, I presume it is poetry. Reciting French poetry to me, which would be wonderfully romantic if I had the first inkling what he was saying.

"You can stop that anytime," I say as I pick my way over a rocky portion of the beach.

"I know."

"Let me rephrase that. Either switch to English or stop that."

"It does not sound the same in English. You cannot simply translate poetry."

"Then try some in English."

"English poetry? Does such a thing even exist?"

I make a face at him.

"I cannot imagine why you should wish me to stop. Have you tired of men wooing you with poetry? I suppose it can become quite dull after a while. All those odes to your golden hair, your soft skin, your . . . truly exceptional buttocks."

I glance back to see him gazing at the body part in question. "You're reciting poetry to my arse?"

"About your arse." He makes a face. "What a terrible word. Do you see what I mean about the English language?"

"The point is that if I don't know what you're saying, I have no idea whether it's complimentary or not."

"Ah. I see the problem. I also see the solution. You will have to learn French."

I turn to him. "Eakingspay ofay arsesay, oursyay isay ulytray ectacularspay."

His brow furrows. "Is that Latin?"

"Dog Latin."

"Dare I ask what you said?"

"No, sorry, you will have to learn Dog Latin."

"There is no such thing. You have made it up."

When I only continue walking, he jogs up beside me. "What did you say?"

"Something about you."

"And it was complimentary?"

"Definitely."

"About what?"

"Is that a cave?" I say, turning. "That appears to be an opening there. We ought to check it out. You'll need a place to store any items we rescue from the ship."

"What did you say about me?"

I head to the opening. "It looks like a cave. Come, take a closer look."

"You will not tell me, will you?"

"Will you tell me?"

"Fine." He stops, arms folded. "Here is part of a poem I recited, by Pierre de Ronsard, translated as best I am able."

My lady woke upon a morning fair,
What time Apollo's chariot takes the skies,
And, fain to fill with arrows from her eyes
His empty quiver, Love was standing there:
I saw two apples that her breast doth bear
None such the close of the Hesperides
Yields; nor hath Venus any such as these . . .

He glances over. "Now yours?"

"I said your arse is spectacular."

He sputters. "I see . . . While I do appreciate the sentiment, I believe mine was somewhat more romantic."

"I was complimenting your posterior. You were complimenting

my breasts. I do not believe you occupy the higher moral ground here, sir. Now, on to the cave."

"Are you asking me to explore your cave, crécerelle?"

"Perhaps later. Unless you continue to annoy me with French poetry."

"Annoy you? I am wooing you. Wait. Did you say yes to my indecent offer? I believe you did."

"No, I said *perhaps*, the likelihood of which is dropping with each moment you delay. Understood?"

"Oui, mademoiselle. I also understand that you said that cave exploration is a delight that may well exist in my near future. It is a decision you will not regret."

"Do you have that letter of recommendation yet? No? Then stop talking and get moving."

17

The cave is perfect for storage, being high enough from the high tide mark, with an easier walk up than his hideaway. With that, Nicolas does set aside the teasing, and he gets to work. We find two more small caves before reaching the ship. Then it is on to the *Temerity* herself, and not a moment too soon. The rocks have torn through her side, and she is listing and taking on water, having crashed into jagged boulders twenty feet from shore. That means we must venture into the water to get to her and then take great care unloading her most valuable cargo.

Nicolas asks me to wait on shore, and I do not wish to agree, but this is the practical solution. He wades to the boat, swimming if necessary, and then rigs up a rope to send goods down to me on the beach, where I can collect them. There is little point in both of us making our way onto a badly damaged ship, especially when only one of us knows our way around it.

The only reason for me to go onboard would be to speak to Andrés, but the boy can still communicate with me—as best he can communicate—by gestures from the ship. I have little else to ask him at this point. He confirms that he seems unable to leave the ship, which is concerning but not unexpected. I assure him we will find him, even if the wreckage is removed. Given how slowly they have tended to the ship thus far, I doubt anyone will be towing it soon. The true issue will be scavengers, and we are doing what we can to minimize that loss.

It is a slow process. Some of the items cannot be transported on our makeshift pulley line, and Nicolas must bring them out by hand. Fortunately, he has found a path that allows him to do so by wading up to his waist, the objects held over his head. He brings various imported goods, such as spices and textiles, and some local ones. And he brings rum. All of the rum.

When we have finished, I insist he warm himself by a fire. Then we divvy up the "treasure" between the three caves and hide the entrances. We consider taking refuge in one ourselves, but if anyone comes to raid the ship, we do not want to give away the location of the goods with smoke or sound.

We take one bottle of rum, a few foodstuffs and dry clothing. Nicolas also brings a satchel. I ask him what's in it, but he replies in French, and we are *not* getting into that again, so I refrain from demonstrating any further curiosity.

We return to our original cave, and Nicolas relights the fire. Then we open the rum, and he digs out a round of cheese. We pass both back and forth a couple of times before he says, "Would you like to know what is in the satchel, crécerelle?"

"Love letters, I presume. Letters from you to a fair English maiden. You wooed her with French poetry, and she sent them all back with a single note. *I cannot read these, you lout.*"

"I deserved that, I suppose. Mais non, they are not letters to or from a lover."

"Pornographic sketches, then. To keep you warm on long voyages across the bitter—and bitterly lonely—seas."

He grins. "Non, though I am certain I could have found those onboard. The men often asked me to—" He stops short and waggles the satchel. "While you were undoubtedly being sarcastic, you did approach a truth, and so I shall grant you that answer."

He opens the satchel, carefully keeping it from my line of sight. One hand slides in and returns holding a pencil and pad of paper. Then he settles back, tilts his head and starts to write.

"If you are scribbling damnable French poetry . . ." I say.

"You shall have to endure it. Mais non, writing is your talent, not mine. I am forced to steal from the pens of others. My poetry is another sort, and it is, admittedly, French, as I can be nothing else."

He continues, pencil moving over the paper in decisive strokes. Then he frowns at it, making a moue of dissatisfaction as he says, "Non, that is not quite right."

"I will not ask what you mean. I am not the least interested—"

He turns the paper around, and I am on it. My face, rendered in quick strokes. It is the face I catch sometimes in a reflective surface, that moment of surprise when I think, "Is that me?" but when I look in a mirror, that woman is gone. It is me, but the angle is not one I see.

"You flatter me," I say.

"Not at all. If anything, the result is underwhelming. That is the limitation of sketch work. Without color, it loses something, particularly with a face like yours. I see eyes that snap and sparkle with wit and curiosity, and these . . ." He taps the paper. "It is too flat a medium, too dull a pencil."

He stretches his legs and flips to the next page to begin again.

"Wait," I say. "When I teased about the pornographic pictures, you started to say the men often asked for something, and then you stopped. They asked you to draw, didn't they? To sketch women in naughty poses."

His lips twitch. "Whatever 'naughty poses' could you mean, crécerelle. Please, be more specific so I may properly answer the question."

I shake my head. "I have not had enough rum for that yet."

He passes me the bottle, and I laugh but take a drink, and he says, "Yes, they asked for women, and they asked for 'naughty poses,' and I would comply under certain conditions."

"Conditions?"

"I would draw an imaginary woman, with a few details imparted by the purchaser. I would *not* draw an unwitting woman from life and render her naked. Nor put her in any lewd posture. Now, there were times, admittedly, when the men would hire a woman to pose for me, and I would draw her, but that is different. She had agreed to it and been compensated. It is quite another thing to say that one fancies a woman in a shop and could I please draw her bending over the counter with her skirts around her hips."

I take another sip of rum.

"You disagree?" he says.

"Not at all. You are correct to insist on that stipulation. Yet now I am rather curious about such a drawing. Is the skirt simply hiked up, giving the impression of an invitation? Or does it reveal her drawers? Is she even *wearing* drawers?"

"The exact nature of the pose depends on what the purchaser of it desires. I am flexible in my art if decent pay is offered. Although, I must say that in my most popular ones, she is indeed wearing her drawers. However, as the legs of a woman's drawers do not join, if you draw her at the right angle . . ." He grins. "It is all about the angle."

My cheeks flush, and I quickly drink more rum.

He lifts his pencil from the page. "Careful, crécerelle. If you over-imbibe, I will be forced to end this conversation, lest it lead places you would not wish it to go." He glances up at me. "Shall we stop discussing my side profession?"

I shake my head.

He returns to his drawing. "Do you have questions about it?"

I certainly do. So many questions, which range from somewhat indiscreet to wildly indiscreet. What comes out of my mouth, though, is, "I presume it was lucrative?"

He laughs. "Onboard a ship? Among men trapped for months at sea? It was even more lucrative than privateering. One thing you must understand about pirate—or privateer—life, crécerelle, is that when money flows, it flows like water, and men let it slip through their hands just as easily. For a sketch done at sea, which might take me an hour's time, they would pay what they could expect to for an entire day in a brothel."

He adds a few strokes. "While openly lewd sketches were my most lucrative, they are not my favorite to draw. They leave too little to the imagination. They are also not to my personal taste. I prefer something more like this."

He turns the sketchpad around, and I blink. It's me, undoubtedly me, captured exactly as I am right now, lounging by a fire. Lounging by a fire in my corset and drawers, hair over my shoulder as I lean on my arm. There is nothing suggestive in the pose, and somehow that makes it all the more sensual, and I find myself blushing fiercely.

He tears the page from the pad and holds it over the fire. "Oui?"

"No," I say, moving to snatch it from his hand.

"You may destroy it if you like," he says.

I shake my head.

"Then, with your permission, may I continue to work on it another time? That is simply a quick sketch. A concept. I would not ever show it to others, and in case it is ever discovered, I can blur your face to be unrecognizable."

"I am not concerned with anyone recognizing me." Especially considering I won't be born for another thirty years.

"Well, I still would not show it. This is a private portrait, sketched in a private moment. I must admit, that bodice you wear is very fetching. It is not a design I have seen before."

I almost say it's French. That's the usual explanation for any unusual item of fashion.

"It is a new style," I say.

"Very fetching, as are the men's trousers."

"I need something to cover my drawers, as you have pointed out their obvious deficiency."

"I would not call it a deficiency."

I laugh and lean down onto my arm. "Still, it would be rather shocking if I stripped down to them. I could not stretch on the floor like this. Or move my legs like this. Or certainly not sit up and cross them like this." I lean forward, hair falling over my shoulders. "Why is your gaze going there, Nico? There is nothing to see but a well-stitched seam."

"Did I mention I have an excellent imagination?"

"Good. Then I shall not need to do anything as scandalous as remove my trousers. You can simply use your imagination."

"I could, and I am, but an artist must always admit that imagination is no substitute for real life. I could be imagining the scene entirely wrong, and that would be a shame. Also, while I was loath to mention it sooner, those trousers are still damp, as I'm sure the drawers are beneath it."

My brows shoot up. "My, my, you do give yourself airs, sir. Imagining my drawers growing damp when you have not laid a finger on me."

He chokes on a laugh. Then his eyes dance in the firelight. "If you think such a thing is not possible, I am tempted to take that as a challenge."

"Oh, I am certain you are." I toy with the button on my trousers. "You are correct about the dampening, though it is purely seawater. I presume you are suggesting I remove these to dry my undergarments."

"It is merely a suggestion. For your own comfort."

I unfasten the trousers and ease them over my hips. Then, demurely keeping my legs as together as possible, I slide off the trousers and inch closer to the fire.

"Better?" I say.

"They will not dry with your knees quite so tightly bound."

"You are full of such practical advice."

I slide my knees apart, one lifting over the other as he tries to get a better view from where he sits. When he goes to move, I warn him back with a raised finger. Then I look around the cave.

"It is too bad we lack a table," I say. "I could replicate that pose you mentioned. See whether I have it correct in my mind. I do like to be correct."

"Give me five minutes, crécerelle, and I shall build you a table."

"No need." I stretch onto my back, letting my knees fall half-open. "I am certain you are quite tired of seeing women in that particular pose."

"I do not ever draw that one from life. It would . . ." He clears his throat. "As the artist, I must maintain some degree of professionalism."

I laugh softly. "I wondered about that. Having women in all states of undress, striking all sorts of poses, while you must sit there and wield a pencil instead of . . ."

I make a gesture with my hand, one that nearly has him toppling over with gasps of laughter.

"Oh, chérie, I do truly think I love you. Yes, I must admit there are times when it is quite . . ."

"Hard?"

Another snorted laugh. "Very hard, crécerelle, and I will stop there at the risk of saying anything I should not in front of a lady I am wooing."

"You are wooing me?"

"Most ardently."

My gaze drops to the front of his trousers. "I see that. I will not press for details, but you need not worry about offending me with tales of past exploits. It is all fodder for my insatiable curiosity."

He grins. "A most refreshing stance on the matter. I shall remember that."

"If you have not tired of seeing women in that pose, then perhaps I can attempt it? For the sake of satisfying my curiosity?"

I walk to the wall, face it and rest my hands on a jutting piece of rock. "Like this?"

"There is more bending."

"Ah." I lean to rest my forearms on the rock. "This?"

"That is very"—he swallows—"evocative."

"However still not quite right, as I believe my knees are, once again, in too close proximity to one another."

"Oui, if I might offer that slight criticism."

"A constructive one. So I should be more like . . ."

I spread my legs, bend further, and raise my rear, feeling the chill of the night air on those most private of parts.

"Like this?"

He answers with a string of French, his voice husky enough that I do not chide him for it. Then he says, "May I come closer?"

"That depends. Is it for closer inspection or . . . the ultimate purpose of this particular pose?"

"Non, chérie, not for that. I have nothing for protection, and even if I did, I do not think you would wish me to move quite so quickly."

"I would not."

"You would like me to take my time?"

I twist to meet his eyes. "Please."

"Good, because that is exactly what I intend to do. However, I believe I made some promises earlier on how I should like to make you swoon, and I am suddenly very eager to do so, if I may."

Do I sound like an innocent if I admit I am not quite certain what he means? Oh, I know the carnal arts, having read extensively of them, but I am not quite certain which of them he intends, as the majority of what I have read—and all of what I have experienced—centers around the pleasure of the man. That does not seem to be what he's suggesting, and so I nod.

I stay where I am as he walks over. He bends behind me and kisses the back of my calf, the thrill of such an unexpected touch darting through me. I try to relax and lean into the wall and simply experience without trying to guess what he has in mind.

His lips and tongue tease up my calf, tickling at the back of my kneecap before moving onto my thigh, pushing up the drawers as he goes.

When he reaches the top of my inner thigh, he pauses.

"Oui, crécerelle?" he says, his voice hoarse. "This is all right?"

"Yes," I say, even if I am still not quite certain what I am agreeing to.

His mouth moves back to my thigh and inward and then— Oh! Oh, my. I— Oh *my*.

My education was sorely lacking.

Sorely lacking indeed.

Oh, Nico. You *are* a wonder.

18

Afterward, Nicolas lowers me to the floor by the fire, and I barely notice. I am lost in the aftermath of something I have never experienced except by my own hand, and even then, it was not like *that*.

When I finally lift my head, still dazed, I say, "I will write you that letter of recommendation."

He throws back his head and laughs. "I may accept that offer, only because I cannot wait to see what you write."

"Superlatives. A page of superlatives."

He kisses my nose. "Careful, crécerelle, my confidence does not need inflation. I am pleased if you are suggesting that my performance exceeded that of previous contenders."

When I don't reply, he shifts to look at me. "There were previous contenders, non? I am surely not the first in that particular regard."

My cheeks heat. "I am not a virgin, as I said. However, no one has ever"—I clear my throat—"done that."

He shakes his head. "Men can be remarkably reticent when it comes to that particular pleasure, while they fully expect the woman to do the same for them. I am sorry to hear that they overlooked it in their repertoire."

"I do not think they had a repertoire."

The words come before I can stop them, and he looks down even more sharply.

"Please tell me they did *something* for you?"

My cheeks heat more.

"Did they, at the very least, ensure you enjoyed the act they *did* perform?"

My face is red-hot now, and it takes everything I have not to bury it in his chest. An odd shame washes over me, as if it were my oversight for not insisting.

"I was inexperienced," I say carefully. "I knew that I should expect more from intimate relations, and when I did not receive it, I decided I had chosen my partner poorly. So I tried again twice more and discovered that the *sort* of man did not appear to be the issue. As my sole purpose in taking lovers was to enjoy the experience, it was . . . disheartening."

"I can only imagine."

"I may not have been clear enough on what I expected. I tried to be, but it was difficult to make my wishes known. Even the most considerate of the three found such discussion embarrassing."

Nicolas sighs and pulls me to him. "We tie ourselves in such knots on matters that should be natural. If we were not intended to take pleasure in the act, why would such pleasure be possible? I blame the Puritans, of course, though I must also lay some blame at the feet of doctors, who are remarkably loath to develop better methods of preventing procreation and the spread of venereal disease. Instead, we ask women to shoulder the responsibility by teaching them to fear intimate relations."

He glances down at me. "That was a bit of a lecture, was it not?"

"Only to a receptive audience." I prop onto his chest to look down at him. "It is a quandary, and I have not known how to resolve it. My efforts have been met with nothing but frustration."

"Then it is Fate who has brought us together, as I have already decided. You may discuss anything with me, crécerelle. You may ask any questions, and I will answer as best I can, on the under-standing that I am only a student slightly farther along in his studies. I may talk as if I am a man of vast experience, but as much as I enjoy intimacy, I . . ."

He trails off and rubs his mouth. "At the risk of saying more than I should, I consider intimacy an intimate act, as the name implies. I was an eager student in my youth, taking lessons from those with whom I did not intend to form any attachment, much the same as I believe you did, but once I had mastered the basics . . ." He shrugs. "As I grew older, my needs changed."

"You speak as if you are five-and-fifty."

He chuckles. "Non. I speak as a relatively young man who was introduced to such matters at a definitively young age."

"Lucky lad."

He lets out a laugh. "True enough. Most lads are luckier in such matters than lasses, having far vaster opportunities. But now you have an opportunity of your own, with a man possessing a decent amount of experience and ample quantities of enthusiasm, which is at least as important."

"Enthusiasm is very important. As is reciprocity, as you have said. Pleasure for both partners. I believe *that* is what we are lacking here tonight."

He pushes my hair behind my ear as he smiles. "You do not need to worry about that tonight, crécerelle."

"You do not want me to reciprocate?"

"I do not want you to feel that my actions bore the expectation of reciprocity. I wanted to give."

"Understood. But if I wish to give in return? To further my own education?"

He tilts his head, gaze boring into mine as if to be sure I mean it. Then he says, "All right. What would you like to do?"

"I believe the question is, What you would like me to do?"

"Non, crécerelle. I did what I wished to do, and now you should do the same." He folds his hands behind his head. "I am at your disposal."

I hesitate, uncertain. He waits without a word, letting me take my time, which I appreciate because I am at a loss here. The lovers I have had either did not want my active participation or conveyed their wishes very clearly. The freedom to explore on my own is wondrous, but also new and somewhat daunting.

I sit up, straddling his hips and look down at him. He is truly beautiful, and fresh desire flares, smoldering embers leaping to life.

"What is it that you wish to do to me, crécerelle?" he asks softly.

"Everything." I blurt the word and then feel my cheeks heat.

He gives a husky growl of a laugh. "I do like the sound of that. May I make a suggestion?"

"Please."

"We have all the time you'd like. Time tonight. Time tomorrow night, if you do not tire of me so quickly. You said you wished to proceed slowly. May I suggest that is where you begin?" He takes my hand and traces it down his jaw before kissing my fingertips. "Take your time and get to know me. Would you like that?"

"I would very much like that."

"As would I."

I HAVE NEVER SLEPT WITH A MAN BEFORE. MY EXPERIENCES WERE NOT the sort that ended with a night in bed, and I was glad of that, having no desire to share my bed with anyone. Now I sleep on a thin blanket atop cold rock, and I would not trade it for the most luxurious bed in London.

I did as Nicolas suggested, and my simple—if comprehensive—explorations were all that was required to satisfy him, which leaves plenty of options for later. When I finished, he conducted a little exploration of his own, which I very much appreciated, having discovered there is great pleasure to be found in pleasing another.

After that, we fell into exhausted sleep as the sun began to rise beyond the cave opening. Now it is full daylight, and I am drowsily entwined with him as he sleeps. I use the opportunity to gaze upon him and enjoy the sight of him and to grieve, just a little.

Is it possible to grieve for someone you have not yet left? Before now, I would have rejected such a silly notion. But I am looking at him, and I am feeling more than it is safe to feel, and I am already seeing into the not-too-distant future when he will kiss my cheek and tell me how much he has enjoyed my company, and then we will part ways, never to meet again.

I am trying to focus on the moment. He is here, and I am here, and he is in no hurry to leave. I should not be borrowing grief and regret from the future. And yet, perhaps there is a purpose to such melancholy thoughts. I know an end is coming, and so I will enjoy every moment between now and then. Enjoy it and emblazon it upon my memory.

There is no future between us. It is odd for me to even consider such a possibility, as I never have with a man before. A true partner? A lover of long acquaintance? That is not Nicolas. It cannot be Nicolas. He is a wanted man, repaying a debt before he returns halfway around the world to the island he calls home, where he has family and a future. I am as much a visitor here, out of my time, separated from my world, and I must return there, where I have family and my own future.

I have not been tempted to tell him my truth. There's no reason to do so. He thought my clothing seemed odd but chalked it up to fashion. If he thinks I seem odd—which I am certain I do—he has chalked that up to my quirks of character. I do not need to tell him I have not yet been born. I will never need to tell him that. We will enjoy our time together, and then he will bid me a fond adieu, and we will part with him being none the wiser, which avoids any conversation in which he might need to assess my sanity.

I will not grieve for what is yet to come. Or, if I do, I will allow it only as a reminder that these incredible moments with an incredible man will come to an end, and he will leave me with memories I shall cherish forever.

19

I wake to a most delicious smell, rich and deep and vaguely familiar. I reach for Nicolas, only to find the blanket empty. I crack open my eyes to see him sitting cross-legged on the other side of a low fire. He has what looks like a small cup beside him, steam wafting from it. He's sketching and engrossed in it, biting his lip in a way that makes my heart give a little flutter, it is so boyishly earnest.

I keep watching him until his gaze lifts to mine.

He gives a start. "How long have you been awake?"

"Not long. How do you feel? You must be sore from your fall last night."

He smiles. "Did I fall last night? I scarcely remember. The end to the evening seems to have wiped my memory quite clean of the rest."

My cheeks heat.

"And how are your injuries faring?" he asks.

"Also oddly driven from my mind. You are drawing something?"

"You, of course."

He turns the pad to show a sketch of me asleep on the blanket. I am naked, as I am in life, but he has artfully rearranged my hair and my legs to cover the most private parts.

"It is lovely," I say.

"One cannot do anything else with such a subject. I believe I could draw a hundred of you, chérie, and still not feel I have truly done you justice, nor tire of the attempt."

He says it so simply and honestly that I am doubly flattered, and I must cover my blush by lifting my head to look about.

"What is that I smell?" I ask.

He lifts that tiny cup. "You have not drunk coffee before, crécerelle?"

I make a face as I thump back to the floor. "My brother-in-law is fond of it. Foul stuff."

"Your brother-in-law can easily procure it?" His brows rise. "That is a feat in this country."

I hesitate, confused, until I realize we are a half century before my time, and I quickly say, "He is in shipping. He can easily procure most things, even that dread brew. No offense intended."

"No offense taken. I shall tell myself your opinion is formed by poor beans and poorer preparation."

He rises and bends by the fire, and I have no idea what he's doing because I'm too busy admiring the view, as he has not taken time to dress yet.

He brings over the small cup, that traitorously delicious smell wafting up. "Will you try some?"

I take it and sip. Then I take another sip.

"That is coffee?" I say.

"*That* is coffee, not whatever nastiness your brother-in-law procures."

I drink some more.

"While I am pleased that you enjoy it, I will admit this is not how I intended to begin the morning. I planned to sketch you until you woke and then to crawl back into the blankets with you and while the day away in pleasure, pretending that nothing else requires my attention." He sighs. "I can be terribly selfish for a man who has made a reputation of being good."

I put an arm around his neck and slide onto his lap. "I have a feeling you are far better at imagining being selfish than actually being it. As much as I would also love to spend the day in these blankets, I suspect that will be far more pleasurable after we both feel we have accomplished something more productive with our day."

He drops his head to my shoulder. "You are far too sensible, crécerelle."

"No, I am far too selfish, wanting to protect our time together for when we can both relax and enjoy it."

"True enough." He twists me on his lap to face him. "So, I have goods to deliver, but that is not a matter of urgency. Andrés's death *is*."

"We must learn for certain who killed him so we may free his spirit. Which means I must start by asking a very awkward question. I know whoever told you he was in York is someone you trusted, but—"

Nicolas groans and thumps onto his back. As I am currently on his lap, with his arms around me, I thump down onto him, awkwardly twisted.

"Umm . . ." I say.

"I was being dramatic."

"Understood, but perhaps do not take me along with you?"

I start to rise, and accidentally—yes, I declare it a complete accident—elbow him on my way up. He lets out a soft "oomph" and then pulls me down again, this time onto my stomach atop him.

"You really do not want to get up today, do you?" I say.

"I really do not." He tugs me up so I'm looking down at him. "It was Mademoiselle M."

I say nothing. I do not dare. I have already been suspicious of Miss Jenkins—*Mademoiselle M*—purely because she is infatuated with Nicolas, and that bothers me more than it should.

"Also, Mademoiselle M was the one I was supposed to meet the other day when I encountered Norrington's naval men instead."

"*What?*"

He winces. "Yes, I am well aware of how this looks. I also ought to admit that she is Lord Norrington's niece."

I bolt up and twist to face him. "*What?*"

He grimaces.

"Wait. The young woman I heard you call Miss *Jenkins* is the niece of Lord Norrington—the man who is trying to kill you—and you still did not think she might have betrayed you?"

"It sounds so much worse when you say it like that, crécerelle."

I cross my arms and glare down at him. "You might claim you were not interested in her romantically, but this leads me to believe you were not immune to her charms, having clearly been blinded by them."

He levers up. "Non. I *was* immune. She is a child, and not at all to my taste even if she were older. I did not tell you about the connection because I knew it would look suspicious, and yet it was not like that. When I was to meet Mademoiselle M, it was because her father could not risk arousing Lord Norrington's suspicions further. Her father is the one who rescued me and gave me shelter and who helps with the villagers' plight."

"And her father is Lord Norrington's brother?"

"Brother-in-law. It is complicated, which is why I can trust him."

He crosses his legs again as I settle in front of him.

Nicolas continues, "Here is what I understand. The late Lord Norrington had a daughter, who fell in love with a young clerk—Mr. Jenkins. The elder Lord Norrington forbade the match, and so she eloped. She died giving birth to a daughter, who is Miss Jenkins. The elder Lord Norrington was devastated by the death of his daughter. He welcomed his granddaughter and Mr. Jenkins home. Jenkins works for the family, and his daughter was raised in the big house until her grandfather died. The current Lord Norrington and Mr. Jenkins do not get on, so Jenkins moved into town with Miss Jenkins."

I curl my legs under me. "Your contact is this Mr. Jenkins, who is the brother-in-law of Lord Norrington, but there is no love lost between them."

"None at all. Lord Norrington views Jenkins as an embarrassment, a lowly employee who tricked his way into the family."

"And how does Norrington feel about his niece?"

Another sigh, softer now. "He is very fond of her. He treats her as family and is always concerned for her welfare. It is a matter of some contention in her household. She believes she can help resolve the situation in the village by persuading her uncle to be a better man, and her father knows that would be like expecting the wolf to learn to care for the lambs."

"Is it possible that Norrington used his niece to get close to you? Could she have innocently arranged that meeting on the road at his request, thinking she was helping foster a mediation? As for Andrés, I presume you believe Miss Jenkins does not know what happened to him but was told to pass along that story to you."

"Oui. She is the one who told me Andrés was safely in York."

"And convinced you it would be unsafe to go see him."

"Oui."

I rise and pick up my clothing. "All right, then. Whether or not Miss Jenkins believes Andrés is safely in York, someone told her to pass along that story. Presumably, it was her uncle, but we must determine that for certain. You shall need to seduce her."

I catch his look of horror and shake my head. "I am not asking you to *do* anything, Nico. I mean you must flirt with her." I glance over at him. "Unless you are telling me you have never played on a lady's interest, however gently, to your advantage."

He sighs.

"You are an expert in the art of flirtation," I say. "Handsome, charming, well spoken, witty and respectful."

He arches a brow. "Respectful? I am not certain that turns a lady's head quite as much as the rest."

"Then you are mistaken. Of all the weapons in your arsenal, Nico, that might be your sharpest. What woman cannot help but swoon for a man who takes such care to treat her as an actual person?"

"That is a depressing sentiment, crécerelle."

"But true." I walk over, rise onto my tiptoes and kiss his cheek. Then I kiss it again. "I am going to like doing that."

He puts an arm around me, pulling me to him. "And I am going to like you doing that."

I adjust my cap. "Perhaps not while we are out, though, at least not while I am dressed like this."

He grins. "I would not mind. You do make a very pretty boy."

He tucks my hair under my cap and pats my rear. A low growl, and he moves in front of me, both hands on my rear as he presses me to him.

I set my hand on his chest. "None of that, sir. If I must play the coquette today to keep our mission on track, I shall do it. Perhaps you will like that better than my boldness."

"Never." Another growl as he kisses my neck. "I adore your boldness. It is one of your eleven most attractive traits."

"Eleven?" I say as he begins pulling on his clothing. "That is very specific."

"I have given the matter great thought. There are at least eleven distinct traits I adore about you." He tugs on his shirt and then says, "Would you like to know what they are?"

"Of course."

He hefts his satchel and tosses me an apple that seems to appear from nowhere. I take a bite, and then he says, "*J'adore ton esprit, ton sens de l'humour—*"

I glare at him, take a bite of my apple and march from the cave.

20

We walk to a break in the cliff where it's an easier climb. At the top, we emerge in a small stand of trees and pause to catch our breath.

When I open my mouth, Nicolas lifts a finger. I notice he's gone still, his gaze skipping over the trees.

"Who is there?" he calls.

Two men step out, both armed with pistols. Nicolas backs in front of me, arms out, as if to shield me.

The men step closer. They are the two who ambushed Nicolas on Hood's Lane.

"So it seems the stories are true," a man's voice says from behind the other two. A figure steps out. It is a man in his thirties, with a knife-slit of a thin-lipped mouth and a sleek white wig. I recognize him from the boat last night. Lord Norrington.

Norrington continues, "Rats really do flee a sinking ship."

"As a former admiral, you should know that," Nicolas says. "Though I have heard you spent more time behind a desk than on a deck."

"Is that supposed to insult me, boy? Only a fool wants to be aboard a ship, a thousand miles from home, eating salted meat and sea biscuits."

"Then call me a fool. As for rats, I find them most admirable creatures. I had a pet one for a time. Our cabin boy—Andrés—and I trained it." Nicolas purses his lips and looks thoughtful. "I have often wondered what happened to the young man. You would not know, would you?"

"Would I know what happened to your cabin boy?" Norrington says. "Oddly, I do not keep track of pirates. That is a matter for the law. I only concern myself with those brigands who interfere with my personal business."

"Perhaps Andrés interfered with your business. Then you would know what became of him."

"Do not try to distract me with your nonsense. You like to talk when you ought to be silent, and to be silent when you ought to talk. I have attempted to be fair with you. I have offered you clemency in return for the name of your employer. He is my enemy. Not a boy who plays at pirating."

"Since the Crown executed my captain, I no longer have an employer."

The two navy men lift their pistols, but Norrington waves them down.

"You are fortunate that I am a man of patience," Norrington says. "If I were not, you would be dead."

I rock forward, but Nicolas subtly puts a hand back to stop me.

"I suppose you are going to claim you did not realize I was on that ship last night?" Nicolas says.

"Of course I knew. I was teaching you a lesson, boy. One you seem incapable of learning. I want Robin Hood of the Bay. Now, step aside and introduce me to him."

We both go still. Then Nicolas slowly glances back at me.

"Come, come," Norrington says impatiently. "Do you think we cannot see him right there. He may be short, but he does not quite fit behind you."

The two lackeys snicker.

I take a slow step out, even as Nicolas makes a noise of warning. The trees cast this spot into shadow, and I can only guess that

Norrington and his men cannot see me clearly. Once they do, they will understand their mistake.

Even if they do not realize I am a woman, they cannot confuse me for Nicolas's employer. As a man, I am a whiskerless and pink-cheeked boy.

Yet when I do step out, their expressions don't change.

"You are one of Lancaster's brood, I presume," Norrington says. "You lot cannot keep your noses out of other people's business. Almost as bad as the Thornes. At least *they* do not run about the countryside playing at being Robin Hood. How old are you, boy? Sixteen, yet?"

I stand there, dumbfounded into silence. He hasn't mistaken me for an older man. Not even mistaken me for a *grown* man. He sees a boy. A soft and smooth-cheeked boy. And yet somehow, I am more likely to be Robin Hood of the Bay than Nicolas—ten years older, educated and well spoken, and in the sort of physical condition one would expect of such a hero.

But I am not a man of color. To Norrington, a mere boy, as physically unprepossessing as I appear, is a more likely candidate than Nicolas.

"Speak, boy," Norrington says to me. "I asked your name."

I hesitate only a moment. I want to tell them they are mistaken. Nicolas truly *is* the one they seek. And yet how does that help him? The only reason he corrects their error is out of fear they'll target an innocent. What if, instead, they target a real person . . . one who doesn't exist in this century? A specter for them to chase, leaving Nicolas be?

Then I put my hand on my gladius and stand tall. "I am called the Kestrel."

The two men burst into laughter. Even the corners of Norrington's mouth quirk as he shakes his head.

"I presume you do not know what such a thing is, boy. Do you imagine some terrible bird of prey? It is an American sparrow hawk. Called such because it hunts nothing bigger than sparrows."

I lift my chin. "As you have pointed out, I am small of stature myself. Yet the kestrel is still a bird of prey, and a fierce one, and if I may be so bold, is that not a sparrow on your buckle?"

Norrington looks down.

"That is a grosbeak, crécerelle," Nicolas says. "Yet you are correct. It is indeed akin to a sparrow. Perhaps Lord Norrington should not be so quick to dismiss you. But no, Norrington, this is not my employer. It is a young man of my acquaintance who has no part in my machinations."

Norrington rolls his eyes and tells Nicolas to stop the ridiculous pretense. As they argue, I catch movement to my left. I glance over and give a start. It is the man I saw with Miss Jenkins. Her father, I presumed, or a male member of her household acting as escort.

The older man walks right up behind one of Norrington's lackeys. Then he steps in front of the man, who doesn't even startle. Norrington himself keeps talking to Nicolas.

"You can see me, can't you, child?" the man says. "Can you hear me?"

I give a start myself as I realize he is a ghost. I nod, my gaze cutting back to Norrington.

"Pay my son no mind," the ghost says. "For the moment, he is occupied."

Son? I look from Norrington to the ghost. I see it then. The older man is shorter and stouter, but the resemblance is clear.

This is the elder Lord Norrington, whose death started all the trouble here, as his son seized his inheritance.

"I am sorry for the trouble my son has caused," the ghost continues. "I am sorry for the trouble he continues to cause. I knew he was selfish and arrogant, but I thought he would come to love this area as I did and care for its people—"

The ghost gives his head a sharp shake. "Enough of that. You do not care about my regrets. Your situation—and that of young Nicolas—is the bigger concern right now. My son is calm, and so there is a chance you may be able to resolve this peacefully if you—"

"Enough," Norrington snaps at Nicolas. "You do not know when to shut your mouth, boy. All I need to hear from you is one sentence.

One decision. Do you admit this young man is your employer and allow us to escort him to the authorities? Or do you persist in this madness and insist on accompanying him there?"

When Nicolas opens his mouth, Norrington says, "Answer carefully. Remember who he is and who you are. He is the young son of a nobleman. I will demand compensation from his family, and that will be the end of it. You are a foreign pirate, wanted for treason. You saw what happened to your crewmates. Do you wish to swing?"

I step forward. "Take me to the authorities, sir. Dr. Dupuis had nothing to do with this."

"Doctor?" Norrington snorts. "He's no doctor."

"Not unless he is a witch doctor," one of the other men says, and they both cackle.

"Careful, child," the ghost murmurs. "If you let Nicolas leave alone, I fear he will not get far. I know that any role my granddaughter has played is that of an innocent pawn, and I want to say my son is equally innocent. That he is a man of his word. He is not. The real choices here are whether Nicolas is allowed to run—and be quietly murdered—or turned in and publicly hanged."

I glare at the ghost. "What happened to resolving this peacefully?"

I say the words aloud—I must—but I turn my gaze to Norrington, letting him believe they are for him. He replies that he's trying to resolve it peacefully, sounding exasperated now. I barely hear him. My attention is on the ghost.

"Allow him to take Nicolas with you," the ghost says. "There is a spot along the way where you can escape. I will help you. The trick is to let my son think he's won. He will relax his guard. He expects to win. He always does."

"We will both go with you," Nicolas says. "I will not abandon my friend."

Norrington snorts. "You are a fool, then. Come along."

He waves to his men, who lead us at gunpoint through the trees.

"There is a spot ahead," the ghost says as he follows. "Once we are past the trees and before we reach the cart. His men will bind your hands and feet at the cart. You do not want that."

I only half listen to the ghost. I'm trying to figure out how to communicate with Nicolas, but I cannot get his attention. He's looking from side to side. At first, I think he expects trouble. Then I realize he is looking for a chance to escape, and I relax. We are thinking the same thing, even if we cannot properly communicate.

As the ghost said, Norrington relaxes once we've agreed. He's leading the way, tramping along the path, paying no attention to us. His two men have relaxed as well. Oh, they do not lower the guns pointed at us, but they've taken to taunting Nicolas, saying they cannot wait to see him swing, how they'll bring their families for the entertainment.

Nicolas does not even seem to hear them. He's surveying the woods. When the trees close in, he uses the excuse to brush against me. His hand slides into mine, and he taps my finger. He's trying to tell me something—lay out a plan—but I do not understand. No matter. I will follow his lead. The forest ends just ahead. Once we are out, we can see the lay of the land and—

"Down!" Nicolas shouts, and he shoves me hard into the thick forest.

One of the two men starts to shout, but he's drowned out by a crack of gunfire. Gunfire that comes from somewhere in the forest.

Nicolas half pushes and half drags me until I understand what is happening. An ambush. Someone is shooting—either at us or Norrington and his men. They fire back, but they're armed with short-range pistols firing blindly into the forest.

"Go! Go!" Nicolas whispers, as if I'm not already on all fours, crawling as fast as I can through the thick underbrush.

Behind us, Norrington shouts and snarls at his men. He thinks one of Nicolas's confederates is out there, firing at us. I glance around for the ghost and spot him back with the others. He's looking about wildly, trying to find us. I want to get his attention—he can guide us out of here—but there's no way of doing that without also getting the attention of someone with a gun.

We keep going until we reach a patch of thick broad-leaf plants. I wave to it, and Nicolas nods, and we hide ourselves in the patch.

"Is it your confederates?" I whisper in Nicolas's ear.

He lifts one shoulder in a shrug. Someone loyal to his cause may have known of Norrington's plans and intercepted. It could also be a trap from Norrington himself. He pretends to be taking us to the authorities, only to have us murdered by assassins, and even his own men could honestly attest to that.

Either way, we certainly are not about to find our liberators and throw ourselves on their mercy. If they are indeed friends, we will thank them later.

We wait and listen. As I turn, I see a young roe deer poised about thirty feet away. I whisper to Nicolas. His strained expression eases into a faint smile as he leans over to kiss my cheek.

"I think I love you," he says.

"You keep saying that."

"You keep giving me cause to say it."

I hand him a stone. While I am skilled in many of the martial arts, none of them involve throwing with any accuracy. I hunker down and watch Norrington and his men thump around. Nicolas pitches the rock. It lands on our side of the young deer, and the startled beast takes off, crashing through the forest.

"There!" one of the men shouts. "They are making a run for the road!"

They take off in hot pursuit, with the ghost flying after them as he scans the forest looking for us.

The moment they are out of sight, we move as quickly and quietly as we can in the other direction. The "other direction" leads us back to the cliff, which is not ideal, but it is also the last place Norrington will expect us to go. We climb down and then take off along the shore. We reach a spot where the cliffside has dipped enough for us to climb back up, and we are almost at the top when we hear the clatter of a cart.

21

We duck fast. Nicolas tilts his head and motions for me to wait as he scrambles high enough to peer over the top. Then he drops back beside me.

"I know him," he says to me quickly. "Mr. Walker is a friend. Come."

We climb to the top, where I see an old mule-driver cart. Nicolas hails the driver and motions for the old man to wait. We scamper up the bank, and then Nicolas strides ahead to explain the situation.

"Aye," the old man says in a thick Yorkshire accent. "I spotted his lordship back a way." The man spits and curses and then spots me. "Apologies to the young lad there."

"My friend knows there is no love lost between the lord and people of Hood's Bay."

"That's putting it kindly," the man says with a cackle. "Hop in the back under the hay, and I'll get you to town."

"Only as far as the old church, please," Nicolas says. "Best you not be seen with us past that."

"I don't care what he does to me. Cannot be worse than what he's done already, with his taxes and his bully men."

"Well, I care what he does to you, so you'll leave us at the church."

৩৯৯

WE CRAWL INTO THE BACK OF THE CART UNDER THE HAY PILED IN THERE along with sacks of what smells like dried fish. I do not complain about the smell, but as we settle in, I switch to breathing through my mouth, which has Nicolas chuckling.

"You would not want to get too close to those sacks," he says. "Which is the point. Norrington's men take one whiff of old Walker's cart, and they cannot send him on his way fast enough."

"Meanwhile, he has other goods hidden deep inside them," I guess.

Nicolas grins. "He does indeed." He rips two empty sacks and stretches them over us as the cart lurches forward. Then he covers the sacks in hay and lies down beside me, one hand on my hip.

"Thank you," I say, "for seeing whoever shot at us before they fired."

"I do not even know if they were firing at us."

"Maybe so, but your quick reaction got us out of a very dire situation, meaning you did save my life, and therefore I owe you."

His mouth opens. Shuts. He eyes me. "I was about to say that it was nothing more than you have done for me. However, the mention of recompense stopped me. I fear arguing may not be in my best interests."

"It is not," I say. "I owe you my life and will repay you handsomely."

His smile grows to a grin. "I do like the sound of that."

"You should. I may not be the most skilled at that particular art, but I am eager to improve."

"I think you are quite adept, but it is true that practice does improve any skill."

I sigh. "That is what my sister always says."

He pauses. "You sister advises you on . . . ?"

"Cooking. She is a baker, after all. I cannot promise you the best meal you have ever had, but I promise all my efforts in that regard, in repayment for saving my life."

I catch his look and frown. "You seem disappointed, sir. The growling in your stomach tells me you are quite hungry, and I am offering to feed you." I wriggle closer to him. "Unless there is something else you would like."

"If you were honestly offering me dinner, I would accept with thanks, as I would also tell you that you owe me nothing. However, as you seem to be teasing me, I will admit that I may have been hoping for another form of recompense tonight."

"Tonight?" I widen my eyes. "You do not want it now?"

He shivers and nuzzles my neck. "Do not tease, crécerelle, or I will be in no condition to stand when this cart reaches its destination."

· "I am not teasing. Mr. Walker cannot see us under these sacks. No one can. I presume we have a bit of a ride ahead. Also, I am discovering a very odd thing about narrowly escaping death. It does make me rather . . . libidinous. However, if it has the opposite effect on you . . ."

He takes my hand and pulls it lower, pressing it against the crotch of his trousers.

"Indeed," I muse. "It seems to have the same effect on you. How interesting. Well, the offer stands, sir. If you would prefer your payment at a more reasonable time, in a more reasonable place—"

"I would not."

"Splendid."

I lift my head from the sacks to ensure we are indeed traveling over the moors on an empty road. Then I duck back under and begin wriggling downward. When I reach for the button on his trousers, he sighs and runs his fingers through my hair.

"I may have to marry you, crécerelle."

"Don't be silly," I say. "One does not marry a girl who would pleasure you in a hay cart. One marries a girl who would faint at the thought. Everyone knows that."

"Then everyone is doing it entirely wrong."

"I have always thought so," I say, and then peel down his trousers to begin.

❧

FORTUNATELY, I HAVE FINISHED MY MINISTRATIONS BEFORE WE REACH our destination. Otherwise, that would be terribly embarrassing. I actually finish quite swiftly. Or, I should say, Nicolas does. I credit the situation rather than any skill of mine. If anything, I believe proper skill would ensure it *doesn't* end quite so quickly. I mention that afterward, curled up in the cart with him. He doesn't answer. Just groans and starts whispering in French, nuzzled against my neck. I really do need to learn the language. It is most vexing.

When we do stop, it's at the ruins of a very old church. Nicolas rummages around in his satchel as I pick hay off myself and thank Mr. Walker.

"For your trouble," Nicolas says, holding out a gold coin that winks in the sun.

The old man waves him off. "I did not do it for that, Nick."

"I know, which is why I insist you take it. I put you into a precarious position, and I appreciate that you helped us and would like to compensate you for the risk."

When Mr. Walker still demurs, Nicolas flips it into the hay. "There, it is yours. If you can find it."

"You're a good lad," the old man says. "Too good for most of this lot around here. You need to get back to France before they hang you."

"I fear that would exchange the noose for the guillotine, and I am uncertain which is preferable."

"Not dying at all?" I suggest.

He smiles as Mr. Walker wheezes a laugh.

"I will be gone as soon as I have finished what I began," Nicolas says. "My confederates have a plan to put an end to his lordship's tax nonsense."

"You mean Mr. Jenkins." He waves off Nicolas's protest. "I know the man has been helping your cause, and if anyone knows how to stop his brother-in-law, it is him. I only wish you both luck, and if you need my cart, you know where to find me."

Mr. Walker digs the gold coin from the hay and waggles a finger at Nicolas as he pockets it. Then he's off. Nicolas waits until the cart is out of sight and then laces his arms around my shoulders.

"I do not believe I asked whether you are all right after what happened with Norrington," he says.

"If I was not all right, I wouldn't have offered what I did." I lean in to kiss him. "I'm fine. However, there is something I need to tell you."

I explain to him about the ghost.

He winces. "Oh, I cannot imagine what a terrible thing that must be. Seeing your son destroy the legacy you worked so hard to build. By all accounts, the elder Lord Norrington was a fine man. Firm but fair, and the people mourn his passing still."

"Especially considering who took over in his stead. No matter how 'firm' the elder Lord Norrington may have been, he was undoubtedly a saint compared to his son."

"True enough." He frowns. "If his ghost lingers, does that mean he was murdered?"

"Do you know how he died?"

"An ailment of some sort. No one questioned it."

"Spirits linger for any unfinished business. In his case, it seems most likely that the unfinished business is his legacy and the damage his son is doing to both it and the people here. In any event, he does believe Norrington wants you dead, if you still had any doubts about that."

"I cannot doubt he has murderous intent after what we believe he did to Andrés and what he attempted to do to us on the *Temerity*. I knew better than to let him take you alone and let me go 'free.' I mistrust anyone who offers to set a man free. It is always a trick."

"I did hope he was serious, which is why I tried to accept the role of your employer. I did not mean any disrespect by it."

"You thought that might be my way to freedom. It is not, and so I would ask you not to endanger yourself again on my behalf, please. The kestrel will stay in hiding from now on, watching from a safe tree branch."

"If you really expect me to do that, Nico, you do not know me at all."

He sighs. "I know, but I had to make the attempt. Just do not place yourself between Lord Norrington and me, please. He may think you a nobleman's son, and that may seem to protect you, but I would not bet your life on it."

"Understood."

"Excellent. Now, I have a question, crécerelle. Do you have any fear of small places?"

"Not at all. Why?"

He grins and takes my hand. "I will show you."

W e are in the tunnels that lead to Hood's Bay. I have heard of them. I have even, on one occasion, attempted to find them in my world when locals pretended not to know what I was talking about. Of course, I cannot tell Nicolas that I have heard of the tunnels that are—in his time—still in use and therefore still a secret, as their purpose is smuggling. I must act surprised, though I do not need to feign my delight at the prospect of using them to reach the village.

To access the tunnels at the church, one must crawl under a fallen slab that looks ready to collapse at any moment. Nicolas assures me that is an intentional impression. No one is going to look at that slab and say, "Oh, I should very much like to crawl underneath that."

Before we go in, Nicolas retrieves a small lantern he keeps hidden here. He lights it and crawls under that slab, and I follow to find rudimentary stairs leading down into a room.

"It is the crypt!" I say, peering about. "We are in the old church crypt."

"Yes, and we may return later for better examination, if you are interested. I spent nearly a week hiding in here, and I consider the residents some of my dearest friends." He gestures to a moldering set of bones that has fallen from its berth. "That is Peter. He likes tall women and dark ale. Do not get him started on sheep, or he shall never stop talking."

I smile and follow him through the crypt to the far wall. He bends and unlatches something. Then, with a tug, an entire shelf of bodies comes free from the wall. Behind it, darkness beckons.

"You will need to kneel here," Nicolas says. "We have to crawl hereafter. I hope that is all right."

"As I am not wearing a skirt, which would bunch and bind and restrict my crawling, it is quite all right. Onward."

He drops to all fours and disappears into the tunnel. We enter what becomes a spider's web of them, crisscrossing with no markers to indicate direction.

"That is also intentional," Nicolas says. "Many lead nowhere at all. One leads to a bog. Another heads straight off the cliff. One night, I made the mistake of attempting the tunnels with only a matchstick and found myself hanging off a cliffside. That is when I procured this lantern."

The tunnels are as glorious as I envisioned, and I am somewhat annoyed that I could not find them sooner. I understand the villagers' deceit. I imagine it is quite a trial to have holidayers popping about asking after the tunnels they read of. So I do not blame the villagers, though I do still blame the one utter jackanapes who smirked and suggested I wouldn't fit in the tunnels anyway. I do fit—with room enough that Nicolas could squeeze past me.

I wish I did not dwell on such things. I don't, in my everyday life. My body does everything I ask of it, and so I do not see any reason to change it. I have been plump since birth, and the one time —as a silly young woman—that I surrendered to pressure and became slender, I was both miserable and unwell. So I have accepted my shape, not with resignation but with pride, and I want to laugh off insults, yet some seem to lie like traps waiting to spring.

The point is that the tunnel is quite wide enough, and I will dismiss that man's petty jibe with one of my own, that judging by his own physical condition, he would not have been able to endure this endless crawl. For me, it is a delightful experience, complete with nuances such as a lewd drawing on a bracing post, sheep's teeth set into a macabre signature and a spot where two people traded joking insults, searing them onto driftwood set in the ceiling. From one wall, I even pull the remains of an ancient, hammered amulet, which I pocket.

While I find the amulet on my own, the rest is pointed out by Nicolas, who acts as tour guide. That might be his considerate side, easing a difficult journey, but I think it is also his nature, like mine, our own curiosity thrilled to find one who shares it. I am the eager pupil, asking endless questions, which he happily answers.

We've been crawling for a half hour when he finally twists around to face me.

"We are approaching the home of a friend, whom I must tell of the goods we hid so he may retrieve them. It is his family's home. I am never entirely comfortable with that. It is one thing for a man and his wife to choose to shelter me, but another for his children to be expected to do the same. Yet if I were to ask that they not be involved, he would be insulted, as if I were saying his children cannot be trusted."

"I understand."

He nods. "I wanted to be clear so I do not seem cavalier."

"I could not imagine such a thing, but yes, thank you for explaining."

"I would also like to ask you to remain here, so that I may speak to them and say I have a friend and allow them to decide whether they are comfortable hosting you as well."

"Of course."

"If they choose not, I will return with food, and we will depart as soon as we have eaten. Is there anything else you require?"

"I would say a hot bath, but I will settle for a dip in the ocean when it is possible."

He smiles. "I will ensure it is possible soon, as I am in need of the same. One last question. Is it all right if I tell them you are a woman, or would you prefer to remain a man?"

"If I were a young woman, would that affect how they view me, being alone with you?"

"It is the country, crécerelle. There are none of those silly city rules here, at least not among people like this. I shall tell them you are a young woman related to Lord Thorne, and that will explain everything. They would not expect the usual behavior from you then."

"Good. Then that shall be my story."

NICOLAS'S COMPATRIOTS INVITE ME INTO THEIR HOME. THEY WORK THE sea, with a small fishing boat, and I am reminded again of how fortunate I have been in my birth and my life. Oh, I do not lack for reminders. I receive them whenever I accompany Portia on her medical rounds, visiting the homes of those who do not care whether their "doctor" is a man or a woman, with a school degree or the equivalent informal studies. Yet poverty is not something I will ever inure myself to, nor should I want to. I visit those homes, and the next time I am tempted by a gorgeous pen or a rare book of history, I do not stop myself from buying it, but I find a charitable use for the equivalent of my indulgence.

Like many of the families I have visited, while this one lacks so much that I take for granted, they do not lack the most important parts of a home: love and kindness. That is not to put a pretty face on the poverty I see. There are ten people—parents, five children, two grandparents and an aunt—living in a building smaller than the tiny London townhouse I share with Portia. At least they have outdoor space here, moors to roam and a sea to explore, unlike the city tenement families I am accustomed to.

The Miller family invites us in and plies us with food. That is to say that they quickly prepare fish and heat leftovers from the day before. This is not the home of the nineteenth-century middle or upper class where one can ask the cook to make a meal . . . and the poor woman is left scrambling to prepare supper in an hour rather than the usual half day.

Nicolas dives into his meal with the air of a starving man, which means I do not need to play the dainty lady. We eat our fill while the children pepper him with questions and stare at me. When he is done, he grabs two of the youngest, saying he is going to make them pirates. It is obviously an old and beloved game, and the children shriek and fight him off with wooden swords.

When one child accidentally lands on me, she scurries off, whispering apologies. I take up her discarded sword and execute a few moves, which brings her out again, and Nicolas and I find ourselves giving a mock demonstration, to the delight of the children and their elders. Finally, those elders shoo the children off, and Nicolas imparts instructions for the retrieval of the hidden goods. After that, we sneak out the side door and down a path to the ocean, where we might rest a while and make our plans.

We find a spot on the cliff, hidden by grasses, and we lower ourselves to the ground. Nicolas puts an arm around my waist and slides closer as we look out on the sea.

"You are good with children," I say.

Do I imagine that he tenses, just a little? If so, he covers it with a laugh. "My sisters say it is because I have never grown up myself. I have nieces and nephews, and while I miss my parents and brothers and sisters, the children will be what brings me home. I do not wish to return in five years, a stranger to them."

A brief pause, and then he says, carefully, "I must also admit that, as fond as I am of children, I am not certain I envision having any myself. The sort of life I lead is far more conducive to unclehood than fatherhood, which is why I am exceedingly careful on that account. I am not saying I would never change my mind, only it is not in my near future. Although some—like my family—find that hard to understand when I am, as you say, good with children."

"I am good with horses," I say. "I am also very fond of them. That does not mean I intend to change my life so that I might have one of my own."

"Precisely."

I lean back. "I adore my nephew, and I cannot wait to meet his new little sister or brother. I hope Rosalind has a whole brood of children for me to torment and spoil. Portia wants children, too, and so I will have plenty in my life without needing to have any myself."

The arm around me relaxes as he moves closer still, tight against my side. "You understand, then."

"I do, and I am certain some will call me selfish for not wanting children, but would it not be more selfish to bring them into a life where I might resent the limitations they place on mine?"

"Yes, that is it exactly, crécerelle." He kisses my cheek. "I am glad to see we are of a mind. It will make it so much easier when I finally persuade you to marry me."

I roll my eyes and lean my head onto his shoulder. We sit like that, in comfortable silence, until he sighs.

"I suppose we must talk about Miss Jenkins," he says.

"Yes. Her grandfather is convinced she is an innocent pawn, and you feel the same. Yet if that is true, however cruel it seems, she should continue playing the role of pawn, this time for our benefit. I have several ideas as to how you might . . . curry her favor."

He is silent for a moment. Then he says, "Must I? I hesitate to register my complaint, Miranda, as finding who killed Andrés is my highest priority. I will do whatever it takes. But might I ask to consider other possibilities?"

When I open my mouth, he presses a kiss to it.

"Please?" he says. "I struggle with the idea of seduction, however innocent, and it is not my sense of fairness that protests. Yes, I believe she is a pawn, but I acknowledge she might also have knowingly lied to me about Andrés, on her uncle's behalf. I am not certain I can bring myself to speak to her, much less to flirt with her."

When I do not answer, he shifts in obvious discomfort. "I will if it is necessary, of course."

"That is not why I am silent, Nico. I am silent because I am searching for the words to say that I am sorry for asking you. To admit that I did not even think of how uncomfortable it would be."

"Perhaps I am being overly sensitive."

I take his hand and twist to meet his eyes. "No, I ought to have considered it from your point of view, and I did not. You shouldn't need to speak to her, and you certainly shouldn't need to flirt with her. Earlier, when you thought I was going to protest, I was actually going to say I have thought of a second solution, though it may be more difficult. You said that it is not considered unduly inappropriate for me to be in the moors on my own. What if I were to find a way to encounter Miss Jenkins? I cannot guarantee I could win her confidence on such short notice, but if you could advise me, we could make an effort."

"That may work," he says with some relief. "She is very lonely out here, without other young ladies of her station, so you may be able to win her confidence more easily than you expect. You are very easy to speak to, and while I am not certain what you can learn from her, it would be a start."

"All right. Then let us come up with a suitable story."

WE NEED MORE THAN A STORY. I ALSO NEED PROPER CLOTHING. THE dress I left at Thorne Manor is far too elaborate—and unfashionable in the current time. We are able to cobble together a suitable walking outfit, along with a lovely cape, from Nicolas's goods, which will both cover part of my borrowed dress and look suitably fine for a young lady of means, especially when paired with a gorgeous pin and fancy bonnet, also from his store of goods.

For my story, I will not be related to Lord Thorne, as Norrington has no love for that family. Instead, I have an elderly widowed aunt on holiday in Whitby, and I have wandered into the moors to explore. Without a local relative, I must be able to prove I come from good stock, and so I will do that by my connection to Courtenay Hall and the earl of Tynesford, who would at this time be August's grandfather. I am familiar enough with the house and grounds to prove I am a friend of the family. I will not claim to be fast friends with the Courtenays, but friendly enough to have been there on many occasions, which proves I come from an excellent family.

I also receive an expected advantage from the late Lord Norrington. While we are checking on the mare from yesterday—who seems to be gone—the ghost finds us. We tell him our plan, and he knows exactly how I might approach Miss Jenkins. The young lady likes to walk each afternoon, on a set path through the moors. I need only to meet her there and pray for the best.

23

I am sitting on a moor path, perched on the heather, with one boot in my hand. Sitting and waiting until finally, a bonnet appears, bouncing up the path.

"Oh!" I call. "Oh, hello there!" I push up, hopping to balance on one foot. "Hello!"

There is no need to make a spectacle of myself. I am on the path, and Miss Jenkins is heading straight toward me. I still hop, as if trying to catch her eye.

When she is in sight, I let out a tremendous sigh of relief. "Oh, thank the heavens. I heard someone coming, and I was not certain whether I should appeal for rescue or hide myself. You hear such stories of wicked people out here, but my aunt insisted it was safe to walk, and I did so want to be brave, but then I broke my heel and . . ." I throw up my hands.

Miss Jenkins approaches with a smile. "It is only me, and sadly, I am not at all wicked, though it does sound like fun. Are you injured?"

"No, it is only my boot that has suffered. I must admit that I would not entirely object to meeting with a wicked person on the moors, as long as they were only wicked in an interesting way. Perhaps a handsome highwayman who would demand my pin."

Her smile grows. "And which would you give?"

"It would depend on how handsome he was."

She laughs, and it's a pretty, tinkling sound. "Then we are of accord on that, Miss . . . ?"

"Hastings," I say. "Miranda Hastings."

"You said you are with your aunt?"

"Not at the moment. Sadly, she is an invalid and not actually my aunt, but a dear family friend. We attended the Midsummer Ball at Courtenay Hall, and my parents suggested I continue on to Whitby with Aunt Bess for a fortnight."

Her eyes round. "The Midsummer Ball at Courtenay Hall?"

"Were you there?" I ask. "There were so many people that I fear I was quite overwhelmed."

"I was not, though I heard of it, of course. Did they truly serve iced cream?"

I seize the opportunity to solidify my story, granting her a glimpse into this fabled "Midsummer Ball" that the Millers had mentioned took place last week. I know enough of Courtenay Hall to take her there—to the ponds and the mazes and the follies. The rest I can safely make up, and by the time I finish, she is glowing as if she attended the even herself. She spends the next twenty minutes peppering me with questions.

Nicolas is right. Miss Jenkins is indeed a lonely young woman, and as someone raised with two sisters, I feel a pang of sympathy for her plight, alone here on the moors where none of the local girls would be considered proper companions.

I want to agree with the girl's grandfather—that if she has betrayed Nicolas, it is unwittingly. Yet as sweet and naive as Miss Jenkins seems, I must remember that it could be a false front. Or she truly is that naive and still working with her uncle against Nicolas, believing it the right thing to do.

Whatever the answer, Miss Jenkins accepts my story without question, and she does not think it at all odd that I am walking the moors alone, since she is doing the same.

As we are talking, her grandfather's ghost appears to check on my progress, and he helps by nudging my answers in the correct direction. Soon Miss Jenkins and I are chatting like dear friends. She has helped me "fix" my boot—which was not truly broken—and we have continued walking as we talk. She shows me her favorite spot, from which she can gaze out over the ocean, and I sit with her as she tells me all about life in Hood's Bay. She is desperately lonely, and I am an enthusiastic audience for her chatter. Of course, I am hoping to gain something from that chatter, something that will help our cause. That is not so easily done.

Again, the ghost helps, suggesting questions to ask, steering conversation toward Lord Norrington. Miss Jenkins—*call me Emily, please*—does not wish to discuss him. She gives no sign of disliking her uncle. Quite the opposite. He is "very good to me, and I am very fond of him." He just isn't, to her, an interesting topic of conversation, not nearly as interesting as, say, a young man she knows, one who is a doctor and "just a little bit wicked."

She means Nicolas, though I am not convinced one could ever call him wicked. Well, yes, he has a wicked sense of humor. He is also a wicked flirt. That is not what Emily means, and I suspect she has not seen that side of him. She means that he is a fugitive, a supposed pirate. She does not say that—only that he was a privateer—and very handsome, and very charming and intelligent despite being, yes, a little bit wicked.

Is it strange to hear a young woman swooning over the man I spent the night with? Is it uncomfortable? Yes, but mostly because I fear she may have betrayed him, and I would hope she would never do that to a man of whom she is enamored. Because she is clearly enamored.

If she will not speak of her uncle, then I must encourage this talk of Nicolas to get a sense of whether she might have done him wrong. It is not impossible that she likes him and yet still betrayed his trust. How many girls have swooned over an unsuitable young man only to stand by when their fathers send him running at sword —or gun—point?

Her mother didn't do that. Her mother was the young woman

who followed her heart and stayed true to her unsuitable love. Emily seems so young and sheltered that I can scarcely believe she is already nineteen.

"Do you see?" her grandfather says beside me. "She cannot possibly have schemed against young Nicolas. She is half in love with him. She is like her mother. There is not a duplicitous bone in her body. When my daughter ran off with Emily's father, I told myself she had betrayed me, but I came to see the lie in that, the self-deception. She ran off with him because she could *not* betray him or her own heart. She could not lie to me and promise she would never see him again. That is Emily, too. She has not betrayed Nicolas."

For his sake, I hope that is true. Imagine having a son who betrays your legacy, so you turn all your expectations on your granddaughter . . . only to learn she has done the same.

"You must gain access to my estate," the ghost says. "To my son's quarters."

While Emily glances off at a butterfly, I turn a look on the ghost that makes him laugh.

"Not like *that*, child. I almost wish my son were that sort of man so you might flutter your eyelashes and not need to trick poor Emily. Alas, while my son has many faults, chasing pretty girls is not among them. My granddaughter may no longer live on the estate, but she is welcome there and visits almost daily. Inveigle an invitation, preferably when he is not at home. I can lead you to his office. He is a meticulous recordkeeper."

I answer something Emily says, and then I give her grandfather another dubious look.

"Yes, he keeps immaculate records," he says. "I taught him well in that regard. I also taught him to keep them locked away. I bought an excellent safe for that exact purpose, an impenetrable one with a foolproof locking mechanism."

Now my look has him smiling again.

"You are wondering whether I expect you to be an expert cracker of safes? No, child, because this safe is custom made. To change the combination, my son would need to bring a man up from London."

"Which he has not done," I say, too low for Emily to hear while she's exclaiming over a distant ship.

"Yes. Why would he go through all that trouble to change the lock when the only one who knows the combination is deceased?"

I continue talking with Emily—which involves mostly listening and making appropriate noises as *she* talks—while I work this out. I cannot deny the allure of such an escapade. Getting myself invited to the home of an evil lord so that I may sneak into his offices and steal papers from his safe? It is exactly the sort of adventure I write about. However, it is also the sort of adventure I know is best reserved for works of fiction.

That is not to say Nicolas and I couldn't pull off such a caper. We could and would if the reward was great enough. *Is* it great enough, though? What are we going to find in that safe? I understand the late Lord Norrington thinks this a fine idea, but no matter how meticulous the current Norrington's notes, what *exactly* could we find? A receipt for money paid to "nail the cabin boy in the pantry"?

It *is* possible we could find something to prove Norrington is overtaxing the villagers or placing impossible regulations on local trade. But is that worth breaking into his office when the penalty could be death? We cannot even be certain the Crown would care about the overtaxation.

Wait.

Do we need to find proof of wrongdoing to take to the Crown? Or do we simply need to find proof of wrongdoing that we can *threaten* to take to the Crown? Threaten to deliver to the local authorities. Threaten to hand over to men like Lord Thorne, who would happily take down Norrington and who would not fear repercussions.

That is what we would be looking for. Not proof that Norrington had Andrés killed, but incriminating evidence of any sort that we could use against him. Use it to force a confession regarding Andrés? No, I cannot see either Nicolas or myself playing that particular role. But we can use it to alleviate the dire situation in Hood's Bay.

We will likely find incriminating evidence of overtaxation. If we can also find anything—*anything*—to prove Norrington ordered Andrés's death, then that is only more reason to do it.

Now, how to win myself an invitation to the home of Emily's uncle? If I ask about him again, she may think I am using her to secure a wealthy husband.

Instead, I ask about her own home, the one she shares with her father. What is it like? Does she love it as much as I love my parents' London townhouse? I have the most beautiful rooms there, an entire floor now that my siblings have wed. A bedroom and a sitting room and a bath . . .

Oh, it seems poor Emily does not have quite so grand of quarters in the house she rents with her father. However, she does have them at her uncle's estate . . .

"He allows me to keep my old rooms there," she says. "It is most kind of him. I have an entire wing. Bedroom, sitting room *and* morning room."

"A morning room? I have dreamed of a morning room. That is the problem with London townhouses. They are wonderfully close to everything, but they are also annoyingly close to one another. There is simply no good light. Or perhaps that is just London."

She laughs. "London *is* dreadfully gloomy."

"It is, which may be why I dream of a country morning room where the sunlight streams through." I sigh. "Please tell me yours is like that."

"It is. It has the perfect southern window with a seat."

"A window seat? With cushions?"

We go on like that for a bit. I do not say that I should love to see her quarters. That goes too far. Oh, I suspect she wouldn't notice, but I still do not want her thinking I have wrangled an invitation, which she will later find suspicious. I simply talk about morning rooms and window seats, and we move on to compare our quarters in our respective homes.

"You must visit us in London," I say, clasping her hands. "You do go to London, yes? You've had your season?"

"I am not allowed to yet. Uncle has promised me one, but not until I am twenty-one. *Twenty-one*, can you imagine?"

"That is not so far off, and when you do have it, you will be in London for months, with dress fittings and parties. Oh, the parties. They are wonderful. You must come visit us and—"

"Parties!" she says. Then she claps her hands to her mouth. "Oh, I am so sorry. That was terribly rude of me. I did not mean to interrupt. It is just that, earlier, when you said you had been to the Midsummer Ball at Courtenay Hall, it reminded me that we are to have a dance at my uncle's tonight, and that I should dearly love to invite you, but of course, that would have been most odd, inviting someone I only met moments ago. Yet now that we have spoken properly, I may invite you, yes? It would be proper?"

I am not certain that a two-hour acquaintance qualifies that much more than a two-minute one, but Emily is, again, a lonely girl. Do I feel guilty about taking advantage of that? I would if not for two things. One, she may have betrayed Nicolas. Two, there is more at stake here than protecting a young woman's pride. If she later realizes I laid a trap—and she dove into it—then that will sting, but Andrés and the people of Hood's Bay are more important.

She mistakes my moment of reticence for rejection, and I must hurry to assure her that is not the case, that she is proper in extending the invitation, and I should love to accept, if her uncle will not object.

"He will scarcely notice us," she says. "He will be too busy currying favor with other gentry. Also . . ." Her eyes glitter. "He will not notice you because you will be in a mask."

"A . . . ?"

She grins. "It is a masquerade ball. Well, a masquerade party. Very small, as balls go. Have you heard of such things?"

I feign ignorance, and she races on to tell me how masquerades are all the rage in France and how she persuaded her uncle to turn this country dance into one. While such frivolities do not interest him, he is a man of ambition, and if it is popular in France, then by holding one here, he will be seen as a fashionable man. He saw the value in that, and so he agreed.

I am to attend a masquerade ball in Lord Norrington's house. I will have access to his office during a busy party, when everyone will be hidden behind masks.

How perfect is that?

Wait . . .

"Did you say it's tonight?" I say.

"Yes! Isn't that exciting?"

She resumes her chatter, assuring me that I will not need to have an elaborate costume. A simple dress and mask will do. I can find a mask on such short notice, can I not?

I'm going to have to. And I'm going to have to work fast.

24

I am going to a masquerade. Oh, I have been to them in London, where they are somewhat out of vogue, but I travel in circles where fun is more important than fashion. I have been to simple masquerades and elaborate ones, and I presume this will fall on that simpler end, being so far in the countryside, where guests cannot call in a modiste to make them a costume.

I have my own modiste, in the form of Mrs. Miller. She helped me fashion the walking dress earlier, and now she helps me create a costume. What is the base of it? The dress I wore through the stitch.

Mrs. Miller exclaims at the gown after we fetch it from Thorne Manor. It is so bright and colorful, with so many petticoats. It is practically a costume itself, or so it appears to her eighteenth-century eyes. It needs very little work, and so we can focus on the masks.

Yes, *masks*, as in plural. There is no chance that Nicolas is letting me into Norrington's house alone. I insist that I wouldn't be alone— I have the ghost of the former Lord Norrington to guide me. Yet a ghost is hardly a proper guardian, and so Nicolas insists on going.

I may not argue as much as I should. I want him there. The problem is that no costume will fully conceal his skin color, and there are unlikely to be any invited guests who share it. There are, however, a couple of servants who do. When Norrington retired from his admiralty, he brought two men from London. One is of African descent, the other from India. That means Nicolas will not be the only darker-skinned person in the house. With a decent mask and servant attire, if he stays away from the party, guests will mistake him for staff. He just needs to avoid the *actual* staff . . . and Lord Norrington.

It is not a perfect plan, and I do worry, but if we are going to pull this off, we will need to do it together.

WHILE I HAVE BEEN TO MANY BALLS AND PARTIES IN MY LIFE, VERY FEW were in the countryside. I grew up in London, and my social circle is there. The closest a Londoner usually comes to a country party is one held just outside the city, with grounds for perambulation. I might have claimed to have attended the Midsummer Ball at Courtenay Hall, but that is a lie. First, the earl no longer holds it. Second, the earl would never invite the unsuitable sister of his unsuitable sister-in-law. Third, the earl does not even visit Courtenay Hall any longer, having ceded that right to August. I have, however, attended dinner parties there and many picnics—my sister and her husband being very fond of intimate gatherings.

All this is to say that I do not quite know what to expect from tonight's dance. Also, it is fifty years before any party I have ever attended, and customs will have changed. Nicolas knows no more about Yorkshire country society affairs than I do. Oddly, pirates are rarely invited, even if they come from noble stock.

I do know to expect something less formal than I am accustomed to, and if I did not realize that from Emily's casual invitation, I know it when I am able to walk up to the door and no one wonders where my coach is. There are costumed guests spilling over the lawn, and none notice my arrival. The sun has already set, and the grounds are dimly lit with lanterns.

In size and grandeur, the Norrington estate is midway between that of the Thornes and that of the Courtenays, and again, this is what I would expect. I believe Lord Thorne would occupy the same social status as Lord Norrington, but Thorne Manor is a country estate. Norrington Hall is a primary residence, and as such, it has a central house and outbuildings set on acres of land where generations of gardeners have fought a losing battle to transform the moors into a proper English lawn.

The house is impressive, and I wonder that I have not seen it on hikes in my time. Has it been torn down? Do the Norrington fortunes evaporate when the current lord is financially destroyed by the very people whose livelihoods *he* sought to destroy? That would be a delicious twist to the story, but the truth may simply be that I have not spent enough time in this part of the moors to notice the house.

It is a three-story affair of brownish-gray stone set in the shape of an *H*. A massive drive circles around the front, and every window is alight with candles, flickering in the gathering dark.

I said that no one notices my arrival. That is not entirely true. Emily does. She must be on watch for me because I have barely reached the gathering when she flies from the house.

"Oh!" she says. "That is a lovely costume! I feel quite underdressed."

I laugh softly. "I believe a traveling minstrel would appear underdressed next to me. I decided that if I was coming to a masquerade, I would make the best of it."

I swirl, letting my skirts spin around me, and she claps.

"It is beautiful," she says. "Such bright colors. Wherever did you find them?"

This, I realize, is the true reason why my dress is so much brighter than the current fashion. Not because women here prefer drabber attire, but because they do not yet have the dyes necessary to make the colors that women—and men—in my world prefer.

"That is my secret," I say, laying a finger to my lips. "However, if you like the dress, I could let you have it afterward. The style is hardly fashionable, but you could use the fabric for bonnets or such."

She hooks her arm through mine. "You are kind, Miranda, but I would never ask such a thing."

"Do you think I could wear this dress in London?" I roll my eyes. "No, it is for tonight only, and then you may have it."

As she leads me into the house, I look around to see I am indeed more elaborately dressed than most. In addition to my unusual nineteenth-century gown, my mask covers most of my face, in hopes that if I do encounter Norrington, he'll never recognize me. I also have my hair down. Most of the other guests, not quite knowing what to expect from a "masquerade," have simply paired a normal party dress or jacket with a mask.

Emily wears a gorgeous cream dress with embroidered flowers in rust and orange and green. It's wide at the hip—a style I've only seen in paintings—with a slender bodice and natural waist. She pairs that with a sweeping cape and hood of black lace and a black mask. It is very stylish and flattering.

When Emily says, "Oh! There is my uncle!" my heart gives a stutter, even though I am clearly not the pink-cheeked boy he met with Nicolas.

Norrington is, as Emily said, deep in conversation with other wigged men, as if they are at a business meeting. He isn't even wearing a mask, unless one counts the stony expression on his face.

"He seems busy," I whisper as Emily leads me over. "Perhaps later?"

"Nonsense, he will be no less 'busy' later . . . nor tomorrow nor the next day. My uncle lives in a permanent state of busy. Yet he always has time for me."

She is correct. The moment he sees her, that stone softens, and he even manages something like a smile.

"And here is my dear niece," he says. "The instigator of tonight's festivities."

"Instigator?" Emily says. "That sounds suspiciously like laying the blame, uncle."

His smile grows a fraction, eyes warming. "Architect, then? Is that better?"

"Much." She rises to kiss his cheek. "May I introduce my friend, Miss Miranda Hastings?"

His companions use the excuse to ogle me. Norrington's gaze sweeps over me so fast I doubt he could identify my hair color two minutes later.

"Delighted to meet you, Miss Hastings," Norrington says.

And that is it. He does not ask who I am or where I'm from or what my connection might be to Emily. His niece is a young woman, and I am a young woman, and if she has made a suitable local friend, that is all that matters. He speaks to Emily for another moment, and then she is hooking her arm in mine and leading me off to see the dance floor, which is not yet in use as the musicians are still preparing.

"Do you dance?" she asks. Then, "Oh, that is a silly question. Every girl in London must dance and dance beautifully."

"I will not say *beautifully*. I dance well enough. It is one of those things where my interest outstrips my aptitude."

She grins. "I think I can say that about all my interests. I am also but a fair dancer. I would be better if I had better partners. The choices here are . . ." She looks around the knots of middle-aged men. "Underwhelming."

Before I can reply, she grips my arm. "I am certain *he* would be an excellent dancer."

I follow her gaze but see only an elderly couple. She sees where I'm looking and giggles.

"No, silly, not him. The young Frenchman I told you about." She sighs dreamily. "He is so graceful and charming. I know he would be heavenly on the dance floor. If only he could be here."

Nicolas *is* here, somewhere. Safely here, I presume, as I have not heard any uproar or cries that sent Norrington running. We separated well out of sight of the estate, and Nicolas made his way from there.

I have also seen no sign of the elder Lord Norrington's ghost.

That isn't unexpected. Spirits exist in a nether realm that is not quite the same as ours, and while he is able to travel more than poor Andrés, he will still be restricted in many ways. He had hoped to meet us before I entered the house. I am trying not to fret about that. I will need him for the rest of this adventure.

I will also need to slip away from Emily, which I am quickly realizing will not be easy. She is quite glued to my side.

I let her talk about Nicolas and how wonderful a dancer he would make. I agree—I would love to take a turn on the dance floor with him. Sadly, that will not be happening, and so I listen to her and then steer conversation toward other potential partners. That seems to be the best way to slip from her side—when the dancing starts, I must be sure her card is full. Which would work better if she had a card. Do they come into fashion later? I certainly cannot ask, so I only inquire whether there is a local method of scheduling one's dances.

"Uncle says such things are for London balls and society seasons. I am fortunate he even hires musicians. If he had his way, there would be no dancing. The music does interfere with business conversations, after all."

As if on cue, the musicians strike the first note. And in a blink, there is a young man in front of Emily, asking for the dance. Perfect.

I am about to tell her to have fun when a sweaty-faced man of forty appears in front of me.

"Can you dance?" he says, in the same doubtful tone with which one might inquire whether a sow can fly.

"I fear not," I say. "I have twisted—"

Emily is already being led onto the dance floor and doesn't hear my excuse, interrupting with, "She dances very well, sir. Join us!"

I try not to grimace. Before I can try again, the gentleman has me by the hand, which makes me jump, the casual contact quite untoward in my own world.

"Come on, then," he says, as if he's leading that sow to market.

I have no choice but to dance. And because I do not lack pride, I have no choice but to show him how *well* I dance. I told Emily that my interest outstripped my aptitude. That is only because my interest is "exceptional," and my aptitude is merely "quite good." Quite good in London is different from quite good in the country, and in trying to show this lout that yes, I can dance, I attract far more attention than I intended, and I find myself unable to leave the dance floor, as both Emily and I have a line of prospective partners waiting.

This is most inconvenient. Let it be a lesson to me that there are times when my pride must take the blow. It will survive.

I am on my fifth dance when a figure appears at my shoulder, giving me a start.

It is the ghost.

"You must stop dancing," he says, looking alarmed. "A country dance does not last into the wee hours of the morning. You have work to do."

I try not to glower at him. It's not as if I want to be dancing. Also not as if he's been here, ready to show me around.

He is right, though, that I must get out of this. There is only one thing to do. Swallow my pride and lie.

When the dance ends, I feign breathing heavily, hand to my chest. "Oh my, I have quite overtaxed myself. I fear I must sit down."

When Emily looks over, I make a face that has her laughing. Then I motion toward the edge of the dance floor where there are chairs and small tables, telling her that I will rest there.

I follow the ghost. He leads me through those thronged at the edge of the dance floor. Everyone seems to be inside now, and it is quite crowded, the temperature rising enough that my brow beads in sweat.

I wind through knots of onlookers, so that if Emily is watching, I will seem to simply head into the room where elderly guests are resting and listening to the music.

From there, I pick up my pace, following the ghost down a hall and around a corner. When hands reach from an open doorway, I start to yelp. Then I see the white gloves on those hands and glare as Nicolas pulls me into the room.

He shuts the door behind us and puts his hands at my waist as he kisses me against the wall. I allow the kiss and then rap him on the arm.

"Whatever do you think you are doing, sir? You forget yourself."

He chuckles and kisses me again.

"You do know that we have a robbery to conduct. Also"—I jerk my chin to the side—"we have a spectral audience."

Nicolas bows to the ghost. "My apologies, sir. I simply could not resist a reunion with my beloved, however brief and inappropriate. I was watching her dance and seething with envy of her partners."

"The grandfather with a limp?" I retort. "Or the young man with the unfortunate facial hair?"

"I said *envy*, crécerelle, not *jealousy*. One would think an English-woman—and a writer, no less, would understand the difference. I envied their ability to dance with you when I cannot."

"Good. Jealousy is a tedious emotion, and not at all flattering."

"Even in a very small dose?"

I consider. "The tiniest of doses, perhaps. A fleeting prickle, quickly banished upon the realization it is unwarranted."

"Agreed. Now, if you will follow me, I have already ascertained the safest route to the office."

25

Nicolas may have found the office, but he has not been able to enter.

"We require the key," he says. "I presume the elder Lord Norrington can lead us to it?"

The ghost, who has been silently slipping after us, watching for trouble, now looks at me with dawning horror.

"There is a lock on the door?" He looks at it. "Oh, no. I-I did not see that. It must have been added after my death. I put everything of value in the safe and saw no reason to lock the door."

"That is all right," I say. "Do you know where your son might put the key?"

"On his person. He is endlessly suspicious, which is why I ought to have checked the door and foreseen this. He's the only person with a key, and he will carry it on him at all times."

"No matter," I say. "It is not an overly complicated lock."

I pull a pin from my hair. "It seems we will not be easily able to get a key, Nico, so I will need you to stand guard, with Lord Norrington here, while I prize it open."

Nicolas grins. "Dare I ask how you acquired such a skill?"

"I needed it for a book."

"Naturellement. The experiential method of fiction writing." He kisses my cheek. "You are a wonder. Yes, Lord Norrington and I shall stand guard against, well, against Lord Norrington, as confusing as that may be."

"Call me Lord Thomas," the ghost says. "That shall make things simpler."

I tell Nicolas, and then the two go in opposite directions to stand watch. We are in a quiet part of the house, with the bedrooms and such, and I am able to work in silence. Within moments, I have the door open, and we are inside.

Despite what I told Emily, I do not have a sitting room at home— I have converted it to an office, complete with a massive window and an attached seat for daydreaming. I have a desk, bookcases and an armchair. It is my perfect little space.

This is not that office. This is a cramped room, dark and windowless. There is a small desk, an uncomfortable-looking chair and bookshelves filled with ledgers and boxes that I'd wager contain *more* ledgers, along with receipts and correspondence. If there is a single actual book in the office, I do not see it. What I do see are endless places where Norrington could put important notes. The most likely spot, though, is the black iron box squatting in a corner.

"Do you know how to operate a lock like that?" Nicolas says as we peer down at the safe. "I have never seen one."

"They are rare." *Even in my time.* "But I have opened them."

"Then I will leave you to it."

He scans the office and heads for a row of boxes. I kneel in front of the safe and then glance up at Lord Thomas.

The ghost gives me the first number. I turn the dial, with my ear to the safe, and hear the faintest click of the tumblers. When I tell him, he exhales in relief.

"Good. Then he has not changed the lock. May I give you the rest of the numbers and then stand guard in the hall?"

I take a pen from the desk and write down the remaining numbers. He confirms them. Then he slips through the wall and promises to pace the hallway, letting us know whether anyone even seems to be heading this way.

When he is gone, Nicolas says, "If we are discovered, trouble will come from the main section of the house. We need only run into the next room, where I have left open a window for our escape."

"You are rather good at this."

He smiles over his shoulder. "I am a quick study of that which interests me, and while I never imagined thievery and espionage would qualify, I have discovered I have a knack for them, so long as they are in pursuit of good."

"There is nothing quite as thrilling as misbehaving for a cause."

"Very true. You shall need to show me how to open locks. That is a skill I have not yet attempted."

As we talk, I continue working the safe lock, and he continues searching the boxes. We also keep our voices low. When he says something else, though, I do not hear it. I am too busy frowning at the safe.

"Is something wrong?"

I shake my head. "I must have made a mistake. I heard the clicks for all but the last number, and it is not opening. I shall have to restart."

I do that, and again, I catch the faint sound that signals success with all but the final number. As I peer at the paper, Nicolas comes over.

"That is a six, non? Not a five?" he says. "Non, it could not be a five. You would not have misheard the two numbers in English."

"I had Lord Thomas confirm them. Let me try again. Would you put your ear to the safe, please? The noise is *very* faint, but you might hear it."

I run through the combination again, and again, the last number fails. With a growl of frustration, I rock back on my heels.

"There!" Nicolas says.

"There, what?"

He points at the dial, which is on the seven. Then he turns the door crank, and it opens.

"Something must have shifted in the workings," Nicolas says as he reaches inside.

A flicker beside him, and Lord Thomas appears. He sees the safe open.

"We have done it," I say. "The last—"

I see his face then, agitated and wide eyed, as he flutters his hands at me. "Close it up! They are coming."

"Who's coming?"

"My son and his men. Close it!" He sees Nicolas pulling out papers. "Put it all back! Quickly! You can still get out of this if he does not know what you've done."

"Nico?" I say. "Norrington is coming."

He nods, and we both grab more pages, shoving them into the satchel Nicolas brought, as I ignore Lord Thomas's sputtering and flailing.

"We have an escape plan," I say to the ghost.

We shove in the last of the pages. It is then that we hear the pound of footfalls.

"You do not understand," Lord Thomas says. "He is not simply approaching. He knows Nicolas is here. Someone must have spotted him."

We're already at the door. Then Nicolas stops short, and he curses under his breath.

"Nico?"

The moment I say his name, I hear the problem myself. The footsteps are not coming from the direction of the party. They come from the other way. From our escape route.

26

We peer into the hall. Nicolas said he left open a window in the next room. Except the next room is ten feet away, and footsteps are fast approaching the corner.

"Is there another way out?" I whisper to Lord Thomas.

The ghost nods. "Follow me. Quickly! We'll go through the kitchens."

We are already in the hall, running as quickly and silently as we can. A squeak sounds behind us. The men are about to turn the corner and see us. Nicolas slows.

"This way!" Lord Thomas says, waving down the hall.

Nicolas grabs my arm and pulls me to the left, along the side hall that leads back to the party.

"No!" Lord Thomas says. "You will be spotted! Child, tell him. He cannot hear me!"

I do not tell Nicolas. He knows what he is doing. Yes, we are heading straight to the party, where we will indeed be spotted. However, if we did not turn that corner, we would have been spotted by Norrington as we ran for the kitchens.

"Would you like to dance, crécerelle?" Nicolas whispers as we run as fast as my gown will allow.

I stare at him as if he is mad. Then I choke on a laugh. Yes, of course. We are heading into the party. There is nowhere to go but through it, and if we race in, guests will raise the alarm immediately. How do we sneak through the next room? By hiding in the last place Norrington will look: the crowded dance floor.

We slow as we near the room, and Nicolas reaches up to adjust a lock of his hair. It is not actually his hair, which is short and tightly curled. No, tonight he wears a wig. A white wig with loose curls that cover the back of his neck. He pulls curls over his shoulder, and I help adjust them as we walk.

He is dressed in formal attire, which could work for a guest or a member of the staff. The wig would clearly suggest "guest"—as would the mask—but it is a masquerade, and so it would not seem odd if some of the staff were in costume.

Long white gloves hide his hands and wrists, and his mask covers his entire face. With the wig, that leaves only a sliver of dark skin exposed between his high collar and mask. The curls partly cover it, but his mask is also dark, so unless one looks closely, one is unlikely to notice the color of his skin below.

It was not an adequate disguise for him to attend as a guest, but it would have worked if he were spotted briefly in the house . . . or if he is spotted briefly on the dance floor.

He adjusts the satchel strap around his neck. If it looks out of place, well, it *is* a costume ball, and they will presume he is masquerading as some sort of courier. He otherwise cuts such a fine figure that they will overlook this one oddity in his attire.

We walk into the small ballroom, my hand lifted in his as he escorts me to the dance floor. Our timing is impeccable. The quartet is just striking up a minuet, which is delightfully old-fashioned to me, and Nicolas whisks me into the dance.

So far this evening, I have been within the top echelon of the dancers. It is a country ball, after all, and so it was not that difficult to stand out. Yet Nicolas matches and then surpasses my skill, gliding about the dance floor as if he has graced a thousand in his lifetime. I feel like poor Emily, ready to swoon just watching him.

Does the man possess any actual flaws? Well, he does have an alarming propensity for getting himself into trouble, but I can hardly judge him for that, as I suffer from the same shortcoming myself.

Norrington and his men do not barge into the party looking for us. I am certain they are looking, but not here, and so Nicolas and I agree, in whispers, to half a dance as we slowly make our way to the other side of the floor, where we may slip away and escape.

The dance is hardly an intimate one. We rarely come closer than arm's length. Yet it feels as if we are locked in an embrace. Even when I spin away, our gazes unlatch only a moment before finding one another in the crowd. I see nothing but his face, feel nothing but his gloved hands on my arms, smell nothing but the faint odor of orange-flower perfume from his shirt, hear nothing but his whispers when I pass. Whispers telling me I am beautiful, telling me I am an incredible dancer, telling me more things that I cannot understand because he switches to French for those, murmuring them in the brief heartbeats where we draw close.

I feel something, both a tightness and a fluttering in my chest, a dizziness in my mind, my breath catching each time he passes. I may never have experienced this before, but I instantly recognize it for what it is.

I am falling in love.

Falling in love? No, that implies taking the first careful step off the cliff. I have already fallen, and now I am plummeting, and it thrills and terrifies me.

When we draw near again, he murmurs, "You do realize you have stumbled into my trap, crécerelle?"

I tense, breath gone completely for one irrational second. I can only imagine my expression, but he does not see it as he twirls me again and then leans in to whisper.

"You are apparently unfamiliar with the customs of my country," he says. "When one agrees to a *danse à deux* with a man, one is, in fact, agreeing to marry him."

I stifle a laugh. "I see."

"It is true. I shall need to set the bans for morning. That is what they call it here, do they not? Setting the bans? Reading the bans? Something like that. The point, crécerelle, is that you are now stuck with me."

"What if I do not wish to marry?"

"Hmm. That is a problem. However, I believe the custom only requires that, having engaged in an intimate dance for two, you are bound to me. Skipping the wedding would be simpler, I agree. I could save the expense and use it to buy you a proper sword instead."

"I like the one you already gave me."

His eyes spark, pure devilry behind them. "But I have not given you that, crécerelle. We are taking it slow, non?"

"Taking it slow in that regard? Yet committing ourselves to one another after a mere two days together?"

"Three days."

"I was unconscious for part of one."

"We have known one another for two and a half days, which in my country, is the perfect length of courtship."

"Why do I feel that, if I actually went to your country, I would discover you have not been entirely truthful about it?"

"You shall have to visit it and find out. And to visit it, you shall have to stay with me, so that I may escort you there and introduce you to my family as my beloved."

I roll my eyes. We are approaching the far side of the dance floor, and with one final whirl, we are there.

"The door is straight ahead," he whispers. "I will pretend I am taking you outside for some air."

He lifts my hand again, a courtly and proper escort guiding me through the crowd.

"Miranda?" a voice says behind us.

I do not turn. I recognize that voice, and my heart squeezes with the pain of what feels like betrayal, but I pretend I do not hear her, and Nicolas does the same. Then Emily is in front of us, frowning.

"Miranda, wherever—?"

She sees Nicolas and gives a sharp inhale. "Oh."

"We are stepping out for air," I say as calmly as I can. "We will return in a—"

"Nicolas," she says, and my heart jumps into my throat.

I'm about to deny it, pretend she has mistaken my escort for another.

"Oui, Miss Emily," Nicolas murmurs.

Her gaze turns to me then. I brace for anger, for outrage, but the look in her eyes is worse. It isn't even disappointment. It's acceptance. Sad acceptance, as if thinking this is the obvious answer. I had been so friendly and so kind, and of course I had an ulterior motive. Of course I betrayed her.

I try to remind myself that she may have betrayed Nicolas first. But that hurt in her eyes says she did not. Whatever happened, she was her uncle's dupe, as her grandfather said.

"We must go," I say, my voice low. "I'm sorry, Emily. So very sorry. It was important."

"I know," she says, her gaze dropping. "If you are helping Dr. Dupuis, then you are doing God's work for the people of the bay. Thank you."

Those last two words, spoken without a spark of sarcasm, cut straight through me.

I reach to squeeze her arm. "I am sorry. I will apologize better later, if I can."

"No need." Her gaze goes from Nicolas to me, and her lips twist. "Of course, he would be with someone like . . ." She inhales sharply again. "You must leave."

"We truly must. We were caught and fled to the dance floor."

"And now you're running out the front door?" She shakes her head. "Follow me. There is another way."

"No," says a voice behind us. I glance back to see Lord Thomas's ghost. I'd lost sight of him when we fled, and now he's there, as agitated as ever. "The foreyard is clear. They think you ran out the back."

He says more, but I don't hear it. Nicolas tightens his hand on mine as he tugs me in Emily's wake. I glance at him, my gaze asking whether he trusts her, and he only makes a gesture that is half head-shake and half shrug. He isn't sure of her intentions, only that he agrees we ought not to flee through the front door.

I try to tell him what Lord Thomas is saying, but we're moving too fast, the din of voices and music too loud. Emily opens a door. Beyond it is darkness, and I hesitate, but Nicolas guides me through.

"It is a servant's corridor," Emily whispers. "One that is not in use this evening. There is a door at the end."

"No," Lord Thomas says behind us. "Do not follow her. Please. I don't like this. I do not know what she is up to, but I do not like—"

A crack has my entire body spasming. Nicolas yanks me to him, but it is only the sound of the door opening. Emily pushes it wide and then leans out. From beyond, distant footfalls sound, and Norrington's voice rings out, "Why is everyone out here? Is no one searching the house? I want them *found*. Now!"

Emily keeps looking about. Then she gasps and pulls back. Before we can ask what it is, she peeks out again and nods, as if satisfied.

"What is it?" I ask.

"I thought I saw my—" She shakes her head. "I am mistaken, obviously."

I glance to my side. Lord Thomas is gone. Scouting the way, I presume, in case we are walking into a trap. Did Emily catch a glimpse of his ghost? It is not impossible.

"They are looking for you," she says. "They seem to be searching the back of the estate, expecting you will have fled into the moors."

"Then we shall not flee into the moors," Nicolas says.

"I would suggest you head that way." She points. "Circle past the stables and along the stone wall until you reach the—"

A shout cuts her off. She turns that way, and her eyes widen just as someone yells something about a door.

"They see the door open," Nicolas says. "We must go. Now."

"No!" she says. "I can—" She pauses a heartbeat, as if she was about to say she'd handle her uncle when she realized the futility of that. "Yes. Run. I will distract them."

She darts out the door, skirts hiked, heading in the direction of the voices. Nicolas and I take off. Lord Thomas comes running from the front of the house, quickly telling us he knows a way, but we can see our path, and whatever Emily is doing, it has forestalled anyone coming around that corner of the house.

We make it to the stables. Then we're creeping around it to the pasture when boot clomps sound on the hard earth to our right. Emily calls something, as if in distress, and her uncle shouts for someone to help her while the others circle the house.

We're at the pasture. A trio of horses stares at us.

"Pay no mind to the humans sneaking past your corral," Nicolas whispers.

"Also, if you could stop staring at us, that would help."

The horses do not stop staring. One of them comes trotting to the fence and follows us, whinnying. It takes a moment, but then I see why. It's the mare we used to make our escape yesterday.

I worry at first that she has come home to her abuser, but the other horses are sleek and healthy animals. She must have belonged to one of the men chasing us, rather than Norrington himself. Someone from the Norrington estate found her and brought her here. Now she's whinnying her greeting and trotting along the fence as we run.

"The horses!" a man shouts. "Something is disturbing the horses."

I hitch my skirts higher to pick up my speed, but I am wearing a nineteenth-century gown with endless petticoats, and a jog is even more exhausting than half an hour on the dance floor.

"The mare," Nicolas says. "If she is so eager to accompany us, we should make use of her. Can you ride without a saddle, crécerelle?"

"No, but I can hang onto you."

"And that is all that we require."

Before I can speak, he lifts me as easily as if I were a waif in her shift. He puts me on the stone wall, and then he vaults it. A moment later, he is on the mare, who is not at all concerned by this turn of events. She even tosses her head, clearly eager to be off on a fresh adventure.

Nicolas reaches for me, and I manage to transfer myself from the fence to the mare. I'm getting my grip when a shout sounds, followed by a shot. The shot goes wild, but someone yells.

"The horses, you fool! Do not spook the horses. That is Lord Norrington's prize gelding in there."

"I believe we should spook the horses," I say.

"I believe you are correct," Nicolas says.

He taps the mare's sides with his heels and steers her to the nearest gate. Then he leans down, opens it and guides her toward the other two horses, who have ambled over for a closer look. A gorgeous bay gelding snorts and feints, and when Nicolas gets the mare galloping, the other two horses follow, as if this is a lovely and unexpected game.

We fly out the gate and onto the moor. More shouts sound behind us, but the men can do little else. They cannot catch up on foot, and they dare not discharge a firearm when Lord Norrington's gelding runs alongside us.

We sail over the moor with the gelding beside us, the third horse having already bored of the game and turned back. When we are certain we have lost our pursuers, we send the gelding off in hopes they'll pause to collect him.

We continue on until we spot a farm, which seems like a good location to leave the mare. From there, we continue on foot to Thorne Manor. That is the obvious place to go. Obvious for us, while not obvious for our pursuers. They do not know of any connection between Nicolas and Lord Thorne, so they will be checking every croft and barn in the area, presuming he has holed up in one of them, as he did after I was shot.

It is a good three-mile walk until we see the dark shape of Thorne Manor, perched atop a hill. The evening weather is pleasant enough, but we are both exhausted from our evening, and we share a sigh of relief on spotting the house.

"I will go first, if I may," Nicolas says. "To be sure it is empty. Lord Thorne is not due back for a week, but I would not wish to entangle him in this, and my attire is somewhat more somber than yours."

"Also somewhat less cumbersome," I say. *Not to mention the problem of the current Lord Thorne not being the one I know.* "After two days in men's clothing, I cannot wait to shed this dress and these petticoats."

He shoots a smile my way, his teeth glinting in the dark night. "And I cannot wait to assist you in that endeavor. If I recall correctly, his lordship has a bathing tub."

I shiver with pleasure. "Oh, please tell me he does."

"I am quite certain of it, as I am quite certain you have earned a long bath and an attentive valet to heat the water for your tub."

"The only thing that would make that better is if the tub were large enough for two."

His smile grows. "If it is not, I believe we can find a way to both squeeze in. Now, if you wait here, I will return momentarily."

27

There is no one in the house. Nor is there any sign that the current Lord Thorne has returned. Nicolas also scouts the exterior to be sure we weren't followed. I cannot imagine we were tracked unseen across the open and empty moors, but he is leaving nothing to chance. If we are going to spend the night here—a night where we may be absorbed in one another's company—then we must be confident in our safety.

The moment we are inside, he heads upstairs to start a fire, and I strip off my dress and petticoats, leaving only my shift. Then I collapse, sighing, into a wonderfully deep armchair. I think I have only been there a moment, but when Nicolas appears before me, he is holding a glass of what smells like brandy, along with a plate of dried meat and preserves. He is also dressed only in his tight trousers and open shirt.

"I could get used to this," I say with a sigh as I take the brandy from his hand.

"And I could get used to this." He bends to run his fingers up my thigh, making me shiver. "I do not suppose there is room in that chair for two?"

"If there is not, then we can squeeze in."

I rise and let him take the chair. He tugs me onto his lap, and there is the perfect amount of room, enough that we fit together snugly. I sip the brandy and then pass it to him, and he lifts a piece of preserved lemon to my lips. We rest like that, sitting together in silence, eating and drinking as we relax.

When I set aside the empty brandy snifter, he does the same with the empty plate, and I curl into him, my head on his shoulder, his fingers toying with a lock of my hair.

"I promised you a bath, and I will deliver," he says.

"The bath and more?"

A soft chuckle. "Definitely a bath and more. If you are not in a hurry, though . . ."

"Rest," I say. "We had a long and treacherous evening, and I am not about to expect you to start hauling hot water to a tub."

"It is not that. I would like to talk first, now that we are safe and fed, and I have had a bit of brandy to loosen my tongue."

I snuggle into him. "Talk all you like."

"I know I have been teasing about . . . where we go from here. About marrying you or taking you to Martinique with me, and I may be demonstrating a disappointing lack of my usual confidence, but I must ask . . ." He takes a deep breath. "Would you like me to continue pretending that I am entirely teasing?"

I stiffen. I don't mean to, but I do, and he nods.

"That is what I thought," he says. "You are comfortable with it as teasing."

"It's not that," I say. "There's something . . . There's something I must tell you."

I expect him to tense or to look confused, but he only nods again.

"I thought there might be," he says. "That was my impression, at least. I have been trying to decide what it might be, and I have begun to suspect there is a reason you joked about not wishing to marry. You are already married, are you not? Unhappily wed to one of the men who has proven such an inadequate lover?"

"Certainly not." I sit up. "If you think that my lack of virginity means I am clearly married, or that my lack of interest in marriage clearly means the same—"

He presses a kiss to my lips. "I only thought it was a possibility. I know there are men and women who find themselves in such a situation and lead separate lives, which I thought might be the case."

"I am not married. I was never married—or even engaged—to the lovers I have had, and while I am not adamantly opposed to marriage, I do not feel it is the necessary institution that society claims. I believe in unions of a deeper sort, and while I have seen happy marriages—my parents and my sister—I have also seen ones that are cages rather than places of love and safety."

"I do not disagree, and I am sorry if you are insulted by my supposition, crécerelle."

"I am touchy on both matters, as you can see, and I did not mean to snap."

His arms tighten around me. "Yet that leads us back where we were before I interrupted. You have something to tell me?"

"I do." I straighten in his arms. "I did not mean to keep it a secret, but it is not an easy thing to explain. Three days ago, in this very room, I said that I knew you were about to die on that road. I pretended I could see into the future because that is more believable than what I am about to tell you."

His brows shoot up. "The gift of prophecy is more believable? Now you do have my attention, crécerelle."

"What I need is not merely your attention but your trust. As far-fetched as my story may sound, allow me to finish my explanation before you question my sanity."

"I would never question—"

The front door rattles, cutting him short. We both glance over. All has gone still and silent again.

Nicolas lifts me from his lap, sets me on my feet and buttons his shirt as he creeps toward the front door. While I pick up my dress, the knob turns one way and then the other.

I slide the dress over my head. It does not fit well without the petticoats, but right now, my only concern is being covered in case the current Lord Thorne should walk in. As that knob turns again, I know that is not about to happen. Someone is trying the locked door with great care so as not to alert those inside.

We have not bothered to keep the house in darkness. Lanterns are lit. Smoke pours from the chimney. Nicolas said that the current Lord Thorne has many friends who are welcome to use his home, and so the villagers will not send up a mob if they see someone in residence. Could they be concerned, though? Or could it be a thief come to rob us? We *are* in the time of highwaymen.

There is, of course, another obvious scenario. Yet I do not leap to the assumption that Norrington has found us. We escaped on horseback and then on foot, with no one in pursuit. His first thought will never be to check the home of his distant neighbor in case Nicolas knows the family and has permission to use the house.

And yet we cannot dismiss that possibility, can we? The possibility that someone saw us. Or that Norrington's men encountered someone who spotted lights on at Thorne Manor.

Nicolas stands poised at the door with his head cocked. I position myself along the wall, where I am hidden and can both listen and watch him. When the next sound comes, it is at the back door, and I tense, my mind leaping to that broken door.

No, the door is broken in *my* time, under *that* Lord Thorne, and here, the intruder can only twist the knob this way and then that.

Nicolas drops to a crouch and creeps to the front window. Being careful not to ripple the drawn drapes any more than necessary, he opens a peeping hole. One look, and he's pulling back fast.

"They are here," he whispers. "Men. With guns."

I do not ask whether they are Norrington's men. No one else is going to lay armed siege to Thorne Manor with us inside.

"Let us check the rear door," I whisper. "If we can slip out—"

Something flies through the window with the deafening crash of breaking glass. A rock tumbles to the floor. For a moment, I can only stare at it, outrage erupting. They dare break Lord Thorne's front window?

Of course, that reaction lasts only a moment before I realize the breaking of his window is hardly our greatest concern. By then, voices sound outside the window, the drapes billowing with the night wind as one man warns another to clear the glass before entering.

Nicolas grabs my arm and tugs me toward the back of the house.

"No!" I whisper. "That is what they want us to do."

As I speak, I am already running for the stairs. There is no time to explain, but Nicolas does not need an explanation. Smashing the front window with a rock is hardly a stealthy entrance. They want us to hear it. They want us to run pell-mell out the back where they may scoop us up without fear of confrontation.

Sure enough, as we reach the stairs, the man coming through the window says, "Did you see them?"

I dash up the stairs as quietly as I can. When I reach the top, Nicolas whispers, "Oui! There is a secret passage. I recall Lord Thorne joking about it. You are a genius, crécerelle. You know where it is?"

I do not answer. Yes, I have heard of a secret passage, one that in our time, William Thorne barred up after a tragedy. It would still be open here. Yet that is not where I take Nicolas. I grab his hand, and I race into the spare bedroom.

I am barely through the door when boots thud on the stairs. I whirl to Nicolas.

"Do you trust me?"

He blinks at the question. "Of course."

I grip his hand tight. "Then come. Quickly."

He runs beside me as I cross to the center of the room, my brain whirring to remember exactly the right spot—

I skid to a stop as I stumble over a chest where there had been nothing a moment ago. I am through. I am already—

There is no one holding my hand. I wheel, and my heart seizes as I see Nicolas standing on the very spot that holds the time stitch. He's staring at Bronwyn's desk.

"Do not move," I say.

"I am not certain I dare. The room has changed, has it not?"

"Yes. Now take a large step in my direction, please. Do not

return to that spot."

I am ready to say more, but he doesn't need it. He takes that giant step, and I am just about to speak when the door opens. We both wheel as Nicolas pulls his sword in one smooth move. A head pops around the door, one far lower than we expect.

"Edmund?" I say.

My five-year-old nephew opens the door and stands there, solemnly eying this sword-wielding stranger. Nicolas quickly lowers his weapon as Edmund steps in, wearing a long nightshirt.

"You are not a ghost?" he says to Nicolas.

"I . . . do not think so." Nicolas glances at me. "Please tell me I am not a ghost. There are many strange explanations for what has just occurred, and I am hoping that is not the correct one."

"It is not," I say.

"You are alive, then?" Edmund walks in and closes the door. "That is good."

"I have always thought so," Nicolas says carefully.

My nephew looks up at me. "Did you help him escape the navy knaves?"

"I did."

"Good."

"I believe I am missing some context for this conversation," Nicolas says. "May I presume this is your nephew, Edmund?"

"Yes. Edmund, this is—"

The door flies open, Rosalind racing in. Lady Thorne—Bronwyn —hurries after her. They both stop on seeing us. Rosalind's hand goes to Edmund's shoulder, pulling him back from the man with a sword, and Nicolas quickly sheathes his weapon.

Rosalind seems about to speak. Then she stares at Nicolas, taking in the whole of him before looking at me and murmuring under her voice. "Your pirate ghost, Miranda?"

Nicolas hears and smiles. "Not a ghost, or so I am told, though I am concerned that I keep being confused for one. It is rather troubling."

"Because you died," Edmund says. "We have seen you, Aunt

Miranda and me. On Hood's Lane. Mama was afraid I would see you die, but I only saw you walking, and then the two men came out to kill you."

"I . . . see." He turns to me. "Perhaps a fuller explanation is in order?"

"This is the nineteenth century," I say.

He blinks and looks around.

"You didn't get to that part yet, huh?" Bronwyn says.

"We were being pursued, and I ran through the stitch with Nicolas."

"And you *both* came through?" Bronwyn says. "From the *past*? Okay, that is *definitely* not how it works for the rest of us."

"You are . . . American?" Nicolas asks. "Your accent seems to be."

"She is Canadian," I say. "And it is not simply the accent. She is from the twenty-first century, so her language is different, which I have not heard myself, as they have been pretending she is from my time—the nineteenth century."

"I see." Nicolas shakes his head. "No, that is a lie. I do not see at all."

"Because my sister is not explaining this properly," Rosalind says. "I am Rosalind Courtenay, Miranda's eldest sister. This is Bronwyn Dale Thorne, wife to William Thorne. Miranda has brought you through what we call the time stitch and arrived into the nineteenth century."

She points at the spot. "It is there, by the chest, so be careful not to stumble into it."

"I have stepped through time," Nicolas says slowly.

"Yes," everyone says in unison.

"Ten years into the future."

"More like fifty," I say.

"This is the home of Lord William Thorne, but not the Lord William Thorne I know."

Bronwyn sighs. "They do like their Williams. I'm guessing yours would be my husband's grandfather. Or even father, depending on his age. Yes, the current Lord Thorne is also a William. He is not at home. We were in London with Rosalind when Portia—Miranda's other sister—sounded the alarm."

"I thought Portia was in Oxford for a medical lecture?" I say.

"There was some issue, and she returned home to find you gone. Rosalind feared you had learned of the stitch and used it."

"To help you," Edmund says to Nicolas, having been following the conversation in silence.

"Er, no," I say. "I would love to claim that was my goal, but as far as I knew, the stitch only worked between our time and Bronwyn's."

"As far as *any* of us knew," Bronwyn says.

"So you thought you were going to the future," Nicolas says. "Instead, you ended up in the past, in time to warn me."

"Exactly in time to warn you," I say. "Which is odd, but also extremely fortuitous."

"I think so. Particularly as it means I am not now dead and a ghost."

"You were not truly a ghost," Edmund says. "Aunt Miranda calls them death echoes."

"It can happen in the case of a violent death," I say. "Those with the Sight see a spectral replay, but the ghosts themselves have passed over."

"So I *did* die. You *did* see my death, as you claimed. Rather than looking into the future, you were looking into the past."

"Yes."

"I do not suppose you brought that bottle of brandy with you? I suddenly feel in need of it."

Bronwyn laughs. "I can imagine. Come downstairs, and we'll find you something."

"In exchange for telling us what you were running from," Rosalind says. "Do not think I missed that part."

I roll my eyes. "Yes, Rosie."

"Now, downstairs, both of you. Edmund, since you are clearly not going back to bed anytime soon, you may join us."

28

Rosalind and Bronwyn are in the kitchen preparing a snack, with Edmund recruited to help. I am quite certain that a late-night nibble does not require three people's assistance, but I know they have left us alone for a few minutes of privacy.

We are in the sitting room, and I stand by the doorway, watching Nicolas prowl the room, taking everything in. When he pauses at a stack of books, bending to read the titles, I tentatively walk over.

"Are you all right?" I ask. "I know it is a shock."

He straightens and turns to me. "It ought to be, oughtn't it? I have stepped into another time. I should be still in that upstairs room, frozen in disbelief, and instead I feel as if I have been transported to a wondrous new place brimming with new adventures. I suspect that means I have not fully comprehended what has happened. But I also suspect . . ." He shrugs. "As you quoted when we first met, 'There are more things in heaven and earth, . . . than are dreamt of in your philosophy.' Except that my philosophy has always been exactly that—the world contains more things than I can dream of. And so my reaction?"

He shrugs, bends to the books again and takes out a copy of *The*

Tempest, holding it up as he quotes, "Now I will believe that there are unicorns."

I smile and finish the lines, "That in Arabia there is one tree, the phoenix' throne; one phoenix at this hour reigning there."

"Yes." He glances over. "Are there unicorns? Or phoenixes?"

"Only in books. At least as far as I have seen."

"But if one can travel through time, perhaps there is a past where they are alive, and I have always felt such possibilities are real. That is how I was raised. Believe my own eyes and still dream of more, beyond what I can see. So I accept this as what it is. A wonder."

"It will still be something of a shock, and my blunt approach did not make it better."

He chuckles. "I am not certain how any approach could be better. However it is said, I have discovered that you are from the next century."

"Are you angry with me for not telling you sooner?"

He walks to me, arms going around my waist. "Non. In fact, I am glad that it happened the way it did. Otherwise, I would not have wanted to doubt you, but I would have, and that would have been most uncomfortable for me and upsetting for you. While I am still attempting to understand how such a thing is possible, I accept that it is both possible and wondrous."

I exhale. "I am glad you think so."

He grins. "I am in the future. How could that not be wondrous?" He looks around. "Now tell me about everything." He grabs my hand and tugs me toward a photograph. "Let's start with this. It is not a painting, is it?"

I smile. "It is not. It is a direct likeness. It is created by . . ."

I tell him as much as I can. Then the others arrive, and we tell Rosalind and Bronwyn everything. Well, everything except the death of Andrés, which is not suitable within the hearing of a five-year-old child. My sister may grumble about how much I *do* think is suitable for Edmund, but even I draw a line.

With that cut from the narrative, it is an exciting tale of derring-do, with me swooping in to warn Nicolas, being shot by his would-be killers, nursed back to the health by the pirate-physician and so on, all near-death escapes and pirate ships and masquerade balls and subterranean passages. It does make quite a thrilling tale, though from the looks Rosalind is giving me, she would prefer a story with far fewer near-death escapes. Edmund devours every word. So does Bronwyn, up until I mention the gladius and I show it and, being a historian, she spends the rest of my story enrapt in examining the short sword.

When we bring the tale to a close, I take Edmund to bed. I tuck him in, and he makes me promise Nicolas will be here tomorrow. Then I slip back downstairs and find Nicolas telling the part about Andrés.

"That is . . ." Rosalind blinks back tears, touching her pregnant belly. "I do not have the words."

"It is unbelievably horrific," Bronwyn says. "I am so sorry, Dr. Dupuis."

"Nico, please."

"I am sorry for your loss. I am only glad that you and Miranda can put his spirit to rest. We will do whatever we can to help. I don't think we can travel back to your time, though. I'm still not sure how Miranda got there."

"Providence," Nicolas says with a smile. "She arrived in time to warn me. Just as you passed through to meet Lord Thorne. The stitch, as you call it, sends people where they need to be."

Bronwyn glances quickly at Rosalind. "Not in every case."

"My sister went through accidentally," I say. "She was trapped in the twenty-first century for four years. We thought she'd perished."

"Oh." Nicolas sits upright. "I apologize, Lady Courtenay."

"It's Rosalind, please. While my stay in the twenty-first century was involuntary, I did enjoy their much more relaxed social protocols."

"Which were also more relaxed in the eighteenth century," I say. "I think the current social constraints are all ours."

"Speaking as the Victorian historian, they are mostly yours," Bronwyn says. "Even Georgian England wasn't quite so . . . uptight. As for the stitch, I am starting to believe it is different things to different people. For me, it was a door to William, even when we were children. For you, Miranda, it was a door to warn Nicolas of an ambush and then to return here before you were both captured. For Rosalind, it was"—she shrugs—"an accident. A twist of fate. But it has righted the error and allows her family to pass freely. The point is that while I don't think we can help you directly, Miranda, we can play armchair detective."

"Bronwyn has solved a few murders herself," Rosalind says. "She freed ghosts haunting Thorne Manor."

"And Rosalind helped a ghost at Courtenay Hall," Bronwyn says. "So we are more than happy to offer our services, putting all our heads together to solve this particular murder. You said you found papers in this Norrington's office?"

"Yes," I say. "But we left them in the nineteenth century."

"Non, crécerelle," Nicolas says. "I grabbed the satchel before I passed through. It is upstairs."

"Crécerelle?" Bronwyn says, her lips twitching. "That means kestrel, doesn't it?"

I roll my eyes. "He thinks it suits me."

Bronwyn turns to Rosalind. "It's a small North American hawk. A force to be reckoned with, despite its small size. Seems fitting, I think."

Rosalind grumbles under her breath.

"I will bring the satchel," Nicolas says. "While staying far from that time stitch."

NICOLAS RETRIEVES THE SATCHEL, AND WE DIVIDE UP THE PAPERS WE took from Norrington's safe. In them, we find mostly important business documents that do not aid our cause at all. *Legitimate* business documents. We also find a small stack of what Bronwyn calls "blackmail-worthy" documents. Proof that Norrington knows he is imposing undue regulations on the people of Hood's Bay in an attempt to control the sea trade there. More specifically, he wants to control the harbor itself and turn it into a rival for Whitby. To do that, he must force the fishermen out, as they are using docks. He must also put small rival trading firms out of business.

I do not pretend to understand it all. Nor does Nicolas. He may have spent time on the high seas, but he wasn't engaged in what one might consider legitimate shipping. However, the business William Thorne shares with August does exactly that, and so Rosalind and Bronwyn pore over the papers and find proof that Norrington is trying to force out fishermen and small competitors.

William and August may be able to find even more, along with suggesting strategies for stopping Norrington. Rosalind will send August a telegram in the morning. Bronwyn mutters that she wishes she could just "text them," and I have no idea what that means, but Rosalind heartily agrees. I really do need to visit the twenty-first century at some point.

For now, my concerns are in the eighteenth, with helping Nicolas stop Norrington and free Andrés's ghost. We will return there on the morrow to see what else we might do while awaiting August and William's response.

There is nothing more to be done tonight, and it is quite late, so we retire. Thorne Manor—not being Courtenay Hall—has only two guest rooms. I suspect Bronwyn wouldn't blink if I took one with Nicolas. Rosalind would blink, but only momentarily. It is Nicolas who separates us, saying that he will take the small one if I do not mind sharing my sister's. I do mind, quite a bit, actually, but it seems the alternative would see me alone in the second guest room while he sleeps in the hayloft.

We head off to our rooms. As I shut the door to ours, I whisper to Rosalind that I need to speak to Nicolas.

"Speak to him?" she says. "Or sneak into his room?"

"Sneak into his room."

She sighs. "At least you are honest. I thought it might be like that between you."

"You object?"

She walks over to embrace me. "Nicolas seems like exactly the sort of man I should want for you, Miranda. I cannot say he *is* that man on such short acquaintance, but if he is as he appears, then I do not object at all to the forming of a romantic attachment. If I do object to anything, it is a more practical concern."

"I would expect nothing less."

She raps my knuckles. "Do not mock me. Practicality is a fine trait. It allows me to urge caution where you might be too caught up in a romance to do the same."

"You wish to warn me against falling too hard for him when he is not from my world."

"Actually, no. Is that *your* concern?"

When I don't answer, she says, "Silly question. You may have had lovers, but you have never been in love. Do not look so surprised. You don't need to confide such things in me for me to see them. In that regard, I might actually urge less caution. Follow your heart. Nicolas does not seem the sort of man to abuse it."

"He is not."

"Good, then my concern was far more practical. What do you use for birth control?"

It takes me a moment to understand what she means, the phrase unfamiliar.

"For preventing a pregnancy?" I shake my head. "We are not having the sort of intimate relations that would cause one. Nicolas insists on that until we have French letters, for both protection against pregnancy and disease."

Rosalind smiles. "Then I like him even more. I will also point out that your young physician may benefit from the gift of modern medical texts, which would show that the spread of disease is not contained to intercourse. However, if he seems healthy in that respect—and you do as well—we will temporarily overlook that danger. The twenty-first century has far more effective and more comfortable methods of protection than his 'French letters.' Bronwyn can procure those. Until then, I'm sure you can find plenty of amusements short of that." She waves at the door. "Go. Just watch that you lock the door and do not make enough noise to have Edmund investigating again."

❧❧❧

I SLIP INTO NICOLAS'S ROOM. HE IS AT THE WINDOW, STILL DRESSED, gazing out. When he sees me, he smiles.

"I had hoped you could slip away."

"Rosalind knows where I am, and she does not object. She has also promised us proper methods of birth and disease protection from the twenty-first century."

"That is both wonderful to hear and terrifying at the same time. The thought that one can simply pop into the future to obtain such things . . ."

"Wondrous?"

"Truly wondrous."

He swings me off my feet and carries me to the bed, where he lays me on top and crawls on beside me.

"Should we not draw back the coverlet first?" I say.

"That would suggest I am ready for more than conversation."

I slump onto the bed. "As much as I enjoy your conversation, Nico, I cannot help but feel we may have done enough talking for one night."

"If you are tired, then we will indeed pull back the coverlet. If you are not, then I must beg your indulgence a while longer. There are things I need to say."

I sober and turn on my side to look at him. "I was only teasing. We may discuss whatever you need to discuss."

"Thank you." He slides closer, hands going around my hips. "You came through time for me, Miranda. Yes, you did not intend to, but Fate brought you through time for me, and then you insisted on helping me even when I was far from a gracious recipient of your concern. You did not merely impart a warning. You broke from the room where I rudely imprisoned you, and you pursued me to be sure I was safe, and when you were shot doing so, you continued, badly wounded, to save me. That part was not Fate. That was you. Sometimes, the stitch seems to be whatever the ladies of this house need it to be. It brought you to me, and that is no small thing. I believe it is confirmation of what I already know. That we have found one another, across the centuries. That what I feel is no passing whim. No strange fancy. I am in love with you, and I do not wish to lose you."

When I open my mouth, he stops my words with a light kiss. "I am almost done. I promise. To that declaration, I must add a codicil. You may not feel the same. Even if you do, you may understandably not be ready to commit yourself to a man you've known for three days. I am not asking for that. I am simply circling back to what I was saying earlier this evening. This is more than a lark for me. More than a passing affair. If we are to continue, then I need to know where I stand. Do you intend it as a brief affair? Or are you willing to try for more?"

The answer should be obvious. My heart swells with it, my mind reeling with the dizzying thought that I might *not* lose him in a day or two, a week or two. Yet when I open my mouth, nothing comes.

"Is it the complications of our separate worlds?" he says. "I have read tragic stories about lovers who say they are from different worlds, but it is never so true as with us. Your family and your life are here. My family and my life are there. I believe, with the help of this stitch and permission from the Thornes, we could reconcile that. Do you disagree?"

"I love you."

The words come without thought, and he blinks and then says, with a soft chuckle, "Well, that is good. In fact, I do not think I have ever heard sweeter words. However, they are not quite uttered in the tone I imagined for them, and I believe that suggests the true problem. You are not ready to be in love."

"I . . . It's happening very quickly."

"It is."

"And I did not think . . . That is, I had reconciled myself—or 'reconciled' might not be the correct word . . ."

"You had decided that you would likely not marry, and you were all right with that. I had done the same. I have known women whose company I appreciated, but none I wished to commit myself to in such a way."

"Yes," I say slowly. "Yet at the risk of giving offense, I do not think it is quite the same. Men often immerse themselves in their work or their interests with no intention of marrying, knowing they may change their minds at any point. A man may wed at forty, fifty, even sixty and begin a family. A woman past the years of childbearing is less likely to be seen as a prospect for marriage. Once I decided that I was not ready to wed, I knew it could be permanent, and I had accepted that."

I shift in his arms. "I may be making no sense. I ought to be thrilled."

"You ought to be thrilled that you have met a man who wishes to marry you?" His brows shoot up. "If you honestly believe I would think that, I have represented myself very poorly. This has happened quickly, and it is disconcerting."

"Thrilling," I say firmly. "But yes, also disconcerting. Earlier, Rosalind said that I had had lovers but never been in love, and she cautioned me against being so . . . well, cautious. She was not wrong."

"She is not wrong about this being new and disconcerting, but you may be as cautious as you need to be, Miranda."

"It is frightening."

"Oui."

"You feel that, too? Frightened?"

"Oui."

I exhale, his admission oddly making me feel better. "Then you understand that if I do not throw myself into your arms, declaring I am yours for as long as you'll have me, that does not mean I am not feeling exactly that?"

"Oui." He pulls me to him, lips going to my ear. "You said you love me, and that is all I need. I will not wake to find you gone in the morning."

"Never." I pull back. "Also, that would be very awkward and quite rude, abandoning you with my sister, in someone else's house and someone else's century."

"Very awkward." He kisses me. "We will work this out. And now, you will be delighted to know, I have finished talking."

"Finally." I thump back onto the pillow. "Now I can sleep."

He moves over me and arches a brow. "If you truly wish to sleep . . ."

I roll my eyes. "Sometimes you are really too considerate, Nico."

"Mmm, no, if I were truly considerate, I would let you sleep while pleasuring you so that you might enjoy the best of both." He tilts his head. "Of course, there is no reason why I cannot do that."

"It does sound rather lovely."

"I am certain it does." He reaches to tug up my skirts. "And since, having dressed hastily in my time, you now have far fewer underthings to contend with, I ought to be able to manage it with minimal interruption."

I stretch back onto the pillows. "I would appreciate that."

"Then rest, crécerelle. Rest and enjoy. You have had a very difficult day, and since I could not reward you with a bath, this will need to do."

"It will do very nicely."

29

As one might imagine, I did not fall asleep during Nicolas's ministrations. I would need to be exhausted to the point of sedation to do so . . . or he would need to be far less superb at it than he is. Neither of those things being true, I remain awake while giving myself over to both relaxation and indulgence, and once I am wonderfully sated, I am also quite refreshed enough to return the favor. I insist he crawl into bed and rest while I take charge, and I do not rush the process, which is both for his sake and mine, allowing him to relax while I practice my technique.

We sleep afterward, and I expect to be fully unconscious until daylight, but something nudges at me, and I wake while the moon is still high, moonlight streaming through the open window.

I'm tangled in Nicolas's arms and legs, tight against him, which is a lovely place to be caught, and it is only when that odd sensation prickles again that I force myself to lift my head.

I peer around the room. It is empty, of course. I locked the door when I entered, and while I did teach Edmund how to open locked doors—a lesson I may regret—he would never do it to sneak into Nicolas's room, however curious he might be about our "pirate" guest.

The door is closed, and the house is silent. I decide I am imagining things, and I lay my head down on Nicolas's chest, only to have that sensation slide over me again, urging me up. With a sigh, I extricate myself from his embrace and move to the edge of the bed. I peer around. All is silent and still.

I am about to crawl back into bed beside him when motion flickers near the door. I tense and glance over. Nothing is there.

"Hello?" I say. "If there is a spirit in the room, I would ask that they make themselves known, please."

Another flicker, as if a spirit is trying to do as I asked but is unable to materialize. Before I can speak again, the shape comes clear enough for me to make out a human figure. The figure of a man. I catch the barest glimpse of features and blink in surprise.

"Lord Thomas?"

The figure disappears. I get to my feet, pulling my discarded gown around me, and walk to the spot. It is empty, and the ghost does not reappear, but I am certain it was Lord Thomas.

"Miranda?" Nicolas croaks from the bed.

I tell him what I felt and what I saw. Then I say, "I think it is Lord Thomas, attempting to find us but unable to pass over. He must know his son's men tracked us to Thorne Manor."

Nicolas sits up. "While I would like to say it can wait until morning, I suppose we should not ignore the poor man. He was quite distressed last evening."

"Mmm. I agree that I would also like to ignore it, but I would also prefer he not materialize in our bedroom while we are naked in bed."

"Agreed." Nicolas reaches for his shirt. "Shall we see how easy it is to pop back to my world? If it is as simple as it seems, we can assure him we are well and promise to return on the morrow."

That sounds like a reasonable plan, and so we find the rest of our clothing and make ourselves decent for Lord Thomas.

❦

I WRITE OUT A NOTE FOR ROSALIND, EXPLAINING THAT WE HAVE CROSSED over and that we should be back when they wake, and if not, to convey my apologies to Edmund. We will return as soon as we are able. I write the note while Nicolas is dressing, and then I find another gown in the travel bag I'd hidden here, a plain traveling dress that will better suit the eighteenth century.

We tiptoe down the hall and into the office. I take Nicolas's hand, and we hurry to the stitch. This time, I feel the pull of it when we reach the right spot. The room flickers, and footsteps quick-tap down the corridor.

Bronwyn calls quietly, "Miranda? Is that you? There's something —" but before she can finish, we are in the eighteenth century.

Nicolas glances back over his shoulder, as if Bronwyn could still be there. "Was that Lady Thorne? It sounded as if she wanted to speak to you."

I am about to agree and suggest we return when Lord Thomas appears through the wall, his eyes wide with alarm. When he sees us, he wilts with relief.

"I have been searching for hours," he says. "Wherever were you hiding?"

"There's a secret passage," I say. "We were beset by your son's men."

"Yes, I know. I followed them here, but it is not always easy to travel in this form, and I arrived too late to warn or help you." He looks at Nicolas. "Where is the satchel?"

"In the passage," I say. "We have discovered pages that will prove useful. They confirm that your son is trying to take over Hood's Bay, forcing out the fishermen and smaller shipping companies, with his eye on making it a port to rival Whitby."

Lord Thomas seems to fade, his shoulders slumping. "I admire his ambition. I only wish I had imparted a sense of righteousness along with it. Dare I ask how dire the situation might be? I want to help the people of the bay, but I do not wish to see my son hang for his ambition."

"It will not come to that," I say firmly. "We only wish to use the papers to force him to stop his campaign against the people."

And, if possible, to trick him into doing or saying something that will prove he ordered Andrés's death. I won't say that to Lord Thomas. However disappointed he may be in Norrington, the man is still his son, and he does not need to know the truly reprehensible thing he has done.

"Now," I continue. "I can assure you we are fine and safe in our cubbyhole, and so if you will allow us to return, we can continue poring over the pages and—"

"No." He jumps forward with alacrity. "I was worried about you, but that is not why I have been haunting this house all night. They have taken my granddaughter."

"Emily?" I stiffen.

"My son ordered his men to take her into their custody. He knows she aided your escape, and the mad child . . ." He shakes his head. "She did not deny it. I thought I was going to rip a hole between the worlds, shouting at her to lie. She is a woman of honor, and she told the truth with her chin high."

Pride warms his voice as he continues, "She admitted that she had helped and berated her uncle for his misdeeds. She wanted to be brave. She wanted to do right. But she still does not understand what her uncle is capable of, and now I fear she will find out. She did not realize she was his captive. Such a thought would not cross her mind. To her, it was no more serious than her uncle demanding to know who left the barn door open."

"And it was not like that at all," I say.

"No. Worse, thinking her uncle still a man of some honor, she swore she would do what she could to help the people of the bay and aid Nicolas in his cause, even if that meant standing against her own uncle. She swore that she would inform her father, and he would help her cause."

"What did Lord Norrington do?" I ask carefully.

"Took her away. He's holding her captive in the last place young Dr. Dupuis would ever look for her."

"Where?"
"On the *Temerity*."

30

First, I tell Nicolas that Emily has been taken captive, and that is enough to get us moving quickly out of the house as I relate the rest of the story. The *Temerity* is wrecked on the far side of Whitby—nearly a ten-mile distance. Can we walk that? Of course. But not as quickly as poor Lord Thomas wants us there.

We cannot risk the time or the exposure of finding a driver in High Thornesbury, the town at the foot of the hill. The only solution is one we both hate. We need to steal a horse from Lord Thorne's stable. I would be much more comfortable with that if it were the eighteenth-century Lord Thorne. It is not, and we can hardly bring one of his horses through. No, we must steal from his grandfather, and while Lord Thomas assures us it is only borrowing, it feels like theft.

As this is Lord Thorne's country estate, there are only a few horses in residence. We tell ourselves these are not his favorites—he wouldn't leave a favorite to be tended by the hired help. No, these are working horses, and so we can only make a vow to return the gelding we borrow and, if we cannot return it, repay its worth, however terrible that might feel to say about a living creature. Emily is in danger, and so we stifle our discomfort and set out on the gelding, which we shall be sure to return.

We do not travel as quickly as Lord Thomas would like—he urged us to take two horses, or at least a younger and faster one—but we must minimize our transgression. In any event, we move faster than Lord Thomas, and that must be enough.

When we near the shoreline where we'll find the *Temerity*, we stop near a spring and tie the horse there, with a promise to return. We do not dare let the gelding wander the moors. He is unlikely to be accustomed to such freedom.

We are at the top of the cliff overlooking the shore. It is barely past dawn, or so I presume by the quantity of light, but the closer we get to the water, the less we see of the sun or anything else. Marine fog has rolled in, thick as smoke. While it helps to hide our approach, it also prevents us from knowing exactly where to find the wreck. Fortunately, Lord Thomas catches up and is able to guide us.

"There is a skiff," he says as we creep close to the cliff. "My son headed home long ago, and the boat is there for his return. He has left Emily with a single guard. They are belowdecks, in the captain's quarters."

I relay that to Nicolas, who nods. "An excellent choice of location. Well, excellent for us. They doubtless chose it because it is the most comfortable room on the ship, but it is also situated in a way that will allow us to sneak up."

Before we see the skiff, we hear it, knocking gently against the waves. The *Temerity* looms a hundred feet from shore, a shapeless hulk swathed in fog. While I cannot imagine anyone spotting us in this tiny boat, I am not comfortable rowing straight to it, and neither is Nicolas. He agrees to my suggestion, which is that he will hide as best he can, stretched out at the bottom of the skiff as I row, gritting my teeth so that Nicolas does not notice when my arm begins to ache. I must be the one who rows—if someone spots me, I will look far less menacing a target.

I am not spotted. Lord Thomas, being able to sprint over the water, has reported back that no one else is onboard. It is only Emily and her single guard, both in the captain's quarters. Norrington is confident he has chosen his spot well. Wherever Nicolas chooses to hide, it will not be on the broken and sinking remains of his former ship.

It is only as I speak to Lord Thomas that I realize a flaw in my plan. Not the plan to rescue Emily—Nicolas is working on that, and I will leave him to it, as he knows the ship's layout best. No, I mean my plan to never let Lord Thomas know about young Andrés's fate. They are both ghosts on the same ship.

Will Lord Thomas not see Andrés? I admit I am not entirely certain how that works. I have never been in the company of two ghosts. I presume they exist in the same plane.

Lord Thomas will see Andrés. And then what? Can I ask Andrés not to say what happened to him? Is that fair to the boy? Should I remain silent and hope it does not come up in conversation?

When Lord Thomas flits off, I ask Nicolas, who agrees that I should not mention it. Neither will he, and if Andrés does, we shall deal with that. Perhaps we can at least avoid telling Lord Thomas that we suspect his son of the deed.

For now, Lord Thomas does not mention seeing Andrés. We make it to the rope and up onto the deck unseen. The ship lurches to one side. Her hull is heavily damaged, but the water is too shallow for her to properly sink. From the deck, she appears whole, as if someone has simply tilted her.

I peer about for Andrés, and when Lord Thomas leaves us to check on Emily again, I call to the boy but get no response.

Is Andrés still here? What if he has managed to leave the wreck? If so, how will we find him?

"Miranda?" Nicolas whispers as I pause, crouched on the deck, lost in my thoughts. "Did you hear something? Is it Andrés?"

I shake my head and murmur that all is well. All is *not* well. I am becoming Portia, fretting over eventualities. That isn't like me. No, it *can* be me, just as it can be Rosalind. It is good to consider possibilities and not run headlong into danger. Only there is no grave danger right now. We are safely onboard. So why am I searching for things to fret about?

Because I am unsettled. Something about this bothers me.

"Miss Miranda," Lord Thomas says as he appears from the fog. "My son will return to check on Emily this morning. We must hurry while she is belowdecks with only one guard."

Annoyance sparks. We have been moving as fast as we can, and it is never fast enough for Lord Thomas. *Move faster. Do this. No, don't do that. Quickly!*

Shame douses the annoyance. The man has discovered his only son is robbing his people of their livelihood. Now that son has taken his only grandchild captive. Can I blame him for being in a constant state of panicked excitement? No. He is beside himself with worry, and he is pleading with us to hurry.

With the badly tilting deck, we *cannot* hurry. We need to hold tight to the side as we pick our way. We creep toward the ladder descending belowdecks. I am almost there when a figure flickers to my left. I nearly ignore it, presuming it is Lord Thomas urging us to hurry. Then I see a waving hand, a hand that is certainly not Lord Thomas's pudgy and wrinkled one. I spin, and I have only the faintest impression of Andrés, waving to get my attention before he vanishes again.

"Andrés?" I whisper.

Nicolas turns. "You see him?"

"Briefly and not well. He seems to be trying to say something."

That tension in me coils tighter.

Something is wrong.

Nicolas nods. "No doubt he is trying to tell us there is a young woman captive below. I can only imagine the panic that would cause for him. He doubtless fears she is about to suffer his fate."

That makes sense. And yet . . .

I peer down the hatch into the darkness belowdecks.

What if this is not what it seems? What if it is a trap? Yes, Emily could be there, but perhaps she is not a captive but a willing lure. She seemed to be an ally, and my instincts say she is. Do I trust that?

Nicolas has begun descending the ladder. I motion for him to come back up, but he cannot see me. I pause only a heartbeat before climbing down after him.

We're on the first level among the crew quarters. Water pools around our feet, and to my left, the tilted corridor is under several feet of water. That is one reason for Emily's captors choosing the captain's quarters—it is a high point, still almost dry.

I'm about to whisper that we need to speak when voices waft from down the corridor. A man tells someone, "Stop that."

"The rope chafes," Emily snaps. "I wish it loosened."

Nicolas's head jerks up. When I slip beside him, his hand goes out to stop me, as if I were trying to get past.

I lean in to whisper my fears, which this exchange seems to confirm. Emily is a false captive, snapping at her captor to loosen her staged bonds.

"Why don't I just remove it for you, your majesty?" the man says.

"That would be grand. Would you?"

The man snorts. "If you wished to be treated like his lordship's niece, perhaps you ought to have remembered that before you betrayed him."

"I did not betray him. He is behaving monstrously, and I will not sit by and watch it. He has put me here to teach me a lesson. The only lesson I am learning is that he is not the man I thought he was."

Nicolas exhales, nodding as he realizes Emily is truly a prisoner, and we have not stepped into a trap. Yes, as a writer, I am suspicious, always imagining the twists one might add to a plot. The lord's niece is a traitor! No, she is an ally! No, she is a traitor pretending to be an ally!

If I were writing this scene, I might indeed have Emily-the-traitor decry her imprisonment when the hero is within earshot, but my dialogue would be very different from what we just heard.

Emily is indeed a captive, and her reaction is not terror, as one might paint such a damsel, but annoyance and anger, and I credit her for that, even if I worry that she does not quite understand the severity of the situation. How could she? To her, she is indeed merely being taught a lesson.

Nicolas leans to my ear and whispers, "All is well, non?"

I glance at him. "You think she is faking captivity?"

"I do not now. I simply . . ." He looks around and then says again, "You do feel all is well, non?"

"Why do you hesitate?" a voice says behind me as Lord Thomas's ghost hurries past. He turns to face us. "She is right there."

"And she is fine," I whisper. "Annoyed but not in immediate danger. We hesitate because we are uncertain."

"Of what?" he says, voice rising. "My son is on his way. You do not have much time."

I frown. "On his way?"

"Yes, I saw him. That is why I came down here. To urge you to hurry."

Which he has been doing since I first met him.

Hurry, hurry, hurry. Do this. Don't do that. Faster! Why do you hesitate?

That free-floating doubt finally solidifies. What is bothering me about all this? Not Emily. Lord Thomas.

Lord *Thomas*? Everyone says he is a good man. Nicolas may not have known him, but based on his reputation, he did not doubt his intentions.

Lord Thomas is a good man appalled by what his son is doing and trying to stop him. That story makes sense. Everyone agrees.

What if everyone is wrong?

I have been annoyed by Lord Thomas's constant fretting and rushing, while feeling guilty for that. But what does his fretting and rushing do? Keeps us moving forward. Keeps us from stopping to think.

Every time we are in trouble, he is there to help, but—contrary young people that we are—we keep ignoring his advice. He says to go this way, and we go that way. He says do not run there or do that, and we do it anyway. And we are fine. We contradict his advice at almost every turn, and we escape.

What would have happened if we'd listened to him?

But he has helped, hasn't he? He got us into Norrington's study and told us about the safe. Gave us the combination. When the last number was wrong, we blamed the safe.

What if he'd intentionally given it wrong? Given us the first few numbers correctly so that when the last failed, I wouldn't think Norrington had changed the combination—I'd think I'd made a mistake. That would keep me at the safe, working at it, long enough for Norrington to catch us.

Only we'd accidentally gotten it open anyway, and when we did, he flew into a panic.

Lord Norrington is coming! Forget the papers and run! No, don't take those! What are you doing? Run into the kitchens! Don't run onto the dance floor—that is madness. Fine, you are on the dance floor. Do not listen to my granddaughter. I have suddenly decided she cannot be trusted. Go out the front!

We went to Thorne Manor because we were certain we had not been followed. We'd seen no one. What if someone *had* been there? Someone we could not see if he chose not to be seen? He claims he cannot keep up when we are on horseback, but he does seem to get from point to point easily when he wishes.

I turn to Lord Thomas and dip my chin. "You are correct, of course, sir. We are tarrying when your granddaughter's life is at stake, and I apologize for that. We shall rescue her posthaste. If you would not mind watching for your son? We should not wish to run into him as we are making our escape."

Lord Thomas nods. "Certainly. He is still on the road but clearly coming in this direction. I shall stand watch on deck and sound the alarm if I spot him. But you must move quickly."

"We shall, sir."

31

L ord Thomas disappears. I wait until I am certain he's gone. Then I whisper to Nicolas.

"I do not trust him," I say. "I did before, but I have begun to suspect he is playing us wrong."

"As have I."

My brows shoot up.

Nicolas lifts one shoulder. "I did not know the man personally, and while I cannot see or hear him, I have been thinking I ought to broach the matter with you, as it seemed he may be misleading us. His reputation is a fine one, but with men of nobility, sometimes the people they govern are eager to see more goodness than is deserved."

He has a point. There are so many horrible landowners that even common decency can seem grounds for sainthood.

The question now is what to do. We believe we have walked into a trap, and yet Emily is still the unwitting bait. Do we dare presume her uncle will not harm her?

We are leaning together to whisper again when a board creaks overhead. Nicolas's hand goes to his sword as we both look up. Another creak comes. I glance around. He motions for me to follow.

Nicolas opens a door with care and looks inside. The room is on the port side of the ship, meaning it is above the water. We need to physically pull ourselves inside so we don't slide back out again on the tilted floor. Once we are in, Nicolas closes the door all but a crack.

The ladder creaks. Someone is coming down. I long to tug Nicolas back from the door so I can see, but I stifle the impulse and hold myself still.

When he pulls back, he looks alarmed.

"It is Mr. Jenkins," he says.

"Emily's father?"

He nods. "He is sneaking along the corridor. He can hear Emily in the captain's quarters, and now he is heading that way."

I curse under my breath.

We have a decision to make here. Emily's father has come to her rescue. We should let him do that, should we not?

An easy choice if Mr. Jenkins knows what exactly is happening. If he knows his brother-in-law is behind the abduction. If he is prepared to fight for his daughter.

"Is he armed?" I whisper.

"He has a sword but . . ." Nicolas makes a face. "I do not wish to be insulting, but I have always presumed it is merely an affectation of fashion."

Nicolas carries one because he was a privateer and he is a fugitive; he knows how to use it. It could be a holdover from when doctors carried swords as a sign of status, but for him, it is mostly a weapon.

I've noticed men in the area wearing them, more than I would expect. Is that another holdover, this one in a more rural part of the country? Is it because Norrington—being a former admiral—wears one? All I know is that it seems to be part of the local couture. For men like Mr. Jenkins—a middle-aged clerk—it might not even be a usable weapon.

Sword or not, I suspect Jenkins is ill-equipped to fight for his daughter. From the look on Nicolas's face, he agrees.

"Do we . . . leave him to it?" I ask hesitantly.

"In good conscience, I cannot."

I exhale. "Nor I. It is agreed, then." I clasp my gladius. "We must at least warn him."

While I watch Nicolas's back, he eases open the door. There's an intake of breath from the hall, and I wince, but it isn't loud enough to alarm the guard, who seems to be still dealing with his difficult prisoner.

Nicolas waves Jenkins into the room with us. On seeing me, the man stops short, his brow furrowed in confusion. I do the same, with a momentary fear that Nicolas has somehow mistaken one of Norrington's men for Emily's father. That, of course, is impossible, as Nicolas knows Jenkins. However, I still pause in my own momentary confusion.

Two days ago, on spotting Lord Thomas's ghost near Emily, I'd thought he might be her father, keeping watch on her. Nicolas said Jenkins was his primary contact, and from that, I had the impression of a man not unlike Lord Thomas. Aging, gray-haired and stout, in need of a young man like Nicolas to do the running and hiding and fighting for the cause, while he handled communication and management. He is a clerk, after all.

The man who walks in could not be less like Lord Thomas. He might even be younger than William Thorne and August, both on the cusp of their fourth decade. I think surely this cannot be Emily's father. Then I calculate and realize he might be only in his late—or even mid—thirties. He met Lord Thomas's daughter when she was a girl and he was a "young clerk." They ran off together and had a baby, who is now nineteen.

I can see why Emily's mother ran off with Mr. Jenkins. He is a handsome man, compact in size but well formed, with sharp gray eyes. Those eyes light on me and then turn to Nicolas in confusion.

"This is my companion," Nicolas says as Jenkins enters the room.

"Norrington said you'd taken up with a young nobleman's son. The Kestrel, he called him." Jenkins jerks his chin at me. "Not a nobleman's *son*, I presume."

Nicolas's lips twitch. "Non. But yes, we shall call her the Kestrel. She knows your daughter, and she has come to help me free her."

Jenkins's shoulders sag. "Thank the saints. There is nothing I would not do for my Emily, but . . ." A rueful smile down at his sword. "The only dueling I do is with numbers and computations."

"Tell me what happened."

Jenkins throws up his hands. "I hardly know. When Emily did not return last night, I presumed she'd stayed at her uncle's estate, where she still has quarters. I wanted to get an early start for York today to sell"—he glances at me and clears his throat—"the goods."

Sell the items from the ship, he means. The goods that help support the people of Hood's Bay.

Jenkins continues, "I was off before dawn, and I did not get a chance yesterday to inform Emily of my plans, so I stopped at Norrington Hall to tell her I would not be home until the morrow. She was not there, and I thought that odd, so I asked to speak to Norrington. He refused an audience, and as I was walking about the house, I overheard one of his men say they had Emily on the *Temerity*. Of course, I thought I must have misheard. Perhaps he meant that Emily had left early to *see* the *Temerity*? To meet with you there? I came, and it did not seem right, so I borrowed a rowboat, crept onboard and heard her. She is truly Norrington's captive?"

Nicolas nods. "It is punishment for her aiding me last evening. She made the mistake of confronting her uncle about it."

Jenkins winces. "She has always seen the best in him. It has put us at odds many a time, and I feared if I pushed the matter too hard, it would drive a wedge between us. At least now she will see him for the man he truly is."

Jenkins looks toward the captain's quarters. "How should we do this? I am at your disposal, sir. I may not be a duelist, but I do not intend to sit back and allow you to take all the risks."

"I will ask—"

Nicolas stops as I turn sharply. Lord Thomas has just entered the room, running through the wall.

Lord Thomas sees Jenkins, and his eyes widen. "Oh, no. Oh dear, no. This is terrible."

I'm sure it is.

"You must tell him to leave," Lord Thomas says. "He ought not to be here. He cannot fight, and he'll only be injured, perhaps even killed."

Ten minutes ago, I would have accepted his concern for what it seems to be—fear that his son-in-law will be harmed. Now I know better. He wants Jenkins gone so that he will not be caught up in this trap. Worse, as Nicolas's ally, Jenkins might come to his aid and complicate our capture.

I wave for Nicolas to continue as I take Lord Thomas off to one side. I tell him not to fear, that we will keep Jenkins out of danger, but the poor man is determined to help. Could Lord Thomas please keep an eye on Norrington? I presume he has not arrived yet. Lord Thomas should do that while we trick Jenkins into staying safely in the cabin while we rescue Emily.

Lord Thomas agrees and flits off, and once he is gone, we begin. Nicolas has arranged the plan, and I am exceedingly pleased by it, as I am not relegated to the side where I will be safe. Nicolas understands I can do more.

I tug my hair into some disarray. Then I scoop water from the corridor to splash onto my dress. Finally, I hike up my skirts and lurch toward the captain's quarters, stumbling about the slanted hallway.

"Hello?" I call. "Please. I heard voices. Is someone here?"

"Yes!" Emily calls. "I am—"

An *oomph*, as if she is physically silenced, and my blood boils at that. The door to the captain's quarters cracks open, and I fall heavily against the wall, as if in a half swoon.

"Oh, thank the Lord," I pant as if catching my breath. "Please. Please, you must come help."

The door stays open only that crack, and I lurch toward it. "Please, miss. I know I heard you in there. I went rowing this morning from Whitby. The young man I was with—" I struggle for breath. "He played me false. He offered a rowing excursion, and the children were so excited that I agreed. Yet the boat was not big enough for the ocean currents, and it has capsized. The children— my charges—oh, miss, the *children*. I dragged them to shore, but little Millie does not breathe."

Is it a ridiculously overwrought story? Of course it is. But even the guard cannot help but open the door another crack. He's young, perhaps younger than me.

"The children," I stagger forward. "Please, sir! Come help the children."

I can see Emily now, behind him, her bound hands lowered as if to hide them. Our eyes meet.

"Oh!" she exclaims. "The poor children. You must help, Rodgers. I shall remain here. Go with the poor girl and help that dying child!"

He glances over his shoulder. "You'll stay here?"

"Yes. You go with the governess, and I will remain right here until you return."

One long pause, and then the guard—Rodgers—awkwardly slides from the captain's quarters while closing the door behind him, blocking me from seeing Emily is a bound captive. I pretend not to have noticed, and I wheel to lead him down the hall.

Jenkins and Nicolas are waiting down that hall. Each is inside a room. Jenkins is the closest to me, hidden behind a half-open door. Nicolas is farther down, his door open. When Rodgers passes that open door, Nicolas will swing out to confront him, and Jenkins will emerge from his hiding spot to run back and free his daughter while I help Nicolas with Rodgers.

I pass the first door where Jenkins waits. It is supposed to be half-closed. It is not. The door is open, and I catch a glimpse of a figure within.

Oh, no. We trusted Jenkins to follow the plan, and he has bungled it. Forgotten to half close the door or—worse—decided he must fight his daughter's captor himself.

I will not look that way. I will keep going in hopes Rodgers does not glance in Jenkins's direction. I am one step past the door when

Lord Thomas flies from the woodwork, charging at me, his face contorted. I stumble. It takes that one heartbeat for me to remember he is only a ghost, but that heartbeat is enough. I fall back. Hands grab me, and a voice shouts, "He is in the next room!"

It all happens at once, a jumble of sound and sight as I'm yanked off my feet by those hands and dragged into the room my attacker sprang from.

I have made an unforgivable error. I saw the door partly open, with a figure within, and I did not look toward it, fearing I would call Rodger's attention to Jenkins. Yet it must not have been Jenkins in that doorway at all, but another of Norrington's men lying in wait, one who subdued Jenkins and now has me and—

That's when I twist to fight off my attacker, and I see his face.

It is Jenkins.

32

A clang of metal sounds from the hall beyond the room where Jenkins has dragged me. Another clang. A grunt. Nicolas's voice, saying something I cannot make out over the clash of swords.

Jenkins whips me around and shoves me against the wall. I kick and snarl, but he has me pinned, rope cinching around my wrists before I can free myself.

I have one last chance. I cannot avoid being bound, but I can push my wrists apart in such a way that when he ties them, I have a bit of room to move. I pretend to strain against the rope, feigning that it is bound tight, as I curse and wriggle and kick back at him.

"No wonder you like wearing men's clothing," Jenkins says when my boot smacks him in the shin. "Not much of a lady, are you? Unnatural little beast."

He shoves me hard into the wall again. I spin on him, ready to kick, before I stop myself. I would do little damage kicking in long skirts. Also, I do not wish to give him any reason to bind my ankles as well. Instead, I lift my chin and channel Portia.

"Do you think your words will sting me?" I say. "I would rather be an unnatural woman than an unnatural *father*."

He strikes me. I do not see it coming. I have suffered many

slights in my life, but no one has ever slapped me, and the shock and outrage leave me gasping.

I grit my teeth. "You were not so quick to strike me before you bound my hands." I spit at his feet. "An unnatural father and a coward."

He slaps me again, but this time, I meet it standing firm, chin up, even turning my face to meet the blow. That infuriates him all the more, and I bite my cheek against a smile of satisfaction as he snarls and calls me an "unnatural woman."

"That is untrue," I say. "I am no more unnatural than every woman who does not conform to your ideas of what a woman should be. I am going to guess that encompasses much of the female population."

His face purples, and he pulls back his hand again, and I turn my cheek to meet the blow when Emily's voice rings down the hallway.

"Miranda? Nicolas?"

I make out Nicolas's voice then. "Crécerelle!"

The clang of metal punctuates the word.

"Crécerelle?" he calls. "Answer me if you can!"

I run for the door. Jenkins grabs me, but I wrench from his grip. While he still manages to catch my skirts, I lunge into the hall, enough to see Nicolas.

Another clang. Nicolas is facing off against the guard, Rodgers. Both men have their swords in hand. Nicolas dances back from a feint and then executes a perfect lunge that catches Rodger in the arm. The guard hisses. I watch the blood stain his sleeve, and my stomach clenches.

This is a duel. An actual sword fight.

I should not be so shocked. Is this not what I've studied? Did I think those swords were for show? For play?

I knew what they were for, but I have never seen them used for such. My lessons are pure play. Sport, at least.

This is something altogether different. Nicolas has already drawn blood, multiple times, and there is a slice through his trouser leg, blood flecking as he dances back out of Rodger's way. Then he sees me. He sees me and falters, and the guard's sword comes swinging at him. I only get the first note of a scream out before Nicolas comes to himself and ducks, just as the sword catches the sleeve of his shirt.

"I am fine," I call. "I am not injured."

"Your nose, crécerelle," he says as he pivots to one side.

I lift my hand and touch blood. One of Jenkins's slaps set my nose bleeding.

"It is nothing," I say. "This coward chose to slap me after he made sure I could not retaliate. Once you are done there, we will show him the error of that. Do hurry, please. This rope chafes terribly."

Nicolas's laugh bubbles up, and his eyes glint as he tosses me a grin. "Have I mentioned that I love you, crécerelle?"

"No, and this does not quite seem the time for it."

"All right, then I will only say that I adore you."

"I am glad you are so amused, Nick," Jenkins says. "You will be less amused when Rodgers runs that sword through your heart. He is a trained swordsman."

"Is he?" Nicolas swings away. "Then I fear he was not trained very well."

Rodgers snarls and lunges, but in his anger, he leaves himself open and Nicolas takes full advantage. While Nicolas gets in a strike, Rodgers is quick to recover and lands one of his own. Nicolas can mock, but the young man is a much better sword fighter than I am. He is a decent match for Nicolas, and my heart hammers as I watch the two.

Jenkins tries pulling me back into the room. I resist, and he shoves harder. I fake a backward stagger, pretend to lose my balance and fall hard on my rump. Jenkins bears down on me, glaring, but I plant myself there and watch him glower as he tries to figure out how to get me into that small room again.

"Drag her by the hair," a voice says behind me.

I startle at that voice, and I twist to see Lord Thomas. He gestures at me. "She has long enough hair. Drag her by it."

Jenkins snorts and shakes his head.

"Why not?"

Jenkins's gaze cuts to the captain's quarters. Emily has gone quiet. She cannot see us, but she can hear. That's why Jenkins wants me back in that room. So she will not overhear anything I might say. He will not listen to his father-in-law—

Listen to his father-in-law . . .

Jenkins can hear Lord Thomas. See him. Jenkins has the Sight.

What proof did I have that Norrington was behind Emily's capture? Lord Thomas said he was. Jenkins claimed to have overheard that. Because they were trying to convince us that Norrington had taken his niece captive, and we had to save her from the monster.

Emily seems to think her uncle is behind it as well, but she has said nothing to suggest she spoke to him directly. Rodgers must have captured her, and he likely is one of her uncle's crew, with the look of a young navy man. Either she presumed it was her uncle's doing or, more likely, he claimed as much.

I glance at Nicolas. He's still fighting Rodgers, still more than holding his own, and the younger man is beginning to tire, missing one opening and then taking another blow. I turn my attention to Lord Thomas.

"Lord Norrington didn't take Emily captive, did he?" I say. "That was you. Your idea. A trap for us."

Lord Thomas's lip curls. "For you? You have too high an opinion of yourself, girl. Dupuis humors you because it is to his advantage. He is a young man, after all, and if a pretty girl is willing to spread her legs for him, he'll tell her whatever she wants to hear."

"My apologies, sir. Of course you don't give a fig about me. The trap was for Nicolas. Bringing him here to free Emily."

I am careful with my words. Jenkins is poised there, ready to leap in if I say anything to alert his daughter to his participation. Do that, and I may very well be dragged away by the hair, which will certainly distract Nicolas from his fight.

I keep my focus on Lord Thomas, who doesn't answer, as if no answer is needed.

"This was a trap," I say. "Like the ambush in the lane two days back. Emily was supposed to meet Nicolas. Instead, an assassin met him."

I remember what I saw in the echo of Nicolas's death. He was killed by a single assailant. Two navy men waited, but it was a third man who shot him in the back. I also remember what happened that day. Yes, Norrington's men stopped Nicolas. They threatened him. They shot at him as he fled. But it was a third man who shot me, and at no time did I see that third man interact with the two others.

A third man of a slight build. Compact in size.

I look at Jenkins.

"Did you set Norrington up?" I say. "Have his men there to take the blame for Nicolas's death? Or did they obtain the same information and arrive on their own?" I wave off my own questions. "No matter. You were the one who wanted to kill him, Lord Thomas. You sent your lickspit, who is Jenkins. The question is, Why? Why kill Nicolas?"

"Is that actually a question?" Lord Thomas says. "Do you expect I would allow this boy"—he waves at Nicolas, who has landed a strike on Rodgers—"to threaten everything I built?"

"The people of the bay count you as a good man," I say. "A good lord. But that only means you were not a tyrant, likely because you lacked the aptitude for it. Not lacked the cruelty, but the aptitude. That's the problem, isn't it? You seemed good because you didn't have the intelligence to do what your son is doing, destroying their way of life to better his own."

"Lacked the intelligence?" Lord Thomas sputters. "I was educated at Harrow, girl. My father left me with nothing but debts, and I rebuilt our estate and our good name, and I did not have time to do more. My son does. He has the time, the will and the ambition, and I will not see anyone interfere with that."

A hiss of pain sounds down the hall, and I almost leap up before I see that it is Rodgers, pinned to the wall at sword point.

"I presume you are speaking to Lord Thomas's ghost," Nicolas calls to me. "And I presume he is confirming all your suspicions?"

"He is," I say.

"Then continue. I do not mean to interfere."

"There is only one question remaining," I say. "The most important of all."

"Oh," Lord Thomas says. "You have an actual question, girl? You are not simply going to chatter on like a magpie, preening at your own cleverness."

"Am I wrong? About any of it?"

"I do not need to answer to a girl."

"You are correct, Lord Thomas. It's not a question, but a statement." I turn to Jenkins. "You have done so much more than kidnap and connive on your master's behalf. You have killed for him. Killed a boy whose ghost I presume you have frightened off or otherwise suppressed from speaking to me."

"I killed no one," Jenkins growls under his breath, too low for Emily to hear. "The boy spied on a conversation he ought not to have overheard, and Lord Thomas needed to be sure he would not tell anyone."

"By killing him."

"I never killed—"

"You did something worse. You thought to keep your own hands clean, and so you locked him in the pantry and barred the door and let nature take her terrible course. Did you think that would save your soul? Oh no, sir. You are *damned* for what you did."

I spit the words and have to rein in my rage before I can continue. "You are damned, and this old man has damned you. He made you do it so that he would not need to. He thinks that keeps his soul clean, but it does not, as he is about to discover."

I turn to Lord Thomas. "Do you know what happens when I name you both as Andrés's killers? The boy is free, and you are damned. Tell me that is all right. Tell me your conscience is clean enough that you do not mind me doing so."

Lord Thomas lunges at me. I feel a sudden slap of cold dread, chilling me to my marrow. Darkness yawns before me. Endless darkness filled with grief and regret for everything I have done and have not had time to do.

I pull back, gasping and blinking. The darkness wants to fade, to disappear from my memory, leaving me only with overwhelming dread.

I leap up, yanking free from the bonds I have been working on while I talked.

"Yes," I snarl at Lord Thomas. "That is exactly what you face. An eternity of grief and regret and emptiness, and I am pleased to be the one to send you—"

A movement. That is all I see. A movement that stops me short and sends my heart into my throat before I even comprehend what I have seen. I think it must be Lord Thomas and another of his ghostly tricks.

It is not. I am busy facing off against the ghost, and Nicolas has turned his attention back to Rodgers, and Jenkins takes advantage of our distraction, pulling a pistol from his jacket and spinning toward Nicolas.

33

"Nico!" My scream and the shot shatter the air at once.

Nicolas dives at the last second. The shot passes him and hits Rodgers, who stands against the wall as if frozen there by shock. The shot strikes him in the throat. His eyes widen, hands going to his neck, and perhaps later I will wish I had done something to help him, but in that moment, I do not care. I cannot care. I only care that the shot passed Nicolas, and he is safe. Jenkins will need to reload, so there is time to disarm him. I run at him, gladius raised.

Jenkins points the gun downward and rotates a lever. Then he's lifting and pointing it again. It is already reloaded? How is that possible?

What matters is that it *is* reloaded, and Nicolas is still scrambling out of its path. There's movement behind him. Emily, lurching from the captain's quarters, her hands still bound. She's right behind Nicolas, and that gun is rising.

My blade strikes Jenkins in the arm. His gun still fires, but the shot veers to the side. It hits Nicolas in the forearm, sending him staggering back. There is a gasp. A gasp that is not from Nicolas. Emily stands behind him, her hands going to her chest, blood seeping through her fingers.

For a moment, no one moves. Then Emily is slumping to the floor, clutching a bloody spot on her bodice, and Nicolas is dropping beside her.

"You shot your daughter," I snarl at Jenkins. "Your own daughter."

He stares at Emily. He blinks. Then he blinks harder, pulling back, and then lowering his gun and opening the chamber. It takes a heartbeat for me to realize what he's doing. To comprehend what he's doing. His daughter is on the floor, shot, and he is reloading his pistol.

With my sword, I strike Jenkins's arm again, and I would sever it if that would make him drop the gun, but the blow hits wrong, the broad side striking the first wound. He cries out, and the gun drops, and I race between him and the weapon, forcing him back at sword point.

He goes for his sword, and a better fighter might know how to stop him before he draws it, but I am half in a panic, hearing Emily gasping, seeing Nicolas wounded, thinking only of getting Jenkins farther away from them so that Nicolas might tend to her.

Before I can speak, Jenkins's sword arcs toward me. I parry, but I do it wrong, and the reverberation rings down my arm.

Out of the corner of my eye, I see Nicolas reach for his own sword, his gaze on Jenkins's, his muscles poised to leap up. I also see that he's reaching for his sword . . . as blood soaks the sleeve of his forearm. He can fight, but he should not fight, especially not when he is needed so much more where he is.

"No," I say. "Please. Help Emily."

He hesitates, and then as he pulls his sword, I'm about to plead again, but he only lifts it for me, giving me the longer blade. I dart in to take it, sheathing my gladius, and as Nicolas presses his sword into my hand, his fingers grasp mine for a moment.

"You have this, crécerelle," he whispers. "I know you do."

I sidestep Jenkins's next attack and drive him away from Nicolas and Emily with one of my own. Behind me, Nicolas speaks to Emily, urging her to stay alert, to stay with us. I concentrate on Jenkins.

Earlier, I dismissed the man's sword as a mere fashion affectation. I only wish it were so. He is not as accomplished a swordsman as Rodgers, but he is better than me, and I am already distracted by Emily's and Nicolas's injuries. Jenkins lands several strikes. I do not feel them, which means Emily might not be the only one suffering from shock.

Blood wells up on both my arms. He has also struck at my torso and legs, but my gown protects me there, and I would be much gladder of that if it did not also inhibit my movement.

I leap back, only to tangle in my skirts and stumble.

"Miranda!" Nicolas shouts, and there's a scrambling, as if he is rising.

"I have this," I say. "Look to Emily and yourself. Please."

"Jenkins," Nicolas snaps. "Your daughter is in mortal peril. Do you not care?"

Jenkins doesn't even flinch. "If she dies, then you will have killed her. You and this woman who struck my arm and made my blow go wild."

"Is that what you tell yourself about the boy?" I say. "That you did not do the deed yourself?"

That makes Jenkins stumble, and I get in a blow.

"Emily can hear us," Nicolas says as he tends to her. "Shall we tell her what a monster her father truly is? Shall those be the last words she hears?"

Jenkins swings at me, his face twisted in such rage that the blow goes wild, and I evade it and come back with an attack that has him hissing in pain. I drive him back, and he trips over the outstretched legs of Rodgers, now dead on the floor.

"Then there is Rodgers," I say. "Another death at your door. Or was that also not your fault?"

"Ignore them," says a voice behind us.

I have forgotten Lord Thomas, who has been silently watching. Silently watching as Jenkins tries to overpower me . . . so he can kill the man who is keeping his granddaughter alive. I did not think it was possible to hate them both more. I was wrong.

"They are trying to distract you," the ghost says. "Just kill the girl and be done with it."

"Yes, kill me," I say. "Kill me and be done with it. What's another death at your doorstep? Rodgers, Andrés . . ."

"What did he do to Andrés?" That's Emily, her voice weak. "He told me they had taken the boy to York. That is what I told Dr. Dupuis."

"Enough!" Lord Thomas shouts. "Ignore her, too, Jenkins. They are all trying to distract you. Remember who you did this for. Your daughter. Securing her future."

"Your daughter has been *shot*," I say. "By you, and now you are trying to kill the man saving her life."

"She is fine," Lord Thomas says. "The shot missed her heart, and she is awake and responding. She will forgive you when you are able to send her to London for a season."

I snort as I parry a wild strike. "Did you tell the old man you were doing this for Emily?"

"I am. Everything I have done is for my daughter. Emily. I am sorry—"

"Every penny is going to her?" I cut in. "The old man actually believed that? You are a better actor than I thought. But I suppose you had to be to win the heart of your master's daughter. Why don't we talk about that, Jenkins? About Emily's mother."

Jenkins lunges at me, but I easily evade.

"You thought she was your golden goose, didn't you?" I say. "Win the master's daughter, and since he dotes on her, he will be forced to accept you as his son-in-law. Only it didn't quite work out that way. Then she died in childbirth, and you used her daughter to win your way back, but even then, you were not a member of the family. Not truly. Just an elevated clerk."

I am guessing. It is all guessing, with a generous dose of interpretation, but Jenkins's snarl of rage tells me that particular blow struck true.

"I was his son-in-law," he snaps. "The father of his darling granddaughter. What did it get me? Nothing but a better wage and a room in the back of the house. Then he dies, and Norrington wants me gone. Tries to frighten me off and keep my daughter. So I did what I needed to do. I took Emily away from him. Threatened to move with her to London."

"And when that didn't get you the annual allowance you demanded, you let the old man drag you into his scheme. A scheme that isn't even about helping you. It's paying you to help Lord Norrington. He's the one who counts. The only one who counts. The only one who has ever counted."

As I say that, I ready myself for a frenzied attack. Surely these will be the words to send him over the edge. The realization that he has killed for a man who still sees him as a mere employee, who has damned his immortal soul to help his real son.

But Jenkins only smirks. "Oh, I still have one card to play, girl. One secret that a boy died to keep. His Highness Lord Norrington is going to pay very well for me to continue *keeping* that secret."

What do they think Andrés overheard? I only know he overheard Norrington talking to someone, and Lord Thomas ordered Jenkins to nail him into the pantry to keep from telling anyone.

"Treason," Nicolas says. "My captain was accused of treason. I believed him innocent. He was not, was he?"

Jenkins gives a humorless laugh as he parries. "You were always a fool, Dupuis. A pirate who thought he was a privateer. Thought his crew had been betrayed by the Crown. No, your captain was as guilty as sin. Guilty of selling secrets of the Royal Navy to the French. To your own people."

"The French are not 'my' people."

Jenkins rolls his eyes.

"How would that secret be blackmail for Norr—?" I stop before I finish. "Because he is the one who gave Nicolas's captain the secrets. He was a British admiral."

"*That* secret is worth a lot of money, don't you think?" Jenkins says, and he's so pleased with himself that I lunge too quickly, only to have him back me off with a blow that leaves me gasping.

Lord Thomas is fuming. Shouting at Jenkins to keep his mouth shut, does he know what he just did? I pay no attention to the ghost. I wait until he pauses his tirade.

"A secret that was worth a boy's life, apparently," I say. "Andrés heard nothing. *Nothing.*"

Jenkins blinks. "No, he overheard. Lord Thomas said he did."

"Lord Thomas lied. He thought Andrés might have heard, and that was enough, and so he told you to . . ." I remember Emily, sitting and listening, and I will not do this to her. "Do what you did."

Jenkins wheels on the ghost. "You said he had heard. You were certain he had."

"Thank you, Mr. Jenkins," I say. "That was the final confirmation I required." I raise my voice as I lift my sword. "Lord Thomas Norrington and John Jenkins, I name you in the death of Andrés, the cabin boy whose spirit haunts this ship."

Emily gasps, and I realize I have torn the cloak not only from her father but also from her grandfather. I regret that, but I cannot place her peace of mind over Andrés's freedom.

Lord Thomas shouts behind me, a roar of rage that turns into a garbled cry as he is wrenched from this world to the next.

"Miranda!"

Jenkins lunges at me. I fall back, and I lift my sword, but my skirts—my damnable skirts—snag, and he traps my blade, and as I stumble, his sword knocks mine splashing into the water at our feet.

Nicolas scrambles to his feet, and he charges toward us.

When a groan comes again, I think it is Nicolas—his injury making him cry out. Then the ship rocks behind me and groans anew. A crack, as if she is splitting in two. Nicolas does let out a cry then—a cry as the floor cracks, leaving a gaping hole in his path.

Jenkins's sword tip goes to my throat.

"You ought not to have done that, girl," he says. "Damn my soul, and what reason do I have to live?"

"Every reason, father," Emily's voice is barely audible over the ship breaking. "If you are damned, you do not wish to die a moment before you must."

"If I die, I take this unnatural creature with me. Say a prayer, girl, for it will be your last."

That is dialogue too trite even for me to craft. If my heart were not hammering in my chest, I would laugh and stand tall and say I do not need to pray, that whatever lies in the hereafter, I trust that my deeds will not condemn me to any version of damnation.

That is what I want to say. Instead, even as my heart hammers, my hand creeps down to my waist. My fingers close on the handle of my gladius and—

The ship rocks again, and I stagger, my hold on my gladius breaking. The tip of Jenkins's blade sinks into my throat. Nicolas has backed up, and when he breaks into a run, I realize he is going to try leaping over the gaping hole. I open my mouth to tell him to stay back, stay safe, but Jenkins's sword tip presses in, hot blood welling up as my fingertips frantically search for—

A movement to my left. A blur of motion that charges straight between Jenkins and me. I think it is Nicolas, but when I look, Nicolas is still in flight, leaping. He touches down and starts to topple back, toward the hole. Before I can do more than gasp, he has righted himself.

Then I see the true source of that blur of motion. It is Andrés, wheeling to face his killer. Jenkins falls back, and I slip from his grasp, my gladius rising. As Andrés stalks toward Jenkins, the ship seems to rock and crackle with each step.

"Andrés," I say to Nicolas, my free hand lifting to warn him back. "It is Andrés."

"Good," Nicolas grunts as he scoops up his fallen sword. "That is the problem with being a seer, Jenkins. You cannot escape your victims, even after you have killed them."

Jenkins has stopped, standing firm, chin raised. Nicolas moves up beside me.

"I did not kill you, boy," Jenkins says to Andrés. "You are still here, which means your killer has not been caught. The girl has named the wrong person and stolen your eternal rest."

"Then why is Lord Thomas gone?" I say.

"Because *he* was the boy's killer. He gave the order. You cannot damn a pistol for killing a man. You must damn the person who pulled the trigger."

"You are not a pistol. You are a man. Andrés? Can you see the way home? You should be able to see it now."

Andrés nods and points to his right while keeping his gaze on Jenkins.

"The way is open," I say to Jenkins. "Andrés is choosing not to take it until he is ready. Perhaps he is not prepared to cross over yet. Perhaps he thinks he would rather spend a few years tormenting the man who killed him, the man who can see him."

Jenkins roars and swings his sword at Andrés. Of course, the blade goes right through the ghost, and so Jenkins runs at me, pulling back his blade. Nicolas swings. His sword slices into Jenkins's arm. The man howls, and his hand spasms. With my gladius, I knock his sword free, letting it splash into the water. Then, together, Nicolas and I back Jenkins against the wall, exactly where he had me, our sword tips at his throat.

"Please!" Emily says. "I know he may deserve death, but please do not kill him."

I had no intention of killing Jenkins. I'm not certain I could murder a person unless I had no choice, and that is not the situation here. Still, Emily does not know that and neither does her father. I press my sword tip in until blood trickles down his throat.

"Do you not deserve death?" I say. "To be cast into a realm where Andrés can truly exact his revenge? Where you must choose between his torments and the torments of eternity?"

Jenkins blanches and quavers, and I must restrain the urge to embellish the prospects that lie before him. He understands them well enough.

"No," I say. "I will not kill you."

I lower my blade. Jenkins's gaze shoots to Nicolas.

"You betrayed me," Nicolas says. "You preyed on my good nature and the trusting nature of the town. They saved me, and I wanted to help, and you took advantage. You tried to kill me. You planned to ambush me from behind and let Norrington's men take the blame. You did not seem to mind killing me outright. Perhaps you thought I did not count. I do count, and you will suffer for that in the next life, the intention to kill me and the attempt to kill my companion here. More sins piled on a very high heap." Nicolas pulls his blade back. "I will not add your death to my own heap."

Jenkins sags in relief.

"There is a door to your left," Nicolas continues. "Please step sideways and go through it."

He does as Nicolas asks. Or he does once Nicolas adds the incentive of another sword prick. Once he's through the door, Nicolas slams it shut. Then I turn the key still jutting from the lock.

"Oh," Nicolas calls. "Did I mention that is the brig? I suppose I forgot that part."

"You are captured, Mr. Jenkins," I say. "And the ship appears to be sinking. I do hope you can find a way out in time. But if you do not, please remember that we didn't actually kill you. That part is very important."

Andrés waves his hands, and the ship gives another lurch as Jenkins shouts and bangs on the locked door.

"We must help Emily off the ship," Nicolas pants, "before it breaks apart."

"I do not believe the situation is quite so dire," I say with a wink at Andrés. The boy grins, and the ship gives a shudder before coming to a rest.

"M-my father," Emily whispers from across the gap in the floor. "I know he has done terrible things but—"

Nicolas helps me over the hole. Then I bend beside her and whisper assurances—that Jenkins cannot hear—that we are not going to let him drown. I help Nicolas with her wound. The ball passed under her arm but did not break the ribs. While muscle is torn, and she has lost blood, Nicolas has bound it securely, and she is past her shock.

We get her on her feet and up the ladder. Once we are on the deck, I turn to Andrés, who waits there.

"Are you ready to leave?" I ask.

He nods.

"In that case, I think Nico will want to speak to you alone."

Nicolas protests that I do not need to go, but I insist. I say my final words to Andrés. Then Nicolas leads him to the bow of the ship and says his.

34

I must now do a thing even more dangerous than sword fighting. A thing even I hesitate to do, though I certainly did not say as much to Nicolas when we discussed our next steps. This is a thing that must be done, and he cannot—should not—do it. Not for his safety or for Emily's, who needs him there, tending to her wounds.

What gets me where I need to be is one simple piece of accepted truth. I trust Emily. Others have betrayed our trust. Lord Thomas betrayed mine, and Jenkins horribly betrayed Nicolas's. Yet Emily remained true. She is dedicated to the cause, and she may have grown up sheltered and lonely, but she has an iron core. I owe her, and I trust her, and so I will do this.

I lift my hand and rap on the door. A butler answers, and I announce myself. There is some to-ing and fro-ing within, and then I am escorted to a breakfast room where Norrington sits at his morning meal. When I walk in, he looks up. Then he stops, pushes back from the table and rises sharply.

"You," he says.

"Yes, me."

"You are Dupuis's girl. The one who insinuated herself with my niece and robbed my safe. The one who pretended to be a lad at the cliff."

"Yes."

He snaps down his fork with a clatter. "If you have come to beg pardon for your young man—"

"No. Well, yes, eventually, but I come now on a more pressing matter. Your niece has been injured. Badly injured."

He moves toward me so fast that I must bolt myself to the floor so as not to retreat.

"It was not us," I say quickly. "She was used as a lure for Dr. Dupuis. We were told you were holding her captive on the *Temerity* in punishment for her helping us last night."

"Emily *helped* you last night?"

I realize my error and want to retract it. Instead, I stand firm. "Your niece understands who is right and who is wrong in this dispute, and as much as she loves you, she cannot let you do what you are doing. Which is beside the point right now. She was shot, and Dr. Dupuis is tending to her, but she requires a local physician —the best you have—and a place to recover."

"You are asking me to do that, despite the fact she betrayed me last night?"

I meet his gaze. "You are a terrible lord, but I trust you are not a terrible uncle. Nor a terrible man. I'm asking you because I cannot ask her father, as he is currently being held captive on the *Temerity* himself."

One corner of Norrington's mouth curls. "If you expect me to care about that, you have certainly come to the wrong person. Emily, yes, but not the cad who stole my sister."

"I expect you will care about his fate, though, as he is also the one who shot your niece."

Norrington rocks back. "What?"

"He was aiming at Dr. Dupuis, but he is still the one who took her captive, pretending it had been you. And he killed a cabin boy he thought overheard a conversation you had on the *Temerity*. The boy did not, but Jenkins locked him in the galley and left him to die, which he did."

Now Norrington pales. He blinks as if trying to fully understand what I am saying. "A cabin boy?"

"Yes, he murdered a cabin boy. He attempted to murder Dr. Dupuis both today and three days ago. You are unmarried, with no heirs save his daughter. His fortunes are tied to yours, and so he protected yours." That is a simple version of the truth, and from Norrington's expression, he accepts it.

"Will you take your niece and tend to her wounds?" I ask.

"Of course." He calls for someone, and a man appears. Norrington tells him to fetch the doctor from Whitby and be quick about it.

When the man leaves, I say, "Will you handle Mr. Jenkins, preferably in a manner that does not cause undue trauma to his daughter?"

"I will."

"Will you pardon Dr. Dupuis, as a man who was erroneously targeted for treason—which we both know he did not commit—and who otherwise only acted for the benefit of others?"

"Yes, yes."

"Finally, we have your papers, which prove what you are doing to the people of Hood's Bay. We also know what conversation the cabin boy was thought to have overheard—the truth behind why the *Temerity*'s captain was accused of treason. There has been great damage done here. A boy is dead, and Emily is seriously injured. We do not wish to engage in a campaign of blackmail and threats. May we avoid that and have your word that you will speak to Emily on this matter and come to some agreement with her?"

His brow knits. "With Emily?"

"She knows these people better than we do, and she cares for them more than we can. The situation might change, sir, but for now, she *is* your heir, and I would suggest you think of her as that. She is quite capable of fulfilling the role. Talk to her. Listen to her. It is only the two of you now."

A look passes behind his eyes, one that might actually be grief. Then he nods. That is all he does. He nods.

WE ARE IN EMILY'S ROOMS AT NORRINGTON HALL. THE DOCTOR HAS removed the ball and declared she was most fortunate to have been shot there. I'm not sure I would ever say anyone was fortunate to be shot anywhere, but I understand what he means. The location of the shot means that she has lost blood and will need time to rest and mend, but she is expected to make a full recovery. Her uncle is already preparing to travel to York to find a doctor to confirm the first's opinion and a nurse to tend to her. Whatever else Lord Norrington might be, he is a loving uncle, and I must accept that.

Nicolas has not joined us here. Norrington has promised to see that the warrant is lifted and Nicolas receives a full pardon, but that does not mean he should risk walking into Norrington Hall just yet. He has already talked to Emily, and while they had the longer acquaintance, I feel as if I need to say more, as I was the one who committed the greater betrayal.

"You have known me for less than a day," she says when I apologize. "I understand that you both did what was best. For the people of the bay and for that poor boy."

"Yes, but Nicolas did not mislead you. He was truly your ally and your friend. I tricked you from the moment we met."

"For good cause."

I give her a mock-stern look. "So this is to be my punishment, is it? You will not let me properly apologize?"

She smiles and puts her hand on mine. "All right. I accept your apology even if you did not need to give it. Whatever your reason, you were kind to me, when I must seem to you a very silly girl."

"A very silly girl does not help a fugitive. Does not defy her family to do so."

She rolls her eyes. "It was a small thing."

"You are as bad at accepting compliments as you are at accepting apologies. You are far from a silly girl, Emily." I turn to face her. "While I am sorry that I misled you, I am even more sorry about what you had to hear on that ship. About your father and your grandfather."

"My father and I have always had . . . a difficult relationship," she says slowly. "He was good to me, but we were never as close as I would have liked. At least I no longer have to feel like an ungrateful child for doubting the sincerity of his love."

She pats my hand again. "I will deal with this, both the personal and the rest. I know my uncle is not a good man but . . ."

"He is good to you."

"Yes, and I can use that to advantage, for both my own situation and that of the people of the bay. If I cannot change his mind, then . . ." Her eyes twinkle. "With Nicolas gone, there is an opening for a new Robin Hood of the Bay."

I lean in to kiss her cheek. "And you would fill it admirably."

OF COURSE, WE WILL NOT SKIP OFF, LEAVING POOR EMILY TO CLEAN UP the mess. However, I am a strong believer in allowing people to at least attempt to accomplish difficult things on their own, particularly if they are women, too often raised to consider themselves incapable of such achievements.

Emily and Nicolas have discussed a plan of action, and she wishes to attempt it independently, and so we will leave her to that, returning to check on her later, lest she find herself in trouble. I doubt she will. Her uncle is devoted to her—I saw that firsthand. She will be that soft voice in his ear, guiding him to make better choices. While I doubt she will be able to persuade him to make choices for philanthropic reasons, I'm sure he can be persuaded to make ones that will not land him on a gallows for treason.

There is another reason for us to leave Emily to it. Nicolas is no longer a fugitive, but his captain was a French spy. The authorities may decide to pursue Nicolas again. Clearly, as the son of a French nobleman, he could have been a party to the plot. Either he would hang, or he would be deported to face the righteous wrath of the French revolution. So he must flee to the one place he is safe: the future.

Emily promises to find and care for the mare as well. As I suspected, the horse had wandered to their stables. It'd been Emily herself who'd seen her abused state and insisted on taking her in. Now she will find her again, and if her former owner complains, she will shame him into selling the mare to her.

Mr. Walker takes us in his cart to High Thornesbury, and from there, we slip up to Thorne Manor. We really will need to have a word with the current Lord Thorne—we can hardly expect to be passing in and out of his house regularly without telling him something. For now, he is still gone, and so we make our way to the bedroom where the stitch waits. Then we clasp hands and leap through into—

Into a room I do not recognize. The room of a child.

"This is not your time," Nicolas says as he looks around.

I walk to the dresser. On it is a lamp with a cord leading into the wall. I pull a chain, and the light ignites, making me gasp as Nicolas gives a start.

"Certainly not," I say. "We must be in the future."

"Lady Thorne's time? The twenty-first century?"

I look around. It is the room of a child much older than toddling Amelia Thorne. There is a baton and a white ball of some sort in a corner, along with a pair of shoes that have wheels on the bottom. Unframed pictures cover the walls. Prints that look like giant colored photographs on shiny thin paper. A man with the same skin tone as Nicolas smiles from one. He grips a baton like the one on the floor. The print reads "Jackie Robinson, 1955 World Series." Below, it says "Brooklyn Dodgers versus New York Yankees."

Nicolas comes over and whistles. "Nineteen fifty-five? That is not Lady's Thorne's time."

"It's not."

I look around as he examines the print and then walks back to the window, where he'd been standing, looking out. A boy whoops downstairs. A woman chides him to be careful around the baby.

I hurry to Nicolas. "We must go."

He nods but keeps looking out.

"Nicolas?"

He glances at me. "Do you . . . feel anything? Out there?"

I've barely turned toward the window when something tugs at me, hard and insistent. Something outside this house.

I hesitate. The voices grow louder, and a child's footsteps pound up the stairs.

Nicolas shakes it off. "We must leave. Come."

I still hesitate, but when I do, panic seeps in. The panic of wondering why we did not go home. What if I cannot go home and Nicolas cannot, either? What if we are endlessly bounced through time? Part of me wants to investigate, but a stronger part wants to be sure we can go home.

Nicolas must feel that, too. He takes my hand, and I yank my attention from the window. Yet even as we are leaping into the stitch, it pulls at me.

Why did we end up here?

What were we supposed to see?

Then the room disappears, and it is William and Bronwyn's nineteenth-century office again. That other world is gone, and a voice sounds from below, the distinct tones of my sister and nephew. I hike my skirts in one hand, entwine Nicolas's fingers in the other and go to meet them.

※

PORTIA COMES FROM LONDON TO HELP TEND TO NICOLAS'S INJURED arm, and Bronwyn brings medical supplies from the twenty-first century, including a miracle called "antibiotics." Of course, having twenty-first-century medicine—and an eighteenth-century pirate—in the house meant telling Portia about the stitch. My sister takes it as she takes everything. She assimilates the information and then plows past it to do what needs to be done.

August, William and the Thornes' two little girls come up to the manor, but only briefly, before Bronwyn and Rosalind declare it is all too much and bustle both families off to Courtenay Hall, leaving Nicolas to recover with Portia and me in attendance.

A week has now passed, and I am restless. Nicolas is, too. We have returned to the eighteenth century to ensure Emily is well. She is, and she is negotiating with her uncle like a seasoned professional.

We have visited High Thornesbury and even hired a coach to go to York for the day, but these amusements have started to feel like distractions.

Bronwyn also brought "birth control" from the twenty-first century, and that is one amusement that would *not* feel like a distraction, but we have decided we will continue to take our time in that regard. Also, it is not necessary to be in Thorne Manor to enjoy it. Not even necessary to be in this time, as Bronwyn ensured we have plenty to take with us, wherever we might go.

Wherever we might go . . .

It is the eighth night in Thorne Manor, and I have slipped from Nicolas's side to creep into the office, where I stand across the room, staring past the stitch to the window. When warm arms go around me, I only give the slightest start before letting myself relax into Nicolas's hold.

He nuzzles my neck and whispers in French, and he has been teaching me enough that I understand the gist of it. He is telling me I am a marvel, a wonder, words that bring a blush to my cheeks and tears to my eyes. Tears of joy, of my own marvel and wonder that I have found such a man.

"You are thinking of that room," he says. "The one with the baseball poster."

Baseball poster. That is what Bronwyn called it when we told them about her room. The poster of a famous player in an American sport. There are so many layers there to comprehend, and I am still not quite certain I do, but I want to. I want to know it all, and I cannot help but feel all the answers—twenty lifetimes of answers—wait beyond the stitch.

"I have been thinking about that room," he says. "About what we felt at the window."

"As if someone needed us. As if we were there because we were supposed to do something."

His arms tighten around me. "You have been thinking the same."

I nod. "Perhaps it was simply a mishap. A glitch, as Bronwyn called it. Yet I cannot help but feel . . ."

"The others travel between the same two distinct times. You are different. You came back to my time for me. To save my life."

"To save you? Or to meet you? I feel as if the 'saving' was incidental, and my true purpose was to assist you in that which you could not accomplish on your own, lacking the Sight. I was there to communicate with Andrés so that you might stop his killers."

"Perhaps, yet the core of my theory holds. I believe there is a reason we stopped in that other world, if only briefly. Something this 'stitch' wanted us to see. Someone it wanted us to help." He kisses the back of my neck. "Does that sound foolish?"

"Not to me." I take a deep breath. "What if it was not simply that one thing? What if there is more? An adventure each time we step through? Lifetimes of adventure and—" I stop short. "Now I am the one who sounds foolish."

"Not to me." He kisses my neck again. "Would you like to find out, crécerelle? To step through and see what awaits?"

"Yes."

"Then talk to your sister in the morning."

IT'S MORNING, AND I'M IN THE OFFICE WITH PORTIA. MY SISTER STANDS at the window, having circumvented the stitch with great care. I did not fail to notice how wide a berth she gave it. As she stands at the window, deep in her thoughts, I observe her with a pang of some unnameable sorrow.

When we were growing up, Portia was considered the prettiest of the Hastings sisters. A perfect diamond between two pearls, someone once said, and the phrase has stuck with me ever since. Rosalind's delicate beauty made men stumble over themselves to protect her, only to learn she did not need their protection, thank you very much. To others, Rosalind was a bit too waifish, too delicate, perhaps a sign of ill health. And then there was me, brimming with health and vitality to an unseemly degree.

Portia falls in the middle, taller than either of us, with a figure between ours, honey-blond hair and piercing blue eyes. Today, that beautiful hair hangs in perfect waves, and she wears the most delightfully ornate confection of a dress, with enough lace to decorate three coverlets. This is the real Portia, relaxed and at ease in the privacy of her family. In public, she is altogether different, hair pulled severely back, clothing as dull and plain as a Quaker's, spectacles perched on her nose—spectacles of plain glass. That is my glorious Portia with her light doused under the heavy basket of constraint because it is the only way she can enjoy even the slightest grudging respect as a "medical woman."

The weight of those expectations and demands douses my sister's light in so many ways. She had already been losing that light when Rosalind disappeared, and that only made things so much worse, as Portia insisted on bearing responsibility for me, which I never needed her to do. Then there was what another writer might call "a disappointment in love." I call it a damnable blessing, the hand of fate revealing her love's true nature before she was trapped with him forever.

I never minded the young lawyer my sister had fallen in love with. Yes, he was rather dull, and I'd wanted more for Portia, particularly as I was not convinced it was "falling in love" rather than "settling for the first decent man who wooed her." She had slid into something akin to love and agreed to marry him, and then suddenly she received a letter that he had eloped with another.

He'd fallen madly in love on a business trip and hoped she understood.

The worst of it was that Portia *did* understand. She accepted the public humiliation as if she expected no better—as if she deserved no better.

Now I watch her, in her wonderfully ridiculous confection of a dress, staring out the window, looking just a little bit wistful, a little bit empty.

"You could come with us," I say.

She startles and turns, blue eyes wide with something like horror. "What?"

I walk over and take her hand. "Come with us. Have an adventure."

She pulls from my grip. "I couldn't. I have so much to do."

She lists off a half-dozen patients waiting for her care in London, and a lecture she is sneaking into, and so many obligations and responsibilities that I want to grab her hand and yank her into the stitch. I want to take her away from all this for a little while. I want the Portia I knew once, endlessly curious and endlessly questing, like Rosalind, like me.

"Someday?" I say.

Portia exhales as if relieved that I will not pursue it. "Yes, someday. I should love to see it someday. In the meantime, Bronwyn will bring me books from the future, and you will run off on glorious adventures with a glorious man."

"You *do* like Nicolas?"

She rolls her eyes as she hugs me. "I think he is the most perfect man I could imagine for you. I could not be more delighted." She pulls back, holding me by the forearms. "Do not second-guess, Miranda. Do not doubt yourself or him. If there is cause to doubt, you will feel it in your heart. Do not manufacture it in your mind."

"I won't."

"Then off with you both, on your grand adventure."

"I will be back. I will always be back."

She hugs me again, holding me tight. "I know."

ᴏᴥᴥᴤ

Nɪᴄᴏʟᴀꜱ ᴀɴᴅ I ꜱᴛᴀɴᴅ ɪɴ ᴛʜᴇ ᴏꜰꜰɪᴄᴇ. Pᴏʀᴛɪᴀ ʜᴀꜱ ᴀʟʀᴇᴀᴅʏ ʟᴇꜰᴛ Thorne Manor, hiring a coach to take her to the train station, rushing back to London and her endless responsibilities.

"We will return soon," Nicolas says when he catches me glancing at a photo on the desk, one of Rosalind and Edmund with Bronwyn and Amelia.

"And we'll return to your time, too," I say, "to visit your family. To let them know you are well."

"Well and happy," he says. "Wherever we go, we will always come back to those we love."

He adjusts a satchel over his arm, and I catch a glimpse of a book in it. When I pluck it out, he grabs it back.

"That's mine," I say.

"No, I believe it is Lady Thorne's. Well, no, first it was August's and then Rosalind's, and after they read it, the Thornes did." He gives a mock frown. "They seem to think they know the authoress."

I groan. "The Thornes have read it, too?"

"Everyone has. It seems it is quite a popular novel, this tale of a young pirate woman and her adventures with swords of *both* varieties." He tucks the book back into his satchel. "I cannot wait to finish reading it. I am told there is another volume in the making."

He glances at me. "There is another in the making, is there not?"

"That depends on whether the authoress is too busy having her own adventures to write them for others."

"Oh, I do not think she shall ever be that busy. In fact, I shall make certain she is not."

He readjusts the strap and takes my hands. Then we turn to the stitch.

"Ready?" he says.

We look at each other and grin. Then we run, hand in hand, and at the last second, we jump, leaping into the stitch, to whatever awaits on the other side.

THANK YOU FOR READING!

I hope you enjoyed Miranda and Nico's adventure. If you'd like to know what happened after **A Turn of the Tide**, I have two more stories for you.

The first is a holiday novella. **Ghosts and Garlands** features Miranda and Nico solving a holiday mystery in modern-day London. You'll find the first chapter on the next page.

The second is **A Castle in the Air**, the final book in the series, featuring middle Hastings sister, Portia, who follows Miranda through the stitch on an adventure of her own.

GHOSTS & GARLANDS
SNEAK PEEK

I have always found Christmas to be the most frustrating of holidays, with its overflowing cornucopia of festive delights and impossible choices. Do I arrive at the yuletide ball in a one-horse open sleigh or walk along a moonlit path, snow crunching under my boots? Or do I forgo the ball and join a caroling party with my sister and her family, traveling incognito through the village and passing out baskets brimming with treats? Or do I go dancing and caroling another night and spend this one at home, snuggled in front of the roaring fire with a book and a cup of mulled wine?

This holiday season, I am facing what may be the most impossible choice yet. Do I stand at the hotel window, staring out at the wonders of the twenty-first century . . . or do I stare at the bed where my lover is stretched naked, engrossed in a book? Both are marvels to behold and present an infuriating quandary.

At last, I find a spot where I might greedily devour both—gazing out the window at this strange and beautiful world while watching Nicolas's reflection as *he* greedily devours a book of twenty-first-century medicine. I suppose I could feel a pang of jealousy at the way he is so engrossed in that book when I stand here wearing nothing but a silken robe, but we have already made very good use of the bed, and it will be at least another half an hour before either of us is ready to continue that part of our holiday.

It is a much-deserved break. A "vacation," as Bronwyn calls it. Being from this world, she arranged it for us, right down to seeing us onto the train in York and ensuring a driver met us in London. It is Nicolas's and my first time in the twenty-first century. Not our first time passing through the stitch, though. I went through months ago, expecting to jump from my Victorian world to this one and instead ending up in Nicolas's—in 1790.

We have spent the intervening months on the move. Twice we let the stitch send us where it may—to another time, another person in need. We also returned to 1790 to visit Nicolas's family in Martinique. That was *not* a short journey. I only wish we weren't limited to the stitch in Thorne Manor so that we might come to this world, fly where we need to be and *then* step back in time. Getting to Martinique was a month's journey each way, and that was on the fastest boat we could find. So Nicolas and I have not truly rested since we met. That is the purpose of this trip.

It is also about me donating the Roman gladius Nicolas gifted me shortly after we met. While the short sword is a common soldier's weapon, it is in incredible condition, as if it had been buried before he bought it—quite inexpensively after the seller realized wealthy nobles had no interest in an "old" short sword. Having now been transported from the eighteenth century, the condition is even more incredible, and as much as I long to keep it, I understand the historical value and have agreed to the donation in a world where they will appreciate it.

There is a third purpose for this trip: finally visiting the twenty-first century. Now that I am here, it is nothing short of terrifying. I am rather tempted to stay in this hotel room and only gaze out the window.

"It is overwhelming, *non*?" Nicolas says as he comes up behind me, his hands going around my waist. "Or is that purely my own impression?"

"Purely yours. My word for it is *terrifying*."

He kisses the side of my neck. "I believe yours may be more accurate, *crécerelle*."

His chin rests on my shoulder as he gazes down at the street an impossible distance below, crammed with cars and omnibuses, the honking reaching us even up here.

"I already respected Rosalind immensely," he says, "but seeing this, my awe for her has grown. I cannot imagine what it was like for your sister, trapped in this world."

"Nor can I," I say, tears prickling my eyes.

His arms tighten around me. "But she survived the ordeal, and she now returns to this world despite it. That makes her the second most remarkable Hastings sister I know."

I nod. "Yes, Portia is quite remarkable."

He chuckles under his breath. "You know that I meant you, but I should not set Portia in last place, even if it is a very difficult competition. While I do not know her as well as I do Rosalind, I hope to rectify that at Christmas, if I might lure Portia into conversation. She has been very quiet with me, and I am endeavoring not to take that personally."

"Do not. Portia has been rather reserved for even me these last couple of years. She—" I wave a hand. "I will not burden you with my family troubles."

"It is no burden if I hope to someday be part of that family myself. Perhaps a marriage license would help. Might I sneak that into your Christmas stocking?"

He says it lightly, but I know he is not entirely joking. I twist in his arms and kiss his cheek. "You may consider it for my Easter basket. As for Portia, take that medical book with you, and you shall not be able to get rid of her."

That makes him smile. I have two sisters. Rosalind is the oldest, married with a son and a newborn daughter. Portia is next, and like Nicolas, she is trained as a doctor, though also without the formal schooling. In her case, she has been unable to obtain that formal schooling because of her sex. In his, he was supposed to obtain it in

France, but the revolution put an end to that, and in my own time, as a Black man, he would find it as difficult a goal as Portia does. Still, both are—for all intents and purposes—as qualified as any medical professional, through apprenticeships, practice and study.

"Then I know what I will buy her," he says. He looks down at the road below. "Yet we would need to locate a bookshop."

"Which might be the one thing to tempt me out of this room."

"We will contact Bronwyn with the device she provided."

He means the "cell phone," as she calls it. Rosalind says it's a "mobile phone" here in England. As if things were not complicated enough . . .

The phone sits on the desk. It is a wonder among wonders, and I find myself both spellbound and daunted. Apparently, it does many things—things that make my head ache thinking about them—but for us, it is intended as a way of instantly communicating with Bronwyn or her husband, William, who are in the twenty-first century, preparing for the holidays.

I have only called Bronwyn once, to test it. I also might have been unable to resist randomly hitting numbers until someone answered . . . someone who spoke a language neither Nicolas nor I recognized, and we realized we might have been speaking to someone halfway around the world. My head also hurts thinking about *that*.

"Perhaps we could walk around the block looking for a book-store," I say, as carefully as I might suggest swimming the Thames in my day. "If we stay on this side of the road and do not cross through traffic." I squint down at what looks like water bugs zooming about at dizzying speeds. "And if we hold hands very tightly and do not let go."

Nicolas smiles. "I shall hold your hand as tightly as you hold mine, and together we shall conquer the beast."

We have been into the future before. Our second adventure took us to the 1950s, but only as far as the village near Thorne Manor. While we'd seen marvels, they'd been viewed from a distance, as we had no need to step into a motor vehicle. Since we've arrived in this world, we've been in Bronwyn's vehicle, a train and a sleek black car with a liveried driver, all moving so fast that I lose my breath remembering it.

"We have money, *non*?" Nicolas says. "Sufficient funds for this excursion?"

I nod. Rosalind had given us each two hundred pounds, which seemed ridiculous. Then her husband, August, snuck Nicolas another five hundred "just in case." In case of what? Getting trapped in this world and needing to purchase a small dwelling? Then, on the drive to the hotel, I saw giant signs advertising what looked like apartment flats for the bargain price of a quarter million pounds. Now I am half-afraid to set foot in a bookshop for fear I'll faint when I see the prices. On the other hand, as an authoress— author, Bronwyn would correct—I *do* hope book prices have kept apace.

"I believe we can safely descend into the maelstrom," Nicolas says. "Perhaps, if we work up the courage, we might even slip into a shop for a bite to eat, as it does appear to be nearing teatime."

I am about to answer when a knock comes at the door. We both pivot to stare at it. Or, at least, to stare in the direction of it. The room is big enough to hold a family of six . . . and Bronwyn warned that it was quite small by her North American standards. It has its own water closet, with running water, a tub and a booth for shower-ing. It also has a front hall, where the door is located.

The knock comes again.

"Hello?" I call, chastising myself for the tremor in my voice. That is not the voice of Miranda Hastings. But in this unfamiliar place, I feel as I did when I first stepped onto the shores of Martinique, uncertain and more than a little unsettled.

"Ms. Hastings?" a woman's voice calls back. "It's your concierge service."

The word *concierge* sounds French, and while Nicolas is teaching me his mother tongue, I do not yet know this term. He whispers, "It means the caretaker of the hotel."

He raises his voice. "We are quite fine, thank you."

"Dr. Dupuis?" she says and then rapid-fires a line in French that has his brows rising.

"She says she has a package and a message for us, one that is, as she says, 'time sensitive.'"

ABOUT THE AUTHOR

Kelley Armstrong believes experience is the best teacher, though she's been told this shouldn't apply to writing her murder scenes. To craft her books, she has studied aikido, archery and fencing. She sucks at all of them. She has also crawled through very shallow cave systems and climbed half a mountain before chickening out. She is however an expert coffee drinker and a true connoisseur of chocolate-chip cookies.

Visit her online:
www.KelleyArmstrong.com
mail@kelleyarmstrong.com

f facebook.com/KelleyArmstrongAuthor
X x.com/KelleyArmstrong
◎ instagram.com/KelleyArmstrongAuthor

Made in the USA
Middletown, DE
30 November 2023

44188966R00167